AŚOKA
In History and Historical Memory

AŚOKA

In History and Historical Memory

Edited by
PATRICK OLIVELLE

MOTILAL BANARSIDASS
PUBLISHING HOUSE • DELHI
Email: naraina@mlbd.in • Website: www.mlbd.in
@mlbdofficial
+91 89 2999 9000

*Reprint: Delhi, **2024***

First Edition: Delhi, 2009

ISBN: 978-93-5903-754-7 (Hardcover)
ISBN: 978-93-5903-755-4 (Paperback)

Printed & Published by
Rajendra P Jain *for*
Motilal Banarsidass Publishing House
A-44, Naraina Industrial Area, Phase I,
New Delhi–110 028 (INDIA)
Email: naraina@mlbd.in Website: www.mlbd.in
Tel.: (+91-11)4751 1592
Delhi Showroom:
4637/20, F-2, Hari Sadan, First Floor, Ansari Road, Daryaganj
Delhi–110 002 (Opp. Fire Station) ***Tel.***: (+91-11)4559 7999
Bengaluru Showroom:
1st Floor, 1/2 Rathnavilas Road, Basvanagudi, Next to Pai Vista
Convention Hall, South End Circle Bengaluru - 560004 (India)

Preface

The papers included in this volume were presented at an international symposium on Aśoka sponsored by the Department of Asian Studies and the South Asia Institute of the University of Texas at Austin on February 4, 2006.

Many individuals were instrumental in the success of this symposium and in the production of this volume; to all of them a heartfelt thank you. They include my colleagues Joel Brereton, Janice Leoshko, Martha Selby, Cynthia Talbot, and Oliver Freiberger. I want to thank especially the distinguished participants; their papers were uniformly excellent and their participation enlightening and energetic. Circumstances prevented Harry Falk from attending the symposium, but his paper was read during the symposium. A special thanks to our friend and colleague Richard Lariviere, who as Dean of the College of Liberal Arts at the University of Texas provided generous funds for this symposium.

One of my graduate students, David Brick, helped with the formatting of the volume for publication and the attendant logistics. I also express my gratitude to Mr. N. P. Jain of Motilal Banarsidass for his assistance in publishing this volume.

Patrick Olivelle
Austin, August 21, 2007

Contents

Introduction

PATRICK OLIVELLE

Apart from the founders of religious traditions, the Maurya Emperor Aśoka stands out as the most central political and cultural figure of ancient India. The discovery of the Aśokan edicts for the first time raised an ancient Indian individual from the fog of history and legend into the light of history. Given that the edicts in some way communicated Aśoka's personal messages, cultural historians of ancient India had for the first time an unparalleled source for reconstructing the person and activities of an ancient Indian king.

In 2003 we organized a conference at the University of Texas at Austin with the theme "Between the Empires: Society in India 300 BCE to 400 CE." This conference brought together scholars pursuing advanced research relating to this period and provided them the opportunity to interact with each other over a three-day period. The participants included archeologists, art historians, numismatists, historians, experts in literature, law, and linguistics, philosophers, and historians of religion. This conference and the volume resulting from it (Olivelle 2006) made clear the seminal nature of this period for the rest of Indian cultural history. In the presentations and discussions during this conference Aśoka loomed large.

Recent scholarship in the literature of this period, including the Sanskrit epics (Biardeau 2002; Hiltebeitel 2001, 2005; Fitzgerald 2004) and the Dharmaśāstras (Olivelle 2005, 2006), has shown that these texts can be best understood as responses to the continuing effects and memory of the Aśokan reforms. As Fitzgerald (2004: 120) notes: "It seems fair to conjecture that the emergence of the Mauryan empire generally and Aśoka's dharma campaign in particular were profound challenges to many pious brahmins, and that these events may well have been a strong stimulus to the creation, development, redaction, and spreading of the apocalyptic *Mahābhārata* narrative." The presenting of Yudhiṣṭhira and Rāma as *dharmarājas* can been seen within this interpretation as deliberate challenges to the other king of *dharma*, the Buddha, whose *stūpas* ascribed to Aśoka are significantly called *dharmarājikā* (Strong below p. 98).

It is significant that Aśvaghoṣa's *Buddhacarita*, at least as preserved in the Tibetan translation, concludes not with the death of the Buddha or the establishment of the Buddhist *saṅgha*, but with the erection of eighty thousand *stūpas* enshrining the Buddha's relics by the Emperor Aśoka. The conversion and religious activities of Aśoka, according to Aśvaghoṣa writing four centuries after Aśoka, signal the final triumph of the Buddha's doctrine. The memory of Aśoka remained strong centuries after his death. As Salomon notes in his contribution to this volume (p. 48), Rudradāman's inscription, engraved on the same boulder as an Aśokan edict and mentioning Aśoka by name, shows that "the historical memory of Aśoka was still alive during Rudradāman's reign, some four centuries after his lifetime." Aśoka, then, is significant not only for the history of India during the 3rd century BCE but also for the political, cultural, and religions formations during the subsequent centuries.

Recent theoretical advances in approaches to history and culture, moreover, along with re-evaluations of the archeology, paleography, art, and content of the Aśokan inscriptions and monuments, have prompted renewed interest in Aśoka and his place in Indian history. No historical document, no written history, and no historical reconstruction is free from cultural, social, religious, and political biases. In this light, even Aśoka's own inscriptions do not constitute unmediated and accurate historical sources; they reveal only what Aśoka wanted to reveal. They are political documents, just as a State of the Union address by an American President. Neither can be used without considerable analysis for the reconstruction of the Aśokan regime or the administration of a President.

Historical persons, events, and political formations, however, are created and recreated by historical memory as they are carried forward within the stream of time. As Deeg (p. 109) observes: "what we can get out of the so-called historical sources is the result of a distillation process, as it were, which says more about the time and the people who preserved them than about the time it pretends to describe." Yet, these sources of historical memory are significant not so much for the light they may shed on Aśoka and his time but for the insight they provide into the society, religion, politics, and culture of those who created these sources and presented and re-presented the Aśokan "reality."

The current volume, which contains the presentations at a symposium sponsored by the South Asia Institute and the Department of Asian Studies of the University of Texas at Austin (February 4, 2006) is intended to advance the study of Aśoka both as history and historical memory. The authors of these papers take as historically significant not only the "historical truth" of Aśoka but also the ways in which Aśoka presents himself and his policies to his subjects and the ways in which Aśoka is remembered and used for political, nationalistic, and religious purposes by succeeding generations both in India and in other parts of Asia, especially within the expanding Buddhist communities and nations.

Three of the papers in this volume by Harry Falk, Madhav Deshpande, and Richard Salomon reassess the Aśokan inscriptions themselves. Falk, who has just published a major volume on the Aśokan inscriptions and archeological remains (Falk 2006), analyzes in detail the actual process that mediated Aśoka's messages and commands and the actual carving of rocks and pillars across the subcontinent. In other words, what in these inscriptions can be called "Aśokan"? We often see the intervention of intermediaries, possibly the *lipikaras*, who, according to Falk, are not simply stone engravers but the regional administrators in charge of inscriptions, that shaped, and often changed, both the form and the content of the imperial messages. Deshpande studies the history of the crucial term *devānāṃpriya,* both in the pre-Aśokan Vedic literature and in the grammatical and other literature post-dating Aśoka, while Salomon evaluates the significance of the Aśokan edicts, the first inscriptions in the Indian subcontinent, with respect to the "epigraphic habit" in India during the succeeding centuries.

These studies, along with that of Janice Leoshko, who reexamines the artistic remains from the Aśokan period, highlight some unique features of Aśoka's activities, both epigraphic and artistic. Although Aśoka introduced writing and inscriptions into India, inscriptional activities of subsequent rulers did not follow his lead in most aspects of their proclamations. Leoshko's work shows the pitfalls of merely looking at foreign influences on Aśokan artistic production. "Why is influence perceived in a manner that implies subordination?" she asks (p. 62). It can be seen also as a "creative manipulation," and when viewed in this manner the Aśokan pillars "offer intriguing evidence of Aśoka's engagement with international definitions of kingship." The possible connection between Aśokan pillars and Egyptian obelisks "allows us to consider issues of agency that are increasingly featured in studies of this monarch. We might consider how the Aśokan pillars reflect the crafting of identity, an issue that relates to ideas of Near Eastern kingship and an issue that might have especially mattered in the environment of greater Greek presence in South Asia after the time of Alexander the Great" (Leoshko, p. 61).

Klaus Karttunen looks for evidence of Aśokan memory in the Greek classical accounts of the Hellenistic period, while John Strong's paper looks at that memory as it was articulated in later Buddhist texts, especially the *Lotus Sūtra*. Strong (p. 100) finds "some significant reverberations between the *Lotus Sūtra*, the edicts, and the legends of Aśoka, in both Sanskrit and Pali traditions." Indeed, we can detect such reverberations also between the Buddhist and the Brahmanical texts of the period, especially when the 84,00 *stūpas* of the *Lotus* finds echoes in the Sanskrit epic also with the enigmatic term *eḍūka*, which probably refers to Buddhist *stūpas* containing the Buddha's relics (*Mahābhārata* 3.188.64-67). The epic considers the proliferation of these *stūpas*, which the Buddhist tradition ascribes to Aśoka himself, as a sure sign of the end of the *yuga*. Finally, Max Deeg surveys the historical memory and the representation of Aśoka in a wide variety of texts spread across Asia and analyzes how Aśoka was reinvented again and again to sustain different political and religious establishments.

We hope that this small contribution to Aśokan studies will be of use to scholars and students of ancient India and perhaps spark further reflection and study of this unique individual from India's past.

Bibliography

Biardeau, M. 2002. *Le Mahābhārata: Un récit fondateur du brahmanisme et son interprétation. Vol 1*. Paris: Éditions du Seuil.

Falk, H. 2006. *Aśokan Sites and Artefacts: A Source-Book with Bibliography*. Monographien zur Indischen Archäologie, Kunst und Philologie, 19. Mainz: Von Zabern.

Fitzgerals, J. L. 2004. *The Mahābhārata: 11. The Book of the Women, 12. The Book of Peace, Part One*. Chicago: Chicago Universitiy Press.

Hiltebeitel, A. 2001. *Rethinking the Mahābhārata: A Reader's Guide to the Education of the Dharma King*. Chicago: Chicago University Press.

———. 2005. "Buddhism and the *Mahābhārata*." In *Boundaries, Dynamics and Construction of Traditions in South Asia*. Ed. F. Squarcini, pp. 107–131. Firenze: Firenze University Press.

Olivelle, P. 2005. *Manu's Code of Law: A Critical Edition and Translation of the Mānava-Dharmaśāstra*. New York: Oxford University Press.

———. 2006. "Explorations in the Early History of Dharmaśāstra." In *Between the Empires: Society in India 300 BCE to 400 CE*. Ed. P. Olivelle, pp. 169-190. New York: Oxford University Press.

The Diverse Degrees of Authenticity of Aśokan Texts

HARRY FALK

Aśoka is the earliest author who has left us texts written on stone in any comprehensible Indian script. There may have been reports about similar inscriptions in Achaemenid Iran; in India, however, Aśoka had no local precursor in this respect and, therefore, he had to experience many difficulties in the beginning. After having had inscribed the Minor Rock Edicts (henceforth MRE), he complained in the last of his Rock Edicts (henceforth RE) about scribes not transporting what he had thought would be written. He mentions two mistakes by name: First, some people may have thought that some facts mentioned are not suitable as to time or place. Second, he found undeniable mistakes made by the *lipikara*, literally the "document-maker," who should be regarded as the formulating "clerk" rather than as the stonemason who mechanically chiseled the letters, as we will see.

So, there are Aśokan texts transporting words or ideas not corresponding to what Aśoka himself wanted to say. In his eyes, the concerned phrases were not authentic. For us, however, it is difficult to find out the exact cases where the points of disagreement occur. In addition to this age-old disagreement, we in our times encounter a much larger series of problems which I will try to outline here.

1. Non-Aśokan Texts Called Aśokan

There are some texts called "Aśokan" which do not deserve this label. Cunningham (1877: 28f., 102) in his first edition of the Aśokan texts included a stone inscription from Deotek, which no one today would link with Aśoka. An inscribed doorframe found at Amarāvatī is often referred to as Aśokan, but there is no proof that it really is (Sircar 1963/64). Much clearer are the two inscriptions from the Laghman valley in eastern Afghanistan. They are written in Aramaic script and language and contain a reference to Aśoka, but only as a means of dating them to his regnal years 10 and 16. Because of his name and because of the difficulties of this script, scholars were tempted to find references to Aśokan ideas in them (Davary and Humbach 1974, Itō 1979). On the other side, we have some studies on these texts from specialists in Aramaic who show that they are the results of law cases, the verdicts of which the winners have put in stone to demonstrate their claims in public (Teixidor 1971: 479; Rosenthal 1978: 99*). Without rock walls, this habit survived for more than a millennium at least when verdicts were put on transportable stone slabs in Kashmir and the mountains to the south of it.

Another case comes from Taxila, where a slab was found in a city built 200 years after Aśoka, again mentioning his name. There have been many attempts at finding Aśokan ideas in this text (Bogolûbov 1976, Itō 1977); others see nothing but a reference in passing in an otherwise non-Aśokan context (Donner and Rölling 1962: 52, 1964; In der Smitten 1971).

Once we exclude the Taxila and the Laghman texts from those epigraphs inscribed by order of Aśoka, we get an interesting picture regarding the distribution of scripts: In the Taxila area and in Gandhara proper (i.e., up to the Khyber Pass), only Kharoṣṭhī was used by his own scribes. Aramaic, however, was still used by professional clerks, local judges or law-seekers outside the fold of Aśokan administration. Aramaic for true Aśokan purposes appears only west of Gandhara, Nangahar (Pul-i Darunte) and in Kandahar, where Kharoṣṭhī is evidently absent. This divide may have some relevance to the question of who had Kharoṣṭhī designed for which realm. The new script spread in Taxila and Gandhara in the late 4th century BC, but not in Nangahar where Kharoṣṭhī was introduced only much later.

Non-Aśokan texts are important when seen this way: They demonstrate the use of scripts by completely different groups of people for very different purposes.

2. Non-Aśokan Texts With Aśokan Contents

There is one text which is regarded as truly Aśokan although it seems to me that it is an addition by one of his clerks, formulated with best intentions, but possibly not meant to be inscribed anywhere. This is the so-called MRE 2, found only in seven places which come in three groups separated by less than 70 km as the crow flies. The first ("southwestern") group south of Bellary in Karnataka comprises Jaṭiṅga-Rāmeśvaram, Siddapur and Brahmagiri, all within a circle of 1 km. The second ("northwestern") group includes Niṭṭūr and Uḍegolam north of the same Bellary, themselves separated by less than 1 km. The two groups are different in three respects:

a) The southwestern group presents the official greetings from the headquarters at Suvarṇagiri, near Eṟṟaguḍi, to the local officials, preceding MRE 1. The northwestern group starts with the Aśokan text proper.

b) The southwestern group continues with MRE 2 right after MRE 1 without indicating the difference; the northwestern group keeps both texts separate, inscribing each one on a different boulder, MRE 1 at the more prominent place and MRE 2 at a place more out of the way.

c) The southwestern group ends with a statement written in Kharoṣṭhī letters saying that it is the *lipikara* Capaḍa who wrote this. The northwestern group skips this reference.

The third ("eastern") group consists of Eṟṟaguḍi and Rājula-Mandagiri, 70 km to the east of the two Bellary groups, themselves separated by about 20 km. In this case we have striking proof that both texts of MRE 2 were copied from a single written master-document, as they do not even change the length of the lines (Andersen 1991; for a corrected version and visual comparison, see Falk 2006: 71).

Taken together we see that the southwestern group blends all sorts of texts: Introduction, MRE 1, MRE 2, *lipikara*. The eastern group likewise adds MRE 2 to MRE 1 without a break sign. Only the northwestern group relegates MRE 2 to a less prominent position in the field and removes all other side dishes.

Compared to MRE 1 with its enigmatic references to mingling gods and Aśoka's own relationship to an unnamed *saṅgha*, MRE 2 uses clear terms and presents the rules of public conduct Aśoka wanted to have established. Therefore, I take MRE 2 as the attempt of an influential clerk to translate Aśoka's ideas into comprehensible language. This was to be pronounced and made public according to the will of the *lipikara*, but it was not meant to be inscribed the same way as the main text.

The text traveled in written form, as mentioned above; nonetheless, all three groups containing MRE 2 are based on separate master-texts, each with its own additions, omissions, and transposals. Linguistically, all three groups diverge from Aśoka's own language in that they do not convert *r* to *l*.

All over northern India, from Delhi and Bairāṭ to Sahasrām and Ahraurā, nothing but *l*-forms are used in the MREs. In the South, at Pāṅgurāria, Gavīmaṭh and Palkiguṇḍu an *r* is (almost) always restored. At all other places, in the Vindhyas down to Maski, *r*-forms prevail, but every single scribe introduced— or preserved— one or more of the original *l*-forms. The seven places in the South which contain MRE 2 restore *r*-forms throughout. There is but one telling exception. Niṭṭūr and Uḍegolam, both being redacted at the same source, get confused at almost the same place in MRE 2, sentences (O) and (P). Niṭṭūr twice has *ācāliya* for *ācāriya*, and Uḍegolam writes *yathālahaṃ* for *yathārahaṃ*. These glaring exceptions at almost the same place in MRE 2 may reflect an instruction about the *r*- and *l*- differences given by one superior to two scribes, who later went to Niṭṭūr and Uḍegolam respectively. While giving examples of where *l*-forms are to be kept and where they are to be reconverted to *r*-forms, one scribe got confused and introduced *ācāliya*, whereas the other mixed up right and wrong when it came to *yathālahaṃ*.

It is customary to attribute *l*-forms to an "eastern" form of Middle Indic. Focusing on the MREs alone, we must say that *l*-forms are "northern," where "North" covers the full Gangetic plain from Delhi down to Magadha. A need to restore *r* is felt only south of the plains and the further south the more intensely.

Usually, the *lipikara* Capaḍa is regarded as the stonemason who outlined and chiseled the letters into the rocks of the southwestern group of MRE 2, it being supposed that he chiseled all three texts of the southern group where his name appears. However, there were clearly at least two scribes at work, one at Brahmagiri and one or two at the two other sites. The style of the letters at Brahmagiri is so different from that of the other sites that it is impossible to assume that one scribe is behind all three inscriptions. With at least two scribes mentioning one Capaḍa, we must remove the *lipikara* from the actual sites and elevate him to a more important place in a superior position, probably at Suvarṇagiri, i.e., Eṟṟaguḍi, from where the texts went to at least seven sites not more than 70 km distant from each other.

3. Aśokan Texts With Non-Aśokan Contents

There is a whole range of shades when it comes to "non-Aśokan contents." Aśoka's own statement in RE 14, cited above, refers to cases that came to his knowledge in the 3rd century BC. Other cases include what I will call "invented," "misread" and "redacted" texts. They make us aware of the many pitfalls awaiting us when taking Aśokan "edicts" at face value.

3.1 Invented Text: Ni-Li

Texts make sense only in our minds; an accumulation of unknown letters does not speak to us without instruction or a medium. A pilgrim facing the inscriptions on Aśokan pillars in the middle of the first millennium AD was not in a position to read the letters. He was forced to believe the words others pronounced claiming to reproduce what the chiseled letters stood for. We have a place where Chinese pilgrims report about an Aśokan inscription. This is Ni-Li, south of the palace at Pāṭaliputra, where Faxian around AD 400 describes a mutilated inscription on a huge pillar saying that Aśoka donated the inhabited world thrice to the Buddhist *saṅgha* and bought it back with money three times (Giles 1923: 48). More than 200 years later, in the early 7th century, Xuanzang tells exactly the same story (Beal 1884, II: 91). We have reliable information about people not being able to read Aśokan Brāhmī at that time. Xuanzang, on the other hand, is not an independent source; very often he uses older reports and it seems that here he simply copied Faxian. Irrespective of whether there are one or two reports, a statement about a triple donation sounds unreliable and the whole "reading" may rather be an invention of the local priests with the intention of demonstrating their once all-encompassing royal patronage.

3.2 Misread Texts

The texts on the surfaces of the polished pillars are very clearly legible and misreadings are extremely rare. Things are different when it comes to the rough rock walls of the MREs and some of the REs, which produce rubbings that are very difficult to read.

3.2.1 Misread: Gujjarā

The MRE at Gujjarā near Jhansi provides a good example of how easily a text can be misread although each *akṣara* is 10 cm high. The rock at Gujjarā is so uneven that the published rubbing is rather useless. Even while inspecting the rock, the letters can only be made out properly with stray light very early in the morning or with a flashlight at night. These circumstances have lead to a strange misreading of the first sentence, which starts allegedly with *devanaṃpiyasa piyadasino aśoka-rājaso*, i.e., with a series of genitives—as does Maski and no other version so far discovered.

Although an *aśokarāja* could be possible if we compare, for example, *tissakumāra* in Pali texts, it still sounds unusual. There are more peculiarities in the first line. When Aśoka joins the *saṅgha*, he usually says *yaṃ ca me saṃghe upayīte*, "when I joined the *saṅgha*," and the next sentence goes *bāḍhaṃ ca me pakaṃte*, meaning "and I took strong efforts." In Gujjarā all the editors have read *yaṃ ca me saṃghe yate ti* in the first case, as if ending a direct quotation with *(i)ti*; and read the second as *ahaṃ bāḍhaṃ ca parakaṃte ti āha*. Now this is really startling because we never find an *ahaṃ*, "I," in this part of India, but only *hakaṃ*. Let us look at the stone.

The first correction is to be made at the beginning: There is no *aśokarāja(sa)*. Where the *–sa* was expected, there is a crack, but it is also clear that the writer stopped short of it and continued well after the crack. There is no genitive *–sa*, but instead we recognize a clear *–e–mātra* in *asoke*. That means that after the initial genitives, something starts anew with two nominatives: *asoke rāja*. But how to construct these nominatives?

Tracing the *akṣaras* on the stone reveals that there is no *ahaṃ* in any MRE, since Gujjarā shows a clear and well-known *āha*. Taking the beginning and end together we now get a regular construction: "(In the name) of Devānaṃpriya Priyadarśin. Aśoka, the king, says (first *ti aha*) '. . .and more than a year ago I joined the *saṅgha*' and he says (second *ti āha*) 'and I took strong efforts.'"

The meaning is not affected to any degree, but a description of the syntax and vocabulary of Aśoka's language based on this misreading has lead to wrong results.

3.2.2 Misread: Karṇa Caupār Cave in the Barābār Hills

More interesting is a text inscribed on the polished surface of a rock wall in front of the first of the caves in the Barābār hills. This epigraph was partially destroyed in the years after Aśoka. It needed several visits to clarify the reading. Earlier, it was read as:

lāja piyadasī ekunavī
sati-vasā[bh]isi[t]e ja[lagh]o
[sāgama]thāta [me] i[yaṃ kubhā]
su[p]i[y]e kha. . .[di]
nā

Hultzsch's (1925) translation is:

> When king Priyadarśin had been anointed nineteen years, this cave in the very pleasant Kha[latika mountain] was given by me (for shelter during) the rainy season.

After cleaning the stone and inspecting it at close range, I read (Falk, 2007):

> *lāja piyadasī ekunavī*
> *sati-vasābhisite jalūṭhaṃ*
> *āgamithā tata iyaṃ kubhā*
> *su[p]i[y]ekha (ājivikehi) [di]*
> *nā*
>
> When king Priyadarśin had been anointed nineteen years, he went to Jalūṭha and then this cave (called) Supriyekṣā was given to the Ājīvikas.

The differences are obvious. It is clear that the old reading cum interpretation adds facts to the life of Aśoka which cannot be verified and that the new reading adds new material which was absent before. However, as long as there is no alternative, a misreading creates a "reality" upon which everyone has to build.

3.2.3 Misread: Pāṅgurāriā

A still more striking case is the so-called Separate Edict at Pāṅgurāriā, incised away from a MRE by several meters, and chiseled in a unique style. It was read by D. C. Sircar (1971/72) as:

> *piyadasi nāma*
> *rājā kumāra[sa]*
> *saṃvasa māṇe*
> *mades[e] [u]punitha*
> *vihāra[ya]tāy[e]*
>
> The king Priyadarśin [speaks/writes] to Kumāra Śaṃva from [his] march [of pilgrimage] to the Upunitha (or Opunitha) vihāra/monastery in Māṇema-deśa.

An inspection of the site produced a rather different reading:

> *piyadasi nāma*
> *rājā kumār(e) va*
> *saṃvasamāne [i]*
> *maṃ desa(ṃ) [p](ā)punitha*
> *vihāra[v]ātāyā*
>
> The king, who (now after consecration) is called Priyadarśin, (once) came to this place on a pleasure tour while he was still a (ruling) prince, living together with his (unwedded) consort.

Details and a full interpretation are found in another publication (Falk 1997); in any case, this example once again proves that no inscription should be read from rubbings or photographs if the surface is rough or the letters are not clearly visible.

3.3 Redacted Texts

As proposed above, the MRE 2 is not redacted, but a new text by someone trying to use a clearer language than Aśoka does in his MRE 1. However, there is one striking example of what the king called "improper with regard to time or region" in his RE 14, i.e., a text showing that some people felt obliged to redact or to rewrite Aśoka's own text in order to make it easier to digest. This is the MRE of Maski in the Raichur district. The Maski edict was found in 1915 and edited in Haiderabad by H. Krishna Shastri. Soon after, Emile Senart (1916) wrote his last Aśokan article on this text.

The inscribed rock measures about 1 x 2 m, stands upright on its wide side, and is located at the lower end of a huge cave whose sides consist of several boulders and whose roof consists of an immense covering rock. The inscription looks inside.

I would like to present an edition here, contrasted in line a) with the standard phrases as found in most other versions of MRE 1, suitably accessible in Andersen 1990. Andersen's analysis of the text into sentences A to X is followed here. Line b) presents the reading of the Maski version in the best edition published so far, Andersen 1990: 58–61, and line c) shows my readings from the rock at Maski. Square brackets indicate partly legible letters, text given in round brackets is completely gone.

[B]
a) *devānaṃpiye hevam āha*
b) *dev[ā]naṃpiyasa asok[a]sa*
c) *devanapiyasa asokasa*

According to Devānaṃpiya Aśoka.

The introduction here as at Gujjarā is a series of two genitives with the same basic meaning. Seven letters follow of which only the first two are partly visible, without parallels in other versions. Then the usual text continues:

[C]
a) *adhikāni aḍhatiyāni vasāni yaṃ hakaṃ upāsake*
b) - - - - - - - *[a]ḍh[a][t]-[yā][ni] vaṣā[ni] aṃ sumi budhaśake*
c) *[s]ā[tirekāni a]ḍha[tiy]ā[n]i vasāni [-]ṃ aṃ sumi <upāsa/pāsaka>śake*

For more than two and a half years I have been a lay devotee.

The additional *[-]ṃ* is an abandoned *aṃ*, repeated in full immediately, because the stone had flaked off while chiseling.

The *upāsaka* in Maski has been read differently. Most editors (suitably cited in Andersen 1990) prefer *budhaśake or budhupāśake*. The reading is difficult, but we can nonetheless exclude any reference to the Buddha here. For one reason or another the writer had to squeeze the *akṣaras* in more closely than he did at any other place. The congestion starts with *sumi*, where the two letters stand very close to each other. The allegedly written *budha* shows itself to consist of three *akṣaras*. The first is a small hook at the lower left corner of the supposed *bu*. It could be an attempt to write an initial *u*.[1] Next comes a clear *pā* and merging with it is *sa*. So the beginning is *upāsa*, as required. The next three akṣaras are more difficult. The first is a second *pā*, then follows a *sa* with the crossbar of a *ka*. And lastly, more or less clear, is *śake*.[2]

I take these irregularities as a doubly missed attempt at writing *upāsake*, finally reverting to the supposedly correct sibilant, *śa*, meant for spoken /sa/.

[D]
a) *no cu kho bāḍhaṃ pakaṃte husaṃ ekaṃ savacharaṃ*

But for one year, I did not put much effort into it.

Maksi excludes this sentence.

[Ea]
a) *sātireke tu kho saṃvachare yaṃ mayā saṃghe upayīte*
b) - - - - - *[-]ire* - - - *[m]i [sa]ṃghaṃ u[pa]gate*
c) *[sava](chare sāt)ireke (yaṃ) [s]u[m]i [s]aṃgh(e) [u](pa)gate*

More than a year ago now, I joined the Buddhist order.

[Eb]
a) *bāḍhaṃ ca me pakaṃte*
b) - - - *[su]mi u[pa]gat[e]*
c) *[b](āḍhaṃ ca) [su]mi upagat(e)*

And I have put much effort into it.

Maski reads more or less with the other versions. However, both verbs of motion, *upayīte* and *pakaṃte*, have been simplified and leveled in meaning to *upagate*.

[F]
a) *iminā cu kālena amisā samānā munisā jaṃbudīpasi misā devehi*
b) *pure jaṃbu* - - *s[i]* - - - - - - - - *[dā]n[i] misibhūtā*
c) *pure jaṃbu(di)[pas](i)* - - - - - *[t](e) [d](ā)ni misibhūtā*

During this time the people in India, being separated from the gods, came into contact with the gods.

The meaning seems to be that the effort Aśoka put into his being a lay devotee is the proper way to please or worship the gods. A similar phraseology is also attested in younger Vedic texts.

Maski clarifies the conditions by using *pure*, "earlier," and *dāni*, "now."

1 Compare *ya-yate* in Pāṅgurāriā, a mistaken copy of an original *u-pa-yite*.
2 For a close-up, see Falk 2006: 82 fig. 4.

[G]
a) *pakamasa hi iyaṃ phale*

This is the fruit of the effort.

Maski is silent.

a) [H] *no hi iyaṃ mahaptena va sakiye papotave*
b) (I) *na hevaṃ dakhitaviye [uḍā]l[ā]ke v[ā] ima adhigach[e]yā ti*
c) (I) *na hevaṃ dakhitaviye [u]ḍālake v[ā] ima adhigach(e)yā ti*

This cannot be reached only by very important persons.

Aśoka speaks of the "mingling of gods and men," or the proper way to please gods. The Maski text changes the sequence of this and the following sentence, reading the negating statement last. It also changes the meaning by changing the verb again: *na hevaṃ dakhitaviye uḍālake vā ima adhigacheyā ti*, "One should not hold the opinion that only affluent people can understand that." The active "reaching a goal" has been replaced by simple mental "understanding."

a) [Ia] *kāmaṃ tu kho khudakena pi pakamamīnena sakiye*
b) (H) *iya a[ṭhe khuda]k[e] . [pi] dhamayu[t]e[na] sake adhigatave*
c) (H) *iya aṭhe [kh](u)dake[na] [p](i) dhamayu[t]e(na) sake adhigatave*

But this can be reached also by small people if they put effort into it.

Again Aśoka speaks of the gods and the necessary effort to meet their demands. And Maski again changes the verb: *iya aṭhe khudakena pi dhamayutena sake adhigatave*, "This matter can also be understood by small people if they stick to the *dharma*."

[Ib]
a) *vipule pi svage ārādhetave*

They are capable also of satisfying the vast heaven.

Maski ignores this sentence.

[J]
a) *se etāya aṭhāye iyaṃ sāvane sāvāpita*

So, for the following aim, I proclaim this text.

Maski drops this sentence.

[K]
a) *khudakā ca mahāptā ca imaṃ pakamevu ti*
b) *[khudak]e ca - - - lake [ca va]taviyā*
c) *khu[dak]e [ca] ma[h]ālake ca vataviyā*

Small and influential people alike may put forth effort accordingly.

This is the central purpose of the whole text, announced as such by sentence (J). In Maski it is changed to a trivial *khudake ca mahālake ca vataviyā*, "Small and affluent people have to be told."

All editors read *udalake* in this sentence. The lower half of several *akṣaras* is missing. But when we check the upper protrusions, I think that a sequence *ma-ha* preceding the clear *-lake* is more likely than *u-da*. *mahālaka* occurs in several parallel versions.

[L]
a) *aṃtā ca me jānevu*

And also the border tribes may learn from me.

Maski is not interested in complicating things and leaves this out again— or maybe the redactor felt himself already inside the border territory, so that nobody but a borderer would get to know this text anyway.

[M]
a) *ciraṭhitike ca iyaṃ pakame hoti*
b) *hevaṃ ve [k]alaṃtaṃ bha - - - - - - -* *t[ike] ca*
c) *hevaṃ ve kalaṃtaṃ bha[dak]e [h]o(s)i(ti) [c](ira)[th](i)[k](e) ca*

And this effort is long-lasting.

Aśoka seems to speak to his own efforts. The Maski text has been misread in this line. Where I read *bhadake hositi* on the rock, all other editors read or presuppose a reading *bhadake se a*, which makes little sense. This M sentence is considerably altered, reading: *hevaṃ ve kalaṃtaṃ bhadake hositi cilathitike ca*, "And if you act in this sense, it will be pleasant and long-lasting."

The Maski writer wants to say what Aśoka expects people to do, but the only sense someone can draw from all his abbreviations is that by following the *dharma* the gods will be pleased. And this then will be pleasant and everlasting.

[N]
a) *iyaṃ ca aṭhe vaḍhisiti vipulaṃ pi ca vaḍhisiti diyaḍhiyaṃ vaḍhisiti*
b) *va – siti* *cā diya[ḍhi]yaṃ he[vaṃ ti]*
c) *va[ḍhi]siti cā diya[ḍh]iya hositi*

And this matter will grow, will spread wide and increase.

Maski is again rather short by reading *viḍhisiti cā diyaḍhiya hositi*, "And it will grow and increase."

Where I read *hositi*, the editions show *hevaṃ ti* since Senart, Sircar and Hultzsch. The first edition by Krishna Shastri was quite right with *hositi*. But once a Westerner "improved" a reading, there was no way back. The letter *sa* has a wavy outline on top, which possibly was meant to be an *i*-stroke. So, only *hositi* or *hosati* can be read, and these are the only readings that make sense at all.

We have seen that the reading of this text can be improved in many details, once we read it on the rock. But what I deem much more important than correcting a few *akṣaras* is that we also gain a look at the man who wrote at Maski. Compare the lines of the synoptical text:

1. In sentence D, the king speaks of his missing efforts, *pakaṃte*. Maski is silent.
2. At the end of sentence E, Aśoka was diligent. Maski uses the simple *upagate*.
3. Sentence G speaks of the fruit of effort, *pakamasa*. Maski is silent.
4. In sentence I, even small people who show effort can please the gods. Maski speaks about understanding (*adhigatave*) the king's words.
5. In sentence K, the king wants all people to show effort. Maski changes it so that the effort disappears.
6. In sentence M, Aśoka wants his efforts to last long. Maski introduces *hevaṃ ve kalaṃtaṃ*, "if you follow the *dharma*."

There can be no doubt that every place where the term "effort," *pakama*, is alluded to, the Maski writer tried to avoid it. He simply did not want to bother his audience with something Aśoka called "effort."[3]

It seems as if the redactor had a rather low opinion of those about to hear his text. He certainly did not want to correct his master, but nonetheless it occurred to him that such people would more easily be brought to Aśoka's side if they were not burdened with too much philosophy and emphasis on religious austerities. He spoke to simple people. The impression that these people would not understand the standard text may also have led to the rare introduction: *devanaṃpiyasa aśokasa*, avoiding *āha*, which would have implied a verbal quotation.

Can we call the Maski MRE an Aśokan text? Yes, with regard to origins and time; no with regard to its meaning. The most important aspect of personal effort was erased on purpose. Instead of mental and physical endeavor, instead of a change in personal attitude and habits, the redactor wanted people to be followers of an unspecified *dharma* (*dharmayukta*). Following this unspecified *dharma*, even an audience of small people could please the gods. Nobody would have objected.

Why was there this redaction? How should one account for this change in meaning and phrases? Was the redactor himself unconvinced of Aśoka's ideas? We will never know.

3 The difference in terminology was not observed by writers editing the Maski text. Otto Stein (1934; KlSchr: 291) observed the formal difference; however, he thought that *pakama* was synonymous with *dhammayuta*.

Bibliography

Andersen, P. K. 1990. *Studies in the Minor Rock Edicts of Aśoka. I: Critical Edition*. Freiburg: Hedwig Falk.

———. "Notes on the Engraving Procedures for the Erraguḍi Version of Aśoka's Minor Rock Edict." *Indo-Iranian Journal* 34: 267–76.

Beal, S. 1884. *Si-Yu-Ki, Buddhist records of the Western World, Translated from the Chinese of Hiuen Tsiang (A.D. 629)*. London: K. Paul, Trench, Trübner & Co. [reprint Delhi 1969]

Bogolûbov, M. N. 1976. "Aramejskaâ nadpis' iz Taksily." *Voproz Jazykoznanija* 1976,6: 64–69.

Cunningham, A. 1877. *Inscriptions of Aśoka* (CII, 1). Calcutta: Archaeological Survey of India. [reprint Varanasi 1961]

Davary, G. D. and Humbach, H. 1974. *Eine weitere aramäoiranische Inschrift der Periode des Aśoka aus Afghanistan*. Abhandlungen der Akademie der Wissenschaften und der Literatur, Mainz 1974,1. Wiesbaden: Steiner.

Donner, H. and Röllig, W. 1962. *Kanaanäische und aramäische Inschriften. Band I: Texte*. Wiesbaden: Otto Harrassowitz.

———. 1964. *Kanaanäische und aramäische Inschriften. Band II: Kommentar*. Wiesbaden: Otto Harrassowitz.

Falk, H. 1997. "The preamble at Pāṅgurāriā." In *Bauddhavidyāsudhākaraḥ. Studies in Honour of Heinz Bechert on the Occasion of His 65th Birthday*, ed. P. Kieffer-Pülz and J. Hartmann. Indica et Tibetica, 30, pp. 107–21. Swistal-Odendorf: Indica et Tibetica Verlag.

———. 2006. *Aśokan sites and artifacts—A source-book with bibliography*. Monographien zur Indischen Archäologie, Kunst und Philologie, 18. Mainz:

———. 2007. "Barabar reconsidered." In *South Asian Archaeology 1999*, ed. E. Raven. Groningen: Egbert Forsten.

Giles, H. A. 1923. *The Travels of Fa-hsien (399–414 A.D.), or Record of the Buddhistic Kingdoms*. Cambridge: Cambridge University Press. [reprint Varanasi 1972]

Hultzsch, E. 1925. *Inscriptions of Aśoka. New Edition* (CII 1). Oxford: Clarendon Press. [reprint Delhi 1969; Tokyo 1977]

In der Smitten, W. T. 1971. "Eine aramäische Inschrift in Pakistan aus dem 3. Jhdt. v. Ch." *Bibliotheca Orientalis* 28: 309–11.

Itō, G. 1977. "A new interpretation of Aśokan inscriptions, Taxila and Kandahar I." *Studia Iranica* 6: 151–61.

———. 1979. "Aśokan inscriptions, Laghmān I and II." *Studia Iranica* 8: 175–83.

Krishna Sastri, H. 1915. *The Maski Rock Edict of Aśoka*. Hyderabad Archaeological Series, 1. Calcutta: Archaeological Survey of India.

Rosenthal, F. 1978. "The Second Laghmân Inscription." *Erez-Israel* 14: 97*–99*.

Senart, É. 1916. "Un nouvel edit d' Aśoka à Maski." *Journal Asiatique* 11. sér. 7: 425–42.

Sircar, D. C. 1963–64. "Fragmentary pillar inscription from Amaravati." *Epigraphia Indica* 35: 40–43 [repr. 1979: 118–22].

———. 1971–72. "Panguraria Inscription of Asoka." *Epigraphia Indica* 39 (issued 1981): 1–8. [repr. 1979: 94–103]

———. 1979. *Aśokan Studies*. Calcutta: Indian Museum.

Stein, O. 1934. "Neuere Forschungen zur altindischen Sozialgeschichte, Rechts- und Staatsrechtsliteratur III." *Archív Orientální* 6: 15–49. [repr. *Kleine Schriften* 1985: 271–305]

Teixidor, J. 1971. "Bulletin d'épigraphie sémitique 1971." *Syria* 48: 453–93.

Interpreting the Aśokan Epithet *devānaṃpiya*

MADHAV M. DESHPANDE

In this paper, I will briefly look at the use of the expression *devānāṃpriya* in Aśokan inscriptions along with references to *devas* in those inscriptions. Further, I will look at the Vedic precursors of the Aśokan term *devānāṃpriya*, as well as its subsequent history in the traditions of *Purāṇas*, Sanskrit Grammar, and literature. I will also review how this term appears in Sri Lankan inscriptions, chronicles and *Aṭṭhakathās*, as well as its complete absence in the northern Buddhist Sanskrit legends about Aśoka, such as the *Aśokāvadāna*. Most of these dimensions have been covered in the extensive previous research regarding the term *devānaṃpiya*/-*devānāṃpriya*, but there may be nuances that I can add to this discussion.

Occurrence of *devānaṃpiya* and *deva* in Aśokan Inscriptions

In his *Glossary* of Aśokan inscriptions, Woolner (1924, pt. II: 95–96) conveniently lists all occurrences and variants of the term *devānaṃpiya*. Almost invariably associated with the title *piyadasi* of Aśoka, the term *devānaṃpiya* occurs in most of Aśoka's inscriptions, sometimes several times in a given inscription. Geographically, it occurs in all regions where Aśoka's inscriptions are found, as well as chronologically it occurs in all periods of Aśokan inscriptions and in all types, namely the minor rock edicts (c. 258 BCE), major rock edicts (c. 257 BCE), and pillar inscriptions (c. 243 BCE). According to W.B. Henning's (1949: 84) interpretation of Aśoka's Aramaic inscription in Lampaka, the term *devānampriya* gets transcribed into Aramaic as [*dy*]*wnprys* [= *devānapriyasa*]. But Karttunen (1997: 269) says that elsewhere it gets translated into Aramaic as *mārān*.[1] We find no trace of it in Aśoka's Greek inscriptions, while they do transcribe into Greek his personal name *piyadasi* as Πιοδασσης, without translating it (Karttunen 1997: 264, 269). It would thus seem that *devānāṃpriya*, unlike *priyadarśī*/*piyadasi*, was an honorific term, rather than part of Aśoka's personal name. The question of

1 A number of colleagues inform me that the Aramaic word *maran* is made up of *mar* "Lord" and the suffix *-an* "our," and basically means something like "Our Lord." This expression is used with reference to God, Jesus, kings, and high officials, and can have either theological or non-theological meaning, depending on the context. This seems to be similar to the range of the use of the word *deva* in Sanskrit.

whether the expression *devānaṃpiya* was exclusively associated with Aśoka must be answered in the negative.[2] Among the five variant versions of Rock Edict VIII (Cunningham 1877, p. 76) referring to journeys undertaken by previous kings, only the Khalsi version uses *devānaṃpiyā* to refer to these previous kings, while other versions use *ne raya* (Shahbazgarhi), *rājano* (Girnar), *lājāno* (Dhauli), and *lājā* (Jaugada).[3] We must thus agree with D. R. Bhandarkar (1969: 6) that "Devānāṃpriya was an auspicious mode of address used with reference to kings. And, as a matter of fact, the Dīpavaṃsa (XI.14, 19, 20, 25 etc.) applies the appellation Devānāṃpriya to Tissa, the ruler of Ceylon and contemporary of Aśoka, and often employs it alone to denote that king." Bhandarkar further points out that the term *devānāṃpriya* is used in the Nāgārjunī Hill Cave inscriptions to designate a king called Daśaratha, who has been identified to be the grandson of Aśoka. Thus, quite clearly the term is used for several generations within this dynasty to refer to kings. I will later come back to the use of this term in Sri Lankan records.

We also need to look at the use of the terms *deva* and *devī* in Mauryan inscriptions to get some further understanding of *devānaṃpiya*.[4] Of these two terms, the term *devī* clearly seems to be used in the sense of a queen, see *devinaṃ, deviye, devīye*, for queens, and *devikumālānaṃ* referring to princes, sons of the queens, Murti and Aiyangar 1951: 118, 132; also see Woolner 1924, pt. II, p. 96. The term *deva* on the other hand has been variously interpreted especially in the context of the

2 A clearly related term *devāṇuppiya* occurs in Jain texts like *Bhagavatisūtra* (15.7), *Vivāgasuya* (1.11, 1.22), *Ovavāiyasutta* (18), and *Rāyapaseṇiyasutta* (1.7). These are just a few sample references. The term occurs widely. Bollée (2002: 34) translates the term merely with "folks," and offers a philological history on p. 261. G. T. Deshpande (1969: 204, fn. 1) informs: "The term *devāṇuppiya* is equated by Hoernle and Pischel with Deva+anupriya; but most of the scholars take it as a variant of Devānāṃpriya. Prof. K. V. Vaidya equates it so. This use has been noted by E. Hultzsch in his introduction to the Inscriptions of Aśoka, Vol. I, pp. xxix–xxx. It is noted by Barua and Sen also." We should also note that the late Jain tradition does not seem to see any connection between the Sanskrit term *devānāṃpriya* and the old Prakrit term *devāṇuppiya*. Hemacandra (11th century CE) in his *Abhidhānacintāmaṇi* (stanzas 352–3) says that the term *devānāṃpriya* refers to a fool. The terms *devānāṃpriya* and *devāṇuppiya* remind me of the Marāṭhī honorific term *rājamānya* lit. "honored by the king." But in its actual use, it was used only as an honorific. Similar was the Marāṭhī use of *rājaśrī*. Letters in the generation of my grandfather would often begin with the abbreviation "*rā. rā.*," a shortened form for *rājamānya rājaśrī*. However, the term *lokamānya* as a title of Lokamānya Tilak was deliberately coined to contrast those recognized by the kings (of old, including the British rulers) and those new leaders now recognized by the people at large (*loka*). So even the conventional terms do not often lose their basic etymological meaning.

3 Hettiarachchy (1972: 47) further adds: "*Devānaṃpiya* in the Second Separate Edict at Dhauli corresponds to the *lājā* of the Jaugada text."

4 It may be noted that while a number of scholars have suggested that the Achaemenid inscriptions may have provided a template for Aśokan inscriptions, Aśoka's references to *devas* are far too few and generic to stand comparison with the Old Persian inscriptions like the Behistan inscription of Darius: "Saith Darius the King: By the favor of Ahuramazda I am King; Ahuramazda bestowed the kingdom upon me. . . .These are the countries which came unto me; by the favor of Ahuramazda. . . . By the favor of Ahuramazda, they were my subjects. . . .By the favor of Ahuramazda these countries showed respect toward my law. . . . Ahuramazda bore me aid until I got possession of this kingdom; by the favor of Ahuramazda I hold this kingdom." (Kent 1950: 119)

Yerragudi rock edict (*iminā ca kālena amisā munisā devehi te dāni misibhutā*, Murti and Aiyangar 1951: 72) and the Maski Edict (*pure jambu[dipa]si ye amisā devā husu te dāni misibhutā*, Murti and Aiyangar 1951: 86). The statement contained in these edicts, namely that previously the *devas* were not mixed with men, and now they are mixed with men, has been variously interpreted in modern scholarship.[5] Assuming that the term *deva* refers to gods, there is still a question of where exactly do the men and gods mingle. Do the gods appear on earth, as they do in numberless Buddhist stories, to meet holy enlightened men like the Buddha? Or do men, on account of their dharmic behavior go to heaven and there mingle with gods?[6] The Vedic expression *miśrā devebhiḥ* is an exact parallel to the Aśokan inscription, and the Vedic expression clearly refers to gods, rather than to kings. But the word *deva* begins to appear in the meaning of 'king' only in non-Vedic and post-Vedic Sanskrit literature. On the other hand, Sylvain Lévi (1911: 124) suggests that the word *devā* in *amisā devā husu* refers to kings. Considering the widespread use of *deva* for king and *devī* for queen in the Sanskrit and Prakrit/Pali literature, and the conclusive use of *devī* for queen in Aśokan inscriptions themselves, Levi's interpretation is not to be easily cast aside. What Aśoka may be saying is that previously the kings used to stay away from the people, while now under his rule they mingle with the subjects. This is a possibility. Coming back to our main concern with the expression *devānāṃ priya* as seen in Aśoka's usage, the term may then either mean "beloved of the gods" or possibly "beloved of the kings."[7] The second alternative that I have proposed finds support in Vedic passages where one is praying to become dear to gods, kings, and equals:

5 On these passages, see: Lévi (1911), Filliozat (1949), Meile (1949), Schlingloff (1985), and Schmithausen (1992). Norman (2001: 65), after reviewing previous research, comments: "This statement has been variously interpreted, e.g., as processions with effigies of gods, or as public appearances of the king, or as gods actually visiting men on earth. I take it to mean that Aśoka had succeeded in bringing men to heaven, where of course they would be reborn as gods, i.e., mixed with other gods. In this interpretation of the phrase 'mixed, i.e., associated, with the gods' I agree with Schmithausen, who shows clearly that the expression *misaṃdevā* or *misā devehi* refers to the attainment of heaven after death."

6 This second interpretation has clear antecedents in the Vedic literature. Compare: *kramadhvam agninā nākam ukhyān hasteṣu bibhrataḥ / divaspṛṣṭhaṃ svar gatvā miśrā devebhir ādhvam, Śaunakīya Atharvaveda*, 4.14.2, rendered by Whitney as: "Stride ye with the fire to the firmament, bearing in your hands vessel-[fires]; having gone to the back of the sky, to the heaven, sit ye mingled with the gods." Whitney, *Atharvaveda Saṃhitā*, Vol. I, p. 170. Whitney also cites parallels from the *Vājasaneyi Saṃhitā* (xvii.65), *Taittirīya Samhitā* (iv.6.5), and *Maitrāyaṇī Saṃhitā* (ii.10.6).

7 There is a further question of what the word *priya* means in *devānāṃpriya*. Hara (1969: 14), using the analysis of Scheller (1958), proposes: "the word means primarily 'one's own' and not 'dear to' or 'beloved of' as it does in the later Sanskrit literature." Hara takes the term to mean "son of gods" and connects this to the Hindu notion that a king is an incarnation of gods. While Hara's interpretation may find further support in Kushan kings using the epithet *devaputra* to refer to themselves on their coins (see: B. Chattopadhyaya 1967: 32), in my view the meaning "dear, pleasing" for the word *priya* is already present in Vedic passages, and one cannot argue that *priya* in *devānāṃpriya* means something different from the immediately next word, i.e., *priyadarśī* in Aśokan inscriptions. In Pali, the word *piya* is often followed by its synonym *manāpa*, "pleasing."

priyam mā kuru deveṣu, "Make me dear among the gods." *Ṛgveda Khila* 10.128.11a, *Śaunakīya Atharvaveda* 19.62.1a, *Paippalāda Atharvaveda* 2.32.5a, *Hiraṇyakeśi Gṛhyasūtra* 1.10.6a.

priyam mā kuru rājasu, "Make me dear among the kings." *Hiraṇyakeśi Gṛhyasūtra* 1.10.6d.

priyaḥ samānānām bhūyāsam, "May I become dear to my equals." *Śaunakīya Atharvaveda* 17.1.5f.

Aśoka does not use the term *samrāṭ* to put himself above other kings, but just uses the term *rājā/lājā* to refer to himself. If the word *deva* also refers to a king, then a possible understanding of *devānāṃpriya* is that Aśoka would ideally like to rule his empire by endearing himself to the kings he may have subdued as well as his neighboring kings. However, this probably did not preclude Aśoka's contemporaries from reading a theological meaning into this term and reacting to it in their own ways.

Vedic Usage of *priya* with *deva*

In order to get a better sense of what Aśoka may have meant by the term *devānāṃ priya*, and, moreover, how it may have been read by others, both his contemporaries and later generations, we can take a look at the related usages in the Vedic literature. A [convenient electronic] search through Bloomfield's *Vedic Concordance* shows that the Vedic literature is replete with usage of the word *priya* with generic gods, as well as with specific Vedic gods, and others. I am documenting some of this data below:

[A] Usages of *priya* with specific gods and others

priyam indrābhirakṣasi, "O Indra, you protect the one dear to you." *Rgveda* 10.86.4b, *Śaunakīya Atharvaveda* 20.126.4b.

priyaṃ mā kuru rājasu, "Make me dear among the gods." *Hiraṇyakeśi Grhyasūtra* 1.10.6d.

priyaḥ samānānāṃ bhūyāsam, "May I become dear to my equals." *Śaunakīya Atharvaveda* 17.1.5f.

priyāḥ devasya savituḥ syāma, "May we become dear to god Savitṛ." *Ṛgveda* 2.38.10d, *Maitrāyaṇī Saṃhitā* 4.14.6d, *Taittirīya Brāhmana* 2.8.6.3d.

[B][8] Usages of *priya* with generic *deva*, where *priya* precedes *deva*

priyaṃ devānām apy etu pāthaḥ, "Let it go upon the dear path of the gods." *Śaunakīya Atharvaveda* 2.34.2d, *Paippalāda Atharvaveda*

8 G. T. Deshpande (1971: 212–213) cites *priyo devānāṃ . . . bhūyāsam*, and provides *Yajurveda* XVI.1,2 and *Yajurveda* XXXVI.18 as textual references.

3.32.3d, *Kāṭhaka Saṃhitā* 30.8, *Taittirīya Brāhmaṇa* 3.1.1.4d.

priyaṃ devebhyo mā kuru, "Make me dear to the gods." *Paippalāda Atharvaveda* 5.14.7b.

priyaṃ mā kuru deveṣu, "Make me dear among the gods." *Rgveda Khila* 10.128.11a, *Śaunakīya Atharvaveda* 19.62.1a, *Paippalāda Atharvaveda* 2.32.5a, *Hiraṇyakeśi Gṛhyasūtra* 1.10.6a.

priyo devānāṃ, "dear to the gods." *Ṛgveda* 10.16.8b, *Śaunakīya Atharvaveda* 18.3.53b, *Taittirīya Āraṇyaka* 6.1.4b.

priyo devānām, "dear to the gods." *Vājasaneyi Saṃhitā* 26.2, *Ṛgveda* 10.56.1d, *Śaunakīya Atharvaveda* 18.3.7d, *Sāmaveda* 1.65d, *Kāṭhaka Saṃhitā* 35.17d, *Taittirīya Āraṇyaka* 6.3.1d, *Mānava Śrautasūtra* 3.4.1d.

aditiḥ . . . priyā devānām, "Aditi, dear to the gods." *Kāṭhaka Saṃhitā* 1.11.

[C] Usages of *priya* after *deva* with intervening words

tvaṃ devānāṃ bhava priyaḥ, "May you become dear to the gods." *Paippalāda Atharvaveda* 10.2.7c.

[D] The word *devānām* directly followed by *priya*

tvaṃ viśveṣāṃ devānāṃ priyam pātho 'pīhi, "path dear to the gods." *Vājasaneyi Saṃhitā* 8.50, *Vājasaneyi Saṃhitā-Kāṇva* 8.22.4, *Śatapatha Brāhmaṇa* 11.5.9.12, *Taittirīya Saṃhitā* 3.3.3.3, *Maitrāyaṇī Saṃhitā* 1.3.36, *Kāṭhaka Saṃhitā* 30.6

devānāṃ priyeṇa nāmnā, "name dear to the gods." *Maitrāyaṇī Saṃhitā* 1.1.12: 7.17; 4.1.13: 18.8.

devānāṃ priyeṇa dhāmnā, "by the abode dear to the gods." *Kāṭhaka Saṃhitā* 1.11.

From the above sample citations, it is clear that the terms *devānāṃ* and *priya* do not occur as a compound form in the Vedic usage. In preponderant usages, the word *priya* occurs before *deva*, and in a large number of cases where *deva* occurs before *priya*, other words intervene. Even in an example like *devā́nāṃ priyám* [*Vājasaneyi Saṃhitā* 8.50] where each word retains an *udātta* syllable, the accents indicate that there is no compounding. Thus, the Vedic usage gives us no indication of an honorific usage of the term, and yet it gives us some indication how the Aśokan expression could have been read by the followers of the Vedic tradition and how they may have perhaps felt some shock that a king who became a Buddhist was, dishonestly in their perception, calling himself *devānāṃ priyaḥ*. The *Bhagavadgītā* (12.14–20) essentially continues the Vedic usage of "*priya* of god(s)," though indicating the new direction of *bhakti* through frequent use of expressions like *sa me priyaḥ*. In its own way, the *Bhagavadgītā* seems to fulfill the request seen in the

Vedic texts: *priyo devānāṃ. . . bhūyāsam*, "May I become dear to the gods?" If the *bhakti* portions of the *Bhagavadgītā* are post-Aśokan, as is assumed by many scholars, one may see the assertions in the *Bhagavadgītā* as a post-Aśokan revival of the days of devotees/sacrificers returning to the state of being *devānāṃ priya* in a neo-Vedic sense, a neo-Vedic reaction to the use of this expression by the Mauryas. A similar approach is indicated by the *Bodhāyana Gṛhyaśeṣa Sūtra* (1.25.15): *yo devasya priyo vidvān devasya padam āpnuyāt*, "the wise one, dear to God, will go to the abode of God" [cited by Palsule 1969: 138], see *madbhaktaḥ . . . yaḥ sa mām eti, Bhagavadgītā* 11.55.

The reactions of the Brahmanical tradition to the claims of the Mauryas are recorded in the various *Purāṇas*[9].

> *tataḥ kalau sampravṛtte sammohāya suradviṣām / buddho nāmāñjana-sutaḥ kīkaṭeṣu bhaviṣyati // Bhāgavata Purāṇa,* Canto 1, Chapter 3, verse 24.
>
> Then, after the Kali age begins, there will be the Buddha [incarnation of Viṣṇu], son of Añjana, in the region of Kīkaṭa, in order to delude the haters of the gods, the demons.
>
> *devadviṣāṃ nigamavartmani niṣṭhitānām / pūrbhir mayena vihitābhir adṛśyatūrbhiḥ / lokān ghnatāṃ mati-vimoham ati-pralobham / veśaṃ vidhāya bahu bhāṣyata aupadharmyam // Bhāgavata Purāṇa*, Canto 2, Chapter 7, verse 37.
>
> The Lord [Viṣṇu having assumed the form of the Buddha], wearing an appearance that was very attractive and capable of deluding the minds [of onlookers], spoke a great deal of pseudo-*dharma* [to delude] those demons, haters of gods, who were steadfast on the Vedic path and [yet] were destroying the worlds with the flying fortresses, designed by Maya, which were invisible and fast-moving.[10]
>
> *vādair vimohayati yajñakṛto 'tadarhān / śūdrān kalau kṣitibhujo nyahaniṣyad ante // Bhāgavata Purāṇa*, Canto 11, Chapter 4, verse 22.
>
> With his doctrines, [the Buddha-incarnation of Viṣṇu] deluded the Śūdra kings during the Kali age, who were conducting Vedic sacrifices, though actually being ineligible to do so, and finally he destroyed them.

9 Among these *Purāṇas*, some like the *Viṣṇu Purāṇa* are old, while others like the *Bhāgavata Purāṇa*, *Skanda Purāṇa*, and *Agni Purāṇa* are relatively late. However, in many cases the later *Purāṇas* seem to copy the wording of older *Purāṇas*, indicating a degree of continuity of narratives.

10 To a modern Hindu reader, this characterization of the Buddha is so shocking that there is an urge to somehow interpret this verse to save the Buddha as we know him. A. C. Bhaktivedanta Swami Prabhupada, commenting on this verse of the *Bhāgavata Purāṇa* (Second Canto, Part II, p. 396, Bhaktivedanta Book Trust, New York, 1972), says: "This incarnation of Lord Buddha is not exactly the same Buddha incarnation as we have in the present history of mankind. According to Śrīla Jīva Gosvāmī, the Buddha incarnation mentioned in this verse appeared in a different Kali age."

Skanda Purāṇa, Kāśīkhaṇḍa (4), Chapter 58, pp. 403–407.

vakṣye buddhāvatāraṃ ca paṭhataḥ śṛṇvato 'rthadam / purā devāsure yuddhe daityair devāḥ parājitāḥ // rakṣa rakṣeti śaraṇam vadanto jagmur īśvaram / māyāmohasvarūpo 'sau śuddhodanasuto 'bhavat // mohayāmāsa daityāṃs tāṃs tyājitā vedadharmakam / te ca bauddhā babhūvur hi . . . // Agni Purāṇa, 16.1–3.

I will narrate the Buddha-incarnation [of Viṣṇu] that grants the wishes of those who recite it and those who listen to it. In ancient times, in the battles between gods and demons, the gods were defeated by the demons. Saying 'save me, save me,' they took refuge in the Lord [Viṣṇu]. Assuming a form of illusion and delusion, he became the son of Śuddhodana, and deluded the demons, and he made them abandon the Vedic dharma. Thus they became the followers of the Buddha.

With such passages, we see the *Purāṇas* staking a claim that Viṣṇu appeared in the form of Buddha and Mahāvīra to delude the Asuras into believing in the anti-Vedic doctrines of Buddhism and Jainism, and once the Asuras were so deluded, the gods were able to destroy them without any feeling of guilt.[11] The followers of Buddhism and Jainism, especially the kings, are referred to not just as Asuras,[12] they are called *suradviṣ* and *devadviṣ* "haters of gods," quite a contrast from the Mauryan self-description as *devānāṃ priya*, and especially the expression *śūdrān kṣitibhujaḥ* is a clear reference to kings like Mahāpadma Nanda[13] and the Mauryas, who were described by the *Purāṇas* as Śūdras who usurped the rule of the earth: *tataḥ prabhṛti śūdrā bhūpālāḥ bhaviṣyanti, Viṣṇu Purāṇa*, 4.24.21, and *tato nṛpā bhaviṣyanti śūdraprāyās tv adhārmikāḥ, Bhāgavata Purāṇa*, Canto 12, Chapter 1, verse 9.

11 For an insightful study of such Purāṇic narratives, see P. S. Jaini (1977).

12 A. J. Karandikar (1962: 7), a Hindu nationalist historian, finds a "hidden" reference in the *Mahābhārata* to Aśoka as an incarnation of a great Asura named Aśva: *yas tv aśva iti vikhyātaḥ śrīmān āsīn mahāsuraḥ / aśoka iti rājābhūn mahāvīryo 'parājitaḥ //*. This verse is found in the Critical Edition of the *Mahābhārata* (1.61.14). The text of the *Mahābhārata* gives no clue that this is a reference to our Aśoka, and yet Karandikar's attempt reveals how the Brahmanical mind can read such texts. Karandikar (1962: 16) says that from the point of view of the Hindus, the kingdom of Aśoka was not a Rāmarājya, but a Rāvaṇarājya. Karandikar (1962: 44) further relies upon the late Sanskrit grammarians who interpret *devānāṃpriya* to refer to an animal that is offered in sacrifice to gods, and says that by using this title for himself, Aśoka wanted to stop the animal sacrifices. From the Hindu nationalist point of view, Aśoka's *ahiṃsā* weakened the "nation," as did Gandhi's.

13 *mahānandisuto rājan śūdrīgarbhodbhavo balī / mahāpadmapatiḥ kaścin nandaḥ kṣatravināśakṛt // sa ekacchatrāṃ pṛthivīm anullaṅghitaśāsanaḥ / śāsiṣyati mahāpadmo dvitīya iva bhārgavaḥ // Bhāgavata Purāṇa*, Canto 12, Chapter 1, verses 8, 10. Also: *mahānandinas tataḥ śūdrāgarbhodbhavo 'tilubdho 'tibalo mahāpadmanāmā nandaḥ paraśurāma ivāparo 'khilakṣatrāntakārī bhaviṣyati / Viṣṇu Purāṇa*, 4.24.20–21.

Sanskrit Grammarians and *devānāṃpriya*

The history of the expression *devānāṃpriya* in the Sanskrit grammatical tradition is most interesting, and convoluted at the same time. For a detailed and yet convoluted explanation, let me quote from Radha Kumud Mookerji (1962: 108, fn. 3):

> The form *devānāṃ-priya* instead of *deva-priya* would be an epithet of contempt under a rule of Pāṇini [vi.3.21], but is mentioned among the exceptions of the rule by Kātyāyana (about 350 B.C. according to Sir R. G. Bhandarkar), supported by Patañjali (150 B.C.) and even the Kāśikā (A.D. 650). The exception is not, however, allowed by the later grammarian, Bhaṭṭojidīkṣita, who insists on taking *devānāṃpriya* as a contempt term implying a fool (*mūrkha*) devoid of the knowledge of Brahma, and hence addicted only to sacrifices and offerings by which they please gods, as cows please men by offering milk (vide *Tattvabodhinī* and *Bālamanoramā*). Thus a title which was complimentary during the Nandas, Mauryas, and Śuṅgas, suffers a deterioration in sense under later Brahmanical prejudice against the most distinguished Buddhist monarch.[14]

There is no indication in Pāṇini's grammar that he himself was particularly concerned with this expression. But Kātyāyana and Patañjali have paid attention to this expression. One of the first features that begins to appear is the recognition in Kātyāyana's *Vārttika* (*devānāṃpriya iti ca*) on Pāṇini 6.3.21 (*ṣaṣṭhyā ākrośe*) that *devānāṃpriya* is a compound expression (*samāsa*). The exceptional feature of this compound is that the case-ending after the first member of this compound has not been deleted. Pāṇini's rule 6.3.21 says that if the compound expression denotes a sense of *ākrośa* "accusation," then the genitive case-ending after the first member of such a compound is not deleted (*aluk*). The other well-known compound of this type is *dāsyāḥputra*, which is an expression of cursing, rather than literally stating that someone happens to be the son of a maid. The normal compound *dāsīputra* can serve that plain indicative function. What Kātyāyana seems to recognize is that such a non-deletion of the genitive case-ending takes place in some cases even when there is no sense of accusation. The example *devānāṃpriya* is one such example. Kātyāyana suggests that a separate provision for this expression needs to be made. Had the expression any accusatory meaning, one could derive it by the rule of Pāṇini as it stands, and it would not need a special provision. This point is gradually lost in the later versions of this *Vārttika* as seen in the works of Bhaṭṭoji Dīkṣita. On the same rule, Kātyāyana also makes a provision for Vedic names like Divodāsa, that clearly do not have any accusatory meaning. The treatment of *devānāṃpriya* by Kātyāyana makes it clear that the order of words *devānāṃ* and *priya* has now become invariant, and perhaps, like most other compounds, the two words have now

14 The last assertion of Mookerji that the sense of the term changed under later Brahmanical prejudice against the most distinguished Buddhist monarch is shared by Chaturvedi (1935). As I have discussed, there is no evidence to support this view.

developed one single *udātta* accent. These would be the external signs of compounding. While the Aśokan edicts exhibit the invariant order of *devānāṃ* and *priya*, we do not have an attested example in an accented post-Vedic text to verify if the expression developed a single *udātta* accent. There is no sign of such a development in the available Vedic accented texts, and it is most likely a post-Vedic development, perhaps contemporary with the Aśokan Prakrits. The one thing that is clear from Kātyāyana's *Vārttika* is that the word *devānāṃpriya* did not have any accusatory meaning in his opinion, because otherwise it would have been covered by Pāṇini's rule 6.3.21 (*ṣaṣṭhyā ākrośe*).

On the other hand, we see Patañjali adding significant information regarding the use of this expression as an honorific term. Commenting on Pāṇini 5.3.14 (*itarābhyo 'pi dṛśyante*), Patañjali says that the rule should be restricted to a specific group of words beginning with *bhavat* (*bhavadādi*). This group of words is fully specified by Patañjali: *bhavān*, *dīrghāyuḥ*, *devānāṃpriyaḥ*, and *āyuṣmān*, *Mahābhāṣya* (Kielhorn edition, Vol. II, p. 405). From Patañjali's discussion of these words and the usages cited by him, it is clear that the term *devānāṃpriya* is just a plain honorific term, similar to the other words listed by him.

Beyond these two occurrences of *devānāṃpriya*, there is a third occurrence of the term in the *Mahābhāṣya* on Pāṇini 2.4.56 (*ajer vy aghañapoḥ*), a rule that teaches substitution of the root *aj* with *vi* under certain conditions. Here we have an imagined conversation between a chariot-driver (*sūta*) and a grammarian (*vaiyākaraṇa*):

> *evaṃ hi kaścid vaiyākaraṇa āha / ko 'sya rathasya praveteti / sūta āha / āyuṣmann ahaṃ prājiteti / vaiyākaraṇa āha apaśabda iti / sūta āha prāptijño devānāṃpriyo na tv iṣṭijña iṣyata etad rūpam iti /* *Mahābhāṣya* (Kielhorn edn., Vol. I, p. 488)

> Thus a certain grammarian said: "Who is the driver (*pravetā*) of this chariot?" The driver said: "Sir, I am the driver (*prājitā*)." The grammarian said: "[The word *prājitā* for a driver] is incorrect." The driver said: "You, beloved of the gods (*devānāṃpriya*), know only what obtains from the rules of grammar,[15] but not what is actually desired in the usage. This usage (= *prājitā*, instead of *pravetā* of the grammarian) is the desired form.

The grammarian clearly takes offense at this rebuke by the driver (*āho khalv anena durutena bādhyāmahe*) and uses the word *dur-uta* to mean "a bad driver" to refer to

15 Patañjali elsewhere seems to suggest that there are normative speakers of good Sanskrit, the *śiṣṭas*, who do not learn Sanskrit by using the *Aṣṭādhyāyī* of Pāṇini, and yet fluently speak good Sanskrit. To explain this miraculous event, Patañjali says that it must be their innate nature (*svabhāva*) or the grace of some divinity (*daivānugraha*), that these people can speak good Sanskrit without any effort, *Mahābhāṣya* (Kielhon. edn.) on Pāṇini 6.3.109, Vol. III, p. 174. The implication here is those who are graced by a divinity do not need to make deliberate effort. This may also account for the sarcastic use of *devānāṃpriya* in the above passage. The grammarian may think he is graced by a divinity and need not make any deliberate effort to go beyond the rules of grammar to take note of actual usage in the world. That makes him appear foolish.

the driver. But then the driver points out that the word *dur-uta* is incorrect, and that if the grammarian correctly wishes to curse, he should use the word *duḥ-sūta* (*sūta āha / na khalu veñaḥ sūtaḥ, suvater eva sūto, yadi kutsā prayoktavyā duḥsūteneti vaktavyam, Mahābhāṣya*, Kielhorn edn., Vol. I, p. 488). It is quite clear that Patañjali is poking fun at the obstinate grammarian who is not willing to adjust his grammar to the changing usage. The use of *devānāṃpriya* in this passage is clearly sarcastic, and this is similar to Patañjali's sarcastic use of the expression *tatrabhavān*, which is normally used as an honorific:

> *kiṃ ca bhoḥ ślokā api pramāṇam / kiṃ cātaḥ / yadi pramāṇam ayam api ślokaḥ pramāṇaṃ bhavitum arhati / yad udumbaravarṇānāṃ ghaṭīnāṃ maṇḍalaṃ mahat / pītaṃ na gamayet svargaṃ kiṃ tat kratugataṃ nayet // iti / pramattagīta eṣa tatrabhavato, yas tv apramattagītas tat pramāṇam / Mahābhāṣya* (Kielhorn edn., Vol. I, p. 3).
>
> O Sir, are even [cited] verses to be treated as authoritative?
> What is the problem?
> If [all cited verses] are authoritative, then even this verse should be authoritative:
>
> > If drinking a whole chain of a hundred [wine] pots, with the color of figs, does not lead one to heaven, how could it do so when drunk during a sacrifice?
>
> This verse was recited by his honor (*tatrabhavataḥ*) when he was under delusion. A verse recited when one is not under delusion can be authoritative.

In this passage, it is clear that Patañjali is using the word *tatrabhavān* sarcastically, while elsewhere he uses it as a normal honorific (see use of *tatrabhavat* in reference to the sages Yarvāṇastarvāṇaḥ, *Mahābhāṣya*, Kielhorn edn., Vol. I, p. 11). Thus the sarcastic use of a word need not change the basic meaning of a word, since any normal expression can be used sarcastically.[16] There is one interesting indication built in this passage that could be of some significance. What sort of behavior prompted Patañjali to speak sarcastically using a normal honorific expression? It looks like the verse cited questions the validity of Vedic ritual practices, and this seems to invoke Patañjali's ire. Any "honorable" person who speaks in such a manner about Vedic sacrifices must indeed be *pramatta* "deluded, intoxicated." The verse could have come from a Lokāyata, Buddhist, or Jaina author poking fun at the Vedic sacrifices, and Patañjali's response to such insinuations is that these speakers are in delusion, and this prompts his sarcastic use of *tatrabhavat*. As I have discussed elsewhere, Kātyāyana and Patañjali are firm defenders of the Vedic tradition and for them Sanskrit grammar is first and foremost a tool to preserve the Vedas (*rakṣārthaṃ vedānām adhyeyaṃ vyākaraṇam, Mahabhāṣya*, Kielhorn edn., Vol. I, p. 1). If the honorific *tatrabhavat* can be used sarcastically to refer to those heterodox disputants who denigrate the Vedas, one can easily imagine how Brahmans with the mindset of Patañjali may have looked at the use of the term

16 Hara (1969) has examined sarcastic use of other expressions in Sanskrit.

devānāṃpriya in the inscriptions of Aśoka who became a Buddhist and used the royal treasury to construct eighty-four thousand[17] Buddhist *stūpas*. The proclamations of *ahiṃsā* in his inscriptions may have put limitations on the performance of Brahmanical sacrifices involving immolation of animals. We should note that while Aśokan edicts do not expressly show anti-Brahman discourse, it is clear that while there are Mauryan donative inscriptions in favor of Buddhists and Ājīvikas, there is not a single donative inscription that I know that is in favor of the Brahmans.

This is where I would like to mention the four other celebrated references in Patañjali's *Mahābhāṣya*:

> [A] *mauryair hiraṇyārthibhir arcāḥ prakalpitāḥ / bhavet tāsu na syāt / yāḥ samprati pūjārthās tāsu bhaviṣyati / Mahābhāṣya*, Kielhorn edn., Vol. II, p. 429.
>
> [B] *iha puṣyamitraṃ yājayāmaḥ / Mahābhāṣya*, Kielhorn edn., Vol. II, p. 123.[18]
>
> [C] *candraguptasabhā / puṣyamitrasabhā / Mahābhāṣya*, Kielhorn edn., Vol. I, p. 177
>
> [D] *yeṣāṃ ca virodhaḥ [śāśvatikaḥ P.2.4.9] ity asya avakāśaḥ / śramaṇa-brāhmaṇam / Mahābhāṣya*, Kielhorn edn., Vol. I, p. 476.

These passages have been extensively discussed and debated in available research, see: R. G. Bhandarkar (1933: 148ff). Without getting into the textual and philological issues, the cumulative conclusions that can be drawn are as follows. Patañjali's *samprati*, "now, these days," refers to the immediate post-Mauryan period. At the very least the passage indicates that in Patañjali's eye's, the Mauryas—lusting after gold—did something or other to the images of gods. It is not clear what the expression *arcāḥ prakalpitāḥ* exactly means.[19] However, the

17 The number 84,000 for the *stūpas* constructed by Aśoka is not a historical number, but a trope that is shared by the Buddhist narratives of Aśoka with other Buddhist texts like the *Saddharmapuṇḍarīkasūtra* (p. 239) and the *Samādhirājasūtra* (p. 218), which describe other kings and Bodhisattvas building 84,000 (or larger multiples of this number) *stūpas*. John Strong, during his presentation at this symposium, brought out these shared similarities. The connection of the *Saddharmapuṇḍarīka* (p. 239) story with Aśoka is even stronger, since as Strong pointed out, the Bodhisattva constructing these *stūpas* is named Sarvasattvapriyadarśana, a likely allusion to Aśoka's common title Priyadarśin in his inscriptions.

18 For multiple references to Puṣyamitra (varient reading: Puṣpamitra) performing sacrifices, see: *Mahābhāṣya*, Vol. II, p. 34. The *Aśokāvadāna* (133) describes Puṣyamitra, aided by his "non-believer" Brahman minister, planning to destroy Buddhist shrines and monasteries: *rājñāśokena caturaśītidharmarājikāsahasraṃ sthāpitam atas tasya nāma ciraṃ tiṣṭhati / bhavāṃś cet tāni nāśayed bhavato nāma ciratarаṃ sthāsyati /*.

19 The passage is taken by the commentators of the *Mahābhāṣya* to mean that the Mauryans prepared for sale the images of gods. The word "for sale" (*vikretum*) is not there in the text of Patañjali, but supplied by the commentators. For a detailed discussion of these passages, see R. G. Bhandarkar (1933: 148ff). The historical situation of the state of iconography of gods during the Mauryan period is unclear. The Buddha himself is not iconographically represented at this time as a human figure. As against whatever disrespect to Hindu gods shown by the gold-driven Mauryas reported by Patañjali, the inscriptions seem to depict a rather different picture. Von Glasenapp (1970: 19) remarks: "The importance of

subsequent sentence *yās tv etāḥ samprati pūjārthāḥ* clearly seems to suggest that in the post-Mauryan "today" of Patañjali, the images of gods were worshipped or perhaps worshipped again. There is indeed some suggestion of change in the treatment of images of gods from the Mauryan period to that of Patañjali. The passage *iha puṣyamitraṃ yājayāmaḥ* minimally seems to tell us that Vedic sacrifices were being performed by and for Puṣyamitra. While there are clear inscriptions of the later imperial Guptas performing Vedic sacrifices, one must again note that Mauryan inscriptions make no reference to Aśoka or his Mauryan successors performing any Vedic sacrifices like Aśvamedha or Rājasūya. So Patañjali does seem to indicate some sort of neo-Vedic revival under Puṣyamitra. The passage C is a reference to the courts of Candragupta and Puṣyamitra. The non-mention of Aśoka in this passage is perhaps very loud, deliberate and symptomatic of Brahmanical reactions to Aśoka. The later Brahmanical tradition has retained significant memories of Candragupta and Puṣyamitra, as seen in Sanskrit dramas like the *Mudrārākṣasa* and the *Mālavikāgnimitra*, but there is no Brahmanical parallel to the Buddhist *Avadānas* dedicated to stories about Aśoka, even negative ones depicting him as a Kālāśoka or a Caṇḍāśoka from the Hindu point of view. That makes one wonder if this began as a systematic strategy on the part of the *Purāṇa* authors.[20]

The passage D is also revealing for our understanding of Patañjali's attitudes as against what one sees in Aśoka's inscriptions. A. C. Woolner (1924: 140) in his *Glossary* of Aśokan inscriptions lists all the occurrences of the compound *samaṇabambhaṇa* in Aśoka's inscriptions. In all the occurrences, the inscriptions use this compound in plural, and the context seems to indicate that Aśoka is referring to two equally respected groups. The Aśokan usage is parallel to the use of the compound *samaṇabrāhmaṇa* in Pali texts like the *Suttanipāta*: *samaṇabrāhmaṇāse* (nom. pl.), 5.7.3–6; *samaṇabrāhmaṇā*, 3.2.17 and 4.10.12. In Patañjali's usage, the compound *śramaṇabrāhmaṇa* can only be used as a collective *dvandva* (*samāhāradvandva*), in neuter singular, referring to two groups that are in permanent conflict, like the compound *ahinakulam*, "snake-n-mongoose." It seems most likely that here we have two parallel streams of linguistic usage, one represented by the Aśokan inscriptions and the Pali texts like the *Suttanipāta* on one hand, and Patañjali's neo-Vedic Brahmans on the other. For Patañjali, there is a permanent conflict between the *śramaṇas* and the *brāhmaṇas*.

popular belief in gods is confirmed by the edicts of the emperor Ashoka. In the fourth rock-edict the 'Lord Beloved of the Gods' says that he showed his subjects images of gods and columns of flame (perhaps images of the fires of hell) together with processions of elephants, and that this resulted in a considerable uplift of general morals." Perhaps the *Mahābhāṣya* passage is referring to these displays of the images by the Mauryas, but then it is not clear how the characterization *hiraṇyārthibhiḥ* can be explained. Perhaps they collected the offerings made to the images of gods, an aspect not evident from the Aśokan inscriptions. Nonetheless it is clear that the stature of Vedic gods is considerably diminished within Buddhism: "One of their functions is to proclaim the Buddha's glory, and always to venerate him," von Glasenapp (1970: 23). This may have been taken as an offence by the Vedic worshippers of those gods.

20 "It is interesting to note that the Purāṇa says nothing of the Mauryan achievements, or of the westward expansion of the empire." R. Morton Smith (1973: 362).

The next significant landmark in the tradition of Sanskrit grammar as regards the expression *devānāṃpriya* is the comment of Kaiyaṭa, a Kashmiri grammarian of the early 11th century CE, in his commentary *Pradīpa* on Patañjali's *Mahābhāṣya*. Of the three places in the *Mahābhāṣya* where the term *devānāṃpriya* occurs, Kaiyaṭa has absolutely not a word to say where the term is clearly used as a normal honorific title. On the passage of the *Mahābhāṣya* where Patañjali uses the term sarcastically in the conversation between a chariot-driver and a grammarian, Kaiyaṭa, without noting that the word is used sarcastically, offers a straightforward negative interpretation:

> *devānāṃpriya iti / devaśabdo mūrkhavācī / mūrkhāṇāṃ ca priyā mūrkhā eva bhavanti / athavā sukhāsaktatayā śāstre 'nabhiyogo 'nena pratipādyate /* Kaiyaṭa's *Pradīpa*, Nirṇayasāgara edn. of the *Mahābhāṣya*, Vol. II, p. 558, on Pāṇini 2.4.56.
>
> *Devānāṃpriya*. Here the word *deva* refers to fools.[21] Those who are dear to fools can only be fools. Or perhaps this expression indicates non-engagement in *śāstra* [on the part of those beloved of the gods] because they are addicted to pleasure.

It is interesting note that while Kaiyaṭa correctly grasps that the expression *devānāṃpriya* in this context has a negative force, he fails to indicate that this negative force is there because a positive term is being used sarcastically. His explanation seems to make the components of the word itself yield this meaning. What may be the reason for Kaiyaṭa to propose this negative meaning? One possibility is that he may have come across a predominantly sarcastic/negative use of this expression, as against its honorific use. Among the clear predecessors and contemporaries of Kaiyaṭa, Vasubandhu,[22] Śabara,[23] Śaṅkara,[24] Abhinavagupta,[25] and Mammaṭa[26] use this term sarcastically, precisely the way it is used in the

21 This is the most shocking statement. We do not know what basis Kaiyaṭa had to suggest that the word *deva* itself refers to a fool.

22 *prāptijño devānāṃpriyo na tv iṣṭijñaḥ*, *Abhidharmakośabhāṣya*, p. 56; *granthajño devānāṃpriyo na tv arthajñaḥ*, p. 76; both passages are discussed by Hara (1969: 22).

23 *ādityam paśya devānāṃpriya /*, *Śābarabhāṣya* on *Mīmāṃsāsūtra* 1.1.15. Palsule (1969: 143) disputes Ganganath Jha's sarcastic reading of this passage. I believe Jha is correct in his reading. But finally Palsule seems to concede: "This is, then the first instance of the tendency which is clearly noticeable in later scientific literature viz. that *devānāṃpriya*-was to be used (for *tvam*) only when some defect of the person addressed was to be pointed out. Śabara might have understood the Mahābhāṣya passage in an ironical tone and so might have used the word in imitation," Palsule (1969: 143).

24 *idam tāvad devānāṃpriyaḥ praṣṭavyaḥ*, *Śāṅkarabhāṣya* on *Brahmasūtra* 1.2.8.

25 *tasmād adṛṣṭagurubhiḥ apariśīlitaśāstrasampradāyaiḥ svavimarśaśūnyaiḥ devānāṃpriyaiḥ yat kiñcid atrocyate tad upekṣyam / Tantrāloka* (4.172) of Abhinavagupta, cited by V.P. Limaye (1974: 145).

26 *te 'py atātparyajñās tātparyavācoyukter devānāṃpriyāḥ*, *Kāvyaprakāśa* of Mammaṭa, BORI edn., pp. 225–226. Palsule (1969: 148–149) observes: "We will not be much mistaken if we take the expression to have been used here in the sense of 'ignorant' which approaches the *mūrkha* of the commentators. What exactly was responsible for Mammaṭa's idea that *devānāṃpriya* was equivalent to *mūrkha* we do not know for certain. A speculation in this respect has been attempted below. For the first time being attention may be

Mahābhāṣya conversation between a chariot-driver and a grammarian.[27] Though there is also evidence in Bāṇa's usage of this term in his *Harṣacarita* as an honorific,[28] it seems clear that there is a preponderance of the negative/sarcastic use of this term in the literature that may have been available to Kaiyaṭa.

In Vasubandhu's *Abhidharmakośabhāṣya* there is an exact copy of Patañjali's sarcastic words directed at the foolish grammarian: *prāptijño devānāṃpriyo na tv iṣṭijñaḥ.*[29] Vasubandhu's usage is remarkable in that it shows that there is a clear continuity of the sarcastic usage from Patañjali (1st century BCE) to Vasubandhu (about 4th or 5th century CE) and that Vasubandhu is directly imitating the usage of Patañjali. Palsule (1969: 142) discusses Yaśomitra's commentary *Abhidharmakośavyākhyā* on this passage of the *Abhidharmakośabhāṣya*: *ko 'yam devānāṃpriyo nāma / ṛjukajātīyo devānāṃpriya ity eke vyācakṣate / aśaṭho hi devānāṃpriyo bhavati / mūrkho devānāṃpriya ity apare / yo hīśvarāṇāṃ iṣṭaḥ sa na tāḍanena śikṣate iti mūrkho bhavatīti /*, Vol. II, p. 46. Yaśomitra (8th century CE) is to my knowledge the first Sanskrit commentator who explicitly offers both a positive and a negative interpretation as alternatives, the negative interpretation using the word *mūrkha* a few centuries before Kaiyaṭa, but Kaiyaṭa clearly drops the positive interpretation and keeps only the negative interpretation. The question is not whether Kaiyaṭa or Yaśomitra is right or wrong (as posed in Palsule 1969), but that through their comments we have access to changing perceptions of linguistic usage. In Kaiyaṭa's mind, the negative interpretation, most likely because of the preponderance of the sarcastic usage, was the only viable interpretation. Under such circumstances, he perhaps rightly treats the usage not as a sarcastic usage, but as a usage literally indicating negativity. The subsequent history within the grammatical tradition is well known. As Kielhorn (1908: 505) already notes, Rāmacandra in his *Prakriyākaumudī* first adds the word *mūrkhe* to the wording of Kātyāyana's *Vārttika* (*devānāṃpriya iti ca*), and this revised *Vārttika* (*devānāṃ priya iti ca mūrkhe*) makes its way further into Bhaṭṭoji Dīkṣita's *Siddhāntakaumudī* and its commentaries like the *Tattvabodhinī*.[30] During this late period of Sanskrit grammar,

drawn to a coincidence: Kaiyaṭa who was the first to express this view that *devānāṃpriya* meant a fool is said to have been a brother of Mammaṭa."

27 For further discussions of these quotations, see: G. T. Deshpande (1969), Hara (1969) and G. B. Palsule (1969). Also see Kielhorn (1908: 504–5), where he refers to a number of authors (Śaṅkara, Mammaṭa, and Haradatta) who use the expression *devānāṃpriya* sarcastically, but Kielhorn does not note that Kaiyaṭa is the first grammarian to directly interpret the expression to refer to a fool (*mūrkha*). Referring to the *Mahābhāṣya* conversation between the chariot-driver and the grammarian, Kielhorn (1908: 504) says: "I may add that in imitation of this passage of the *Mahābhāṣya* the word *devānāṃpriya* has been used in a similar way by later writers. . . and that to that passage is due in the first instance the meaning *mūrkha*, assigned to *devānāṃpriya* in more modern times."

28 *ihāpi janmani dattam evāsmākaṃ amunā tapaḥkleśena phalam asulabhadarśanaṃ darśayatā devānāṃ priyam / Harṣacarita*, p. 219; *saujanyaparatantrā ceyaṃ devānāṃ priyasyātibhadratā kārayati kathām na tu yuvatijane sahotthā taralatā*, ibid, p. 25.

29 *Abhidharmakośabhāṣya*, p. 56.

30 For details of these subsequent transmissions, see: Kielhorn (1908), G. T. Deshpande (1969) and Palsule (1969). Kielhorn (1908: 505, fn. 2) reads: "It is amusing to see how commentators try to account for this meaning of the word *devānāṃpriya*. The author of the *Manoramā* says: *mūrkhā hi devānāṃ prītiṃ janayanti devapaśutvāt*; to which is added in my

the term *devānāṃpriya* decisively attains a negative meaning, though one should keep in mind, that no one in this tradition at this late period has a clue that this term has any association with the ancient emperor Aśoka.

The term *devānāṃpriya* and the Buddhist Narratives on Aśoka

While the legacy of Aśoka was all but forgotten in non-Buddhist India, the Buddhist tradition kept his memory alive. This is seen in the traditional accounts from Sri Lanka, as well as in the Sanskrit *Avadānas* which were further translated and transmitted to China and Tibet. In most of these Buddhist accounts, there is a common thread that shows that the Buddhist narrators divided Aśoka's reign into two periods, one before his conversion to Buddhism and the second that began with his conversion to Buddhism. The Aśoka of the pre-conversion period is typically described as being a cruel king who was devoted to the heretics, and he is generally referred to as Kālāśoka or Caṇḍāśoka. The post-conversion Aśoka is described as the ideal Buddhist king, and named Dharmāśoka.[31] The stories coming from both the southern and the northern traditions highlight this transformative process, and narrate many episodes in Aśoka's life with a view to giving prominence to Buddhism in his life and his contribution to its propagation. Both of these traditions have been extensively studied by scholars, and I am interested here only in the light these traditions throw on the Aśokan designation *devānāṃpriya*.

To begin with, we may note that not a single Buddhist narrative of Aśoka, southern or northern, has retained any memory whatsoever that Aśoka used the title *devānāṃpriya*. The northern Buddhist tradition codified in various *Avadānas* relating to Aśoka does not use the term *devānāṃpriya* for anyone, while the Sri Lankan tradition uses this epithet for the Sri Lankan king Tissa, who was a contemporary of Aśoka, and for some of his successors, but never for Aśoka, whose close relationship with Tissa is at the same time emphasized in Sri Lankan sources, such as the *Dīpavaṃsa*, *Mahāvaṃsa*, and the *Vinaya Aṭṭhakathā Samantapāsādikā*. Robin Coningham (1995: 226) shows that there is inscriptional evidence from early Sri Lanka that "the king Mahaculika (r. 77–63 BCE) was a member of the royal family which carried the name Devanampiya (friend of the gods)." A number of Sri Lankan inscriptions recorded by Paranavitana (1970, Vol. II., pt. I, nos. 1, 9, 23, and 36) refer to kings of this dynasty using this title for themselves. Especially, the first

MSS. the marginal note *mūrkhā hīti / brahmajñānarahitā ity arthaḥ / te hi paśuvad devaniyamyās tad āha devapaśutvād iti /*. And the *Tattvabodhinī*, in commenting on the above passage of the *Manoramā* has: *brahmajñānarahitatvād saṃsāriṇo mūrkhās te tu yāgādikarmāṇy anutiṣṭhantaḥ puroḍāśādipradānadvārā devānāṃ atyantaprītiṃ janayanti / brahmajñāninas tu na tathā teṣāṃ yāgādyanuṣṭhānābhāvāt / ato gavādisthānāpannatvān mūrkhā eva devapaśava iti /*. Nāgojībhaṭṭa, on the other hand, following Kaiyaṭa, takes the gods themselves to be fools, and appropriately adds that fools are fond of fools."

31 See *caṇḍāsoko ti ñāyittha pure pāpena kammunā / dhammāsoko ti ñāyittha pacchā puññena kammunā // Mahāvaṃsa* (5.189). Also: *āryo mauryaśrīḥ sa prajānāṃ hitārthaṃ / kṛtsne stūpān yaḥ kārayāmāsa loke // caṇḍāśokatvaṃ prāpya pūrvaṃ pṛthivyāṃ / dharmāśokatvaṃ karmaṇā tena lebhe // Pāṃśupradānāvadāna, Aśokāvadāna* (edn. by S. Mukhopadhyaya, p. 55).

Tissa is almost universally called Devānampiyatissa in the early chronicles *Dīpavaṃsa* and *Mahāvaṃsa*, and in the accounts of the *Samantapāsādikā* that rely upon these chronicles. The fact that these Sri Lankan texts use the title *devānaṃpiya* exclusively with the Tissa of Sri Lanka (contemporary with Aśoka) and the fact that only a single inscription of Aśoka (discovered relatively later) names his personal name Aśoka while most inscriptions of Aśoka carry the titles *devānaṃpiya* and *piyadasi* for the king led Princep, the first scholar to decipher the Aśokan Brāhmī characters, to initially assume that these inscriptions belonged to the Sri Lankan king Devānaṃpiyatissa. This initial impression was soon cleared by Tourner who identified Priyadarśin with Aśoka. "He pointed out that the Sinhalese chronicle, the Dīpavaṃsa, gave Piyadassi or Piyadassana as but another name of Aśoka. . . .This identification, it is true, has not since then been called in question, but it was definitively demonstrated only nine years ago when the sixth copy of Minor Rock Edict I was discovered at Maski. . . . For this inscription mentions the name of Aśoka clearly and in the very first line," D. R. Bhandarkar (1969: 4). While the identity of Aśoka as the *devānaṃpiya* of the inscriptions was eventually firmly established, it creates an interesting situation that while we in modern times can make a guess that the Sri Lankan Tissa took the title *devānaṃpiya* for himself to suggest his special relation with the Indian emperor Aśoka, or that Aśoka conferred this title on Tissa, the Sri Lankan sources have no idea that Aśoka himself used this title for himself, and hence the Sri Lankan narratives are clearly not trying to suggest that Tissa took this title for himself in imitation of Aśoka.[32] In fact, the Sri Lankan narratives, on the surface, make it appear as if Tissa was always called Devānāṃpiyatissa.[33] Thus, we have an interesting situation involved here. It would

32 Hettiarachchy (1972: 48): "Opinion is divided as to how this title which was fostered by Aśoka came to be applied to the kings of Ceylon. Paranavitana suggests that the Indian emperor may have allowed Devānaṃpiya Tissa to use his title when the latter was consecrated by the former. But Nicholas, who seems rather sceptical about the emperor Aśoka's connexion with the consecration of Devānaṃpiya Tissa, states that Devānaṃpiya Tissa may have imitated the title of Aśoka." Also: Hettiarachchy (1972: 49): "Although the title *devānaṃpiya* may have carried some glamour and lustre during the time of Devānaṃpiya Tissa when the prestige of the Maurya empire was at its peak, once it had become a family name the title had no implication of power and prestige except [for] those that were associated with the Anuradhapura royal house." We must keep in mind that by the time the Sri Lankan chronicles are put together, there is no surviving memory that *devānaṃpiya* was once also the title of Aśoka. At some time, the term is abandoned in Sri Lanka itself. Hettiarachchy (1972: 50) speculates about its disappearance: "Even before the Christian era the term *devānaṃpiya* (Skt. *devānāṃpriya*) became a term of abuse in India. These ideas may have penetrated to Ceylon which maintained some contact with the subcontinent after the introduction of Buddhism, and this may have been one of the reasons why the title was discarded by the members of Devānaṃpiya Tissa's house, if we take the absence of the title after Mahādāṭhaka Mahānāga as positive evidence." There is no evidence to support Hettiarachchy's claim that the term *devānāṃ-priya* had become a term of abuse in India before the Christian era.

33 See *devānaṃpiyatisso ti vissuto dutiyo suto / tesu bhātisu sabbesu puññapaññādhiko ahu // devānaṃpiyatisso so rājā 'si pitu accaye / tassābhisekena samaṃ bahūnacchariyāna huṃ // Mahāvaṃsa* (11.6–7). Also: *devānaṃpiyatisso ca dhammāsoko ca dve ime / adiṭṭhasahāyassu hi cirappabhuti bhūpatī // Mahāvaṃsa* (11.19). The *Samantapāsādikā* says: *tattha asokadhammarājassa sattarasame vasse idha muṭasīvarājā kālam akāsi /*

seem beyond doubt that Tissa of Sri Lanka took the title *devānaṃpiya* in imitation of the title of Aśoka, and this must mean that historically the Sri Lankans contemporary with Aśoka must have known that Aśoka used the title *devānāṃpiya* for himself. But at the same time, from this early period, sometime along the way, the knowledge that this was a title of Aśoka has been lost or suppressed in the subsequent tradition available to us in *Dīpavaṃsa*, *Mahāvaṃsa*, and *Samanta-pāsādikā*. Considering the fact that the northern tradition of Aśoka legends also does not show this awareness, one may make a guess that the Buddhist proto-narratives about Aśoka had lost this piece of information before these narratives appeared in the specific northern and southern textual forms. The northern tradition codified in Sanskrit texts like the *Aśokāvadāna* also has no awareness that Tissa of Sri Lanka took this title for himself, though the southern versions of stories were clearly not completely unknown in the north, as evidenced by Saṅghabhadra's chinese translation (*Shan-Chien-P'i-P'o-Sha*) of the Pali *Samantapāsādikā* completed in 489 CE. The Chinese translation of *Samantapāsādikā* contains all the same information about Devānaṃpiya Tissa of Sri Lanka and his connection with Aśoka that is contained in the Pali text, and very much like the Pali text, the Chinese version has no information that Aśoka used the title *devānaṃpiya* for himself. One gets the impression that the Buddhist tradition as we know it across the board shares this loss of information about *devānaṃpiya* being an epithet of Aśoka. The occurrence of this term in the *Abhidharmakośa* of Vasubandhu, as discussed before, is clearly in imitation of Patañjali's *Mahābhāṣya*, and shows no sign of any awareness that a Buddhist king may have used this term as his invariant honorific title.

This analysis, if valid, poses important questions regarding the origins and transmission of Aśoka legends within the Buddhist tradition. Under the heading "The Forming of the Tradition," Eggermont (1956: 169) says:

> At the beginning of the tradition there is the historical Asoka figure. Asoka was of such an outstanding significance to Buddhism that the forming of the legend may have started already during his lifetime. The stages of the growth of this legend were traced back by Przyluski in an admirable book. It is useful to recall briefly Przyluski's theory.

devānampiyatisso rajjaṃ pāpuṇi / Vol. I, p. 63. The *Samantapāsādikā* (Vol. I, p. 64) narrates an interesting story of Devānampiyatissa's first encounter with the monk Mahinda. Mahinda addresses him merely as: *tissa tissa ito ehi*, "O Tissa, O Tissa, come here." Devānaṃpiyatissa is shocked: *imasmiṃ dīpe jāto maṃ tissā ti nāmaṃ gahetvā ālapituṃ samattho nāma natthi*, "There is no one born in this island who would dare address me just using my name Tissa." Hettiarachchy (1972: 47): "The *Mahāvaṃsa* gives Devānaṃpiya Tissa as the name of the Sinhalese ruler who ascended the throne of Anuradhapura after Muṭasīva. In one instance the *Mahāvaṃsa* (11.42) states that his name is hidden in *devānaṃpiya* (*devānaṃpiya-vacanopagūḷhanāmo*). The *Vaṃsatthappakāsinī*, commenting on this, states that the king's name is Tissa and this is hidden in the *upapada* of *devānaṃpiya*. That work adds further that the king was known as Devānaṃpiya by the people because he was bent on meritorious work leading to heavenly life. The fact that *devānaṃpiya* is called an *upapada* suggests that it was taken by the king at a later date in his life and was not his original name. However, the inscriptions reveal that *devānapiya* (P. *devānaṃpiya*) was not confined to one ruler but was taken by most of the kings belonging to the first dynasty."

Here is Eggermont's (1956: 169) summation of Przyluski's theory:

> Already in the Moriya period a 'Cycle d'Açoka' arose in Magadha. About the middle of the IInd century B.C. this Cycle became known in Kosambī, at the time an important Buddhist centre. There an *Asokasutta* was written in Pali. From Kosambi, a trade centre, this *Asokasutta* followed the routes of trade. It came to the North West, in Mathurā, a centre of Brahman culture. Here the Pali *Asokasutta* was rewritten in Sanskrit. Thus the *Aśokāvadāna* came into being. At the same time the Pāli Asokasutta reached Ceylon by sea via the trade route Kosambī--Ujjayinī--Bharukaccha. In Ceylon it became the basis of the Asoka tales of the *Dīpavaṃsa* and the *Mahāvaṃsa*. The Asoka legend also extended to the East. . . . From Mathurā the Asoka legend came to the North West of India in the 1st century A.D. The reflection of the Asoka legend in this last form we find in the *Avadānakalpalatā* by Kṣemendra (XIth century A.D.). Another historical work of Kṣemendra, which among other things contained an Asoka biography, was lost.

After reviewing Przyluski's theory, Eggermont (1956: 169–170) concludes:

> To what extent does my study modify and supplement this theory? Firstly a more accurate idea can be formed of the Magadhan 'Cycle d'Açoka,' the starting point of the whole tradition. This Cycle must have had the character of a chronicle, which related the events mentioning the year of reign after the king's anointment. . . . Both the Pāli sources and the *Aśokāvadāna* had drawn freely from the same ancient source.

Eggermont (1956: 169) also asserts, in positing such a proto-chronicle, that "there are so many concurrences between the inscriptions and the tradition." I am not interested in fully examining Eggermont's theory here, but I would like to point out that while there may be strong "concurrences between the inscriptions and the tradition," as pointed out by Eggermont, the glaring absence of *devānampiya* in the tradition and its almost universal presence in Aśoka's inscriptions have not been addressed by Eggermont or any subsequent scholar that I am aware of.

Going back to Przyluski's formulation of the stages of development outlined above, we may focus on a few important points. The first point is that the primary agency in the design of the proto-Asoka narrative is with the Buddhist monks. Secondly, even while admitting Przyluski's notion that at the Brahmanical center of Mathura, the Pali proto-version first became Sanskritized, what may be the role of the Brahmans in the transformation of the story? Do we assume that these are Brahmanical Brahmans, or Brahmans who converted to Buddhism, albeit without renouncing their love for Sanskrit? As we consider these various likely agents in the design and transmission of the Aśoka legend, we can rule out the Brahmanical Brahmans from producing a loving narrative showing Aśoka in a positive light. The evidence from the *Mahābhāṣya* and the *Purāṇas* would assist us in arriving at this conclusion. The Brahmanical Brahmans were probably offended by the use of the term *devānāṃpriya* by a king who became a Buddhist. So who might then be the likely agent for the removal of the term *devānāṃpiya* from an otherwise loving narrative in favor of the Buddhist Aśoka? I cannot think of anyone other than the Buddhist monks themselves, who loved the Dharmāśoka, Aśoka after his conversion to Buddhism, and depicted the Caṇḍāśoka, the cruel Aśoka before his conversion with great contrastive effect. In designing the Aśoka narrative for Buddhist audiences, they probably found the title *devānaṃpiya* rather absurd and inconvenient. In support of my guess, I can point to passages in both the Sanskrit versions and the Sri Lankan Pali versions, where the Buddhist monastic narrators seem to be at pains to point out that before his conversion to Buddhism, Aśoka and his father were devoted to Brahmanical religion, a terrible thing from the Buddhist point of view. The *Samantapāsādikā* (Vol. I, p. 38) says:[34]

> *rājā kira abhisekaṃ pāpuṇitvā tīṇiyeva saṃvaccharāni bāhiraka-pāsaṇḍaṃ parigaṇhi / catutthe saṃvacchare buddhasāsane pasīdi / tassa kira pitā bindusāro brāhmaṇabhatto ahosi, so brāhmaṇānaṃ ca brāhmaṇajātiyapāsaṇḍānaṃ ca paṇḍaraṅgaparibbājakādīnaṃ saṭṭhi-sahassamattānaṃ niccabhattaṃ paṭṭhapesi /*
>
> Having been consecrated to his kingship, only for the first three years did the king accept outsider-heretics. During his fourth year, he developed affection for the Buddhist doctrine. His father, Bindusāra, was devoted to Brahmans. He instituted daily meals for sixty-thousand ash-white ascetics of the Brahman caste and [other] Brahmans.

Such "anti-Brahmanical" passages can be traced in both the southern and northern versions of the Aśoka legends, and in my view they go back in all probability to the proto-narrative that Przyluski was talking about. The above cited passage of the *Samantapāsādikā* uses the words *brāhmaṇajātīyapāsaṇḍa* with absolute contempt, and in such cases, we can contrast the positive non-contemptuous usage of the terms *brāhmaṇa* and *pāsaṇḍa* in Aśoka's own inscriptions: (Rock Edict VII, Girnar version): *devānaṃpiyo piyadasi rājā savata icchati save pāsaṇḍā vaseyu save te sayaman ca bhāvasuddhin ca icchati /*, "Beloved of the Gods, king Piyadasi desires that all religious sects can live anywhere. They all desire self-control and purification of beings."[35] I want to conclude my presentation by saying that the

34 For parallel passages, see: *pitā saṭṭhisahassāni brāhmaṇe brahmapakkhike / bhojesi, so pi te yeva tīṇi vassāni bhojayi // Mahāvaṃsa* (5.34). The account in Tārānātha's *History of Buddhism in India* (p. 53) often depicts Brahmans as demon-worshippers: "Following the advice of the anchorite of the Bhṛku [Bhṛgu] family, the worshipper of *ḍākinīs* and *rākṣasas*, Aśoka accepted for his deity the mother goddesses of the crematorium including Umā-devī. Indulging as he did in lust for several years, he came to be known as Kāmāśoka."

35 Edmund Weber (2001: no page no.): "In the eyes of the Buddhist emperor the true dharma doesn't exclude the gods from the human beings; just the opposite is right: the true dharma demands the close association and even mixture of gods and men. . . . There is no question: Ashoka was not only loved by the gods; he loved them too. . . . He effectuated a restitution of the worship of gods and brahmanas. According to him gods and brahmanas were not contradictory to Buddhism. Rather, they were an essential pillar of a society defined by Bauddha dharma." Weber's statements, sometimes almost seeming to suggest that Aśoka

Aśoka of the inscriptions is a ruler far more rooted in the local cultural tradition and tolerant of the plurality of existing religious traditions and groups, in spite of his clear conversion to Buddhism and his zeal in its propagation. The Aśoka of the Buddhist narratives is a narrow-minded intolerant convert to Buddhism who is yanked away by the monastic authors from his tolerant historical personality and made to be a defender of the Buddhist faith and honor. In his mission of being a defender of the Buddhist faith and protector of its honor, the Buddhist authors tell us that the great Dharmāśoka killed eighteen thousand Ājīvikas in the city of Puṇḍravardhana, burned alive the whole family of a Jain layman because of the report that he had painted the scene of a Buddha image falling at the feet of Mahāvīra, and announced the payment of one gold-coin for each severed head of a Jain monk.[36] The loss of Aśoka's epithet *devānaṃpiya* must, in my view, be attributed to this sectarian rivalry into which the Buddhist Aśokan legends were composed.

The other strategy evident in both the southern and northern Aśoka narratives is an effort to subordinate the *devas* to Buddha, Buddhism, and Aśoka. The subordination of the *devas* to Buddha and Buddhism goes back to early canonical texts of Buddhism and has been examined in detail by von Glasenapp and others. Buddha is often referred to as being the teacher of gods and men (*satthā devamanussānam*) and that gods worship the Buddha (*devā pi yaṃ namassanti*), rather than the Buddha worshipping the gods. Better to say that the *devas* loved Aśoka than saying that he loved them.[37] The *Aśokāvadāna* as well as the Sri Lankan sources seem to tailor the narrative along this direction. Even before Aśoka assumes kingship and is competing with other princes, he declares that if he has any accumulated merit, then an army will manifest for him. As soon as he says that, the *devatās* bring to him an army and weapons (*yadi mama rājyavaipākyaṃ kuśalam*

was a pro-Brahman ruler, may perhaps suggest to us how Aśoka perceived the religious world. But there is clear evidence that the Brahmanical tradition as well as the Buddhist tradition did not see it that way. The texts of these two traditions seem to pull Aśoka into a sectarian personality, viewed negatively by the Brahmanical tradition and positively by the Buddhist tradition.

36 *Aśokāvadāna* (edn. by Mukhopadhyaya, p. 67–68): *tasmiṃś ca samaye puṇḍravardhananagare nirgranthopāsakena buddhapratimā nirgranthasya pādayor nipatitā citrārpitā / . . . śrutvā ca rājñābhihitaṃ śīghram ānīyatām / puṇḍravardhane sarve ājīvikāḥ praghātayitavyāḥ / yāvad ekadivase 'ṣṭādaśasahasrāṇi ājīvikānām praghātitāni / . . . śrutvā ca rājñāmarṣitena sa nirgranthopāsakaḥ sabandhuvargo gṛhaṃ praveśayitvāgninā dagdhaḥ / ājñaptaṃ ca yo me nirgranthasya śiro dāsyati tasya dīnāraṃ dāsyāmi iti ghoṣitam. Mahāvaṃsa* (5.74): *titthiyānaṃ sahassāni nikkaḍḍhitvāna saṭṭhi so / saṭṭhi bhikkhusahassāni ghare niccam abhojayi //*. The Aśokan inscriptions give no evidence that his gift-giving was limited to only the Buddhist monks. The inscriptions show him giving donations to Ājīvikas, contrary to the narratives in the *Aśokāvadāna*.

37 There is an interesting passage in the late Sri Lankan Pali work *Dhātuvaṃsa*: *so āyasmā mahākassapatthero yebhuyyena bahunnaṃ devānaṃ piyo manāpo / therassa hi dānaṃ datvā sagge nibbattānaṃ pamāṇo nāma natthi /*, "The monk Mahākassapa was dear to a large number of gods. There is no counting of numbers of those who were born [as Devas] in heaven as a result of giving *dāna* to this monk," Romanized text file on GRETIL—Göttingen Register of Electronic Texts in Indian Languages (SL Page 013). Here, "dear to the gods" is clearly accounted for in a paradigm that subordinates gods even to Buddhist monks, let alone to the Buddha.

asti sainyapraharaṇam prādurbhavatu / evam ukte kumāreṇa pṛthivyām avakāśo datto devatābhiḥ sainyapraharaṇāni copanītāni / Aśokāvadāna, edn. by Mukhopadhyaya, p. 39). In another passage we are told that Aśoka makes a declaration that if the kingdom legally (*dharmeṇa*) belongs to him, then let the gods tie the band of kingship for him. The gods then tie his band of kingship (*yadi mama dharmeṇa rājyaṃ bhavati devatā mama paṭṭaṃ badhnantu / yāvad devatābhiḥ paṭṭo baddhaḥ / Aśokāvadāna*, p. 41).[38] The story of the gods assisting Aśoka in gaining the kingship and the gods bringing sixteen jars of holy water from Anotatta lake for him is narrated in the *Samantapāsādikā* (Vol. I, p. 37): *tathā upari ākāse anotattadahato aṭṭhahi kājehi soḷasa pānīyaghaṭe divase divase devatā āharanti.* This would probably indicate that the subordination of the *devas* to Aśoka was part of the Buddhist Aśoka narrative from the very beginning, on the same lines that the *devas* were subordinated to the Buddha. In the inscriptions of Aśoka there is no trace of this subordination of *devas* to the king, who seems to look up to them respectfully, in spite of his conversion to Buddhism[39]. Thus, a careful study of the absence of the inscriptional term *devānampiya* in the Buddhist narratives of Aśoka, both southern and northern, allows us to understand how these narratives developed, and how the Aśoka of these narratives gradually moved away from the historical Aśoka of the inscriptions.[40]

38 The *Kuṇālāvadāna* narrates a story told by Upagupta to Aśoka regarding Buddha's birth. When the child was brought to Śuddhodana, a prediction was made that the Bodhisattva would at this place of the Śākyas worship a god (*devam arcayiṣyati*). But all the gods actually fell at the feet of the Bodhisattva (*sarvadevatā ca bodhisattvasya pādayor nipatitā*). Then Śuddhodana realized that his son, the Bodhisattva, is a god of gods, and so he named him Devātideva "god of gods." See *Aśokāvadāna*, p. 83.

39 For the co-existence of worship of *devas* and Buddhism, see: Gombrich (1971: 46ff.).

40 Referring to H. Kern (1896, 1972: 115), Basham (1959: 57) says: "The Aśoka of the Buddhist legends is, in the words of a 19th-century authority, 'half monster and half idiot,' his humanity and practical benevolence overlaid by the accretion of monkish legends of later centuries."

Bibliography

Aśokāvadāna. ed. S. Mukhopadhyaya. Delhi: Sahitya Akademi, 1963.

Bāṇabhaṭṭa, *Harṣacarita*. Bombay: Nirnayasagara Press, 1925.

Bapat, P.V. and A. Hirakawa. tr. 1970. *Shan-Chien-P'i-P'o-Sha, A Chinese Version by Saṅghabhadra of Samantapāsādikā*. Pune: Bhandarkar Oriental Research Institute.

Basham. A. L. 1959. *The Wonder that was India*. [Originally published in 1954 by Macmillan, New York]. First Evergreen Edition, 13th printing. New York: Grove Press, Inc.

Bhāgavatapurāṇa. ed. and tr. A. C. Bhaktivedanta. Multivolume edn. New York: Bhaktivedanta Book Trust, 1972.

Bhandarkar, D. R. 1932. "Aśoka." From the Carmichael Lectures, 1929. [2nd rev. ed. reprinted in 1969] Calcutta: University of Calcutta.

Bhandarkar, R. G. 1928. *Collected Works of Sir R.G. Bhandarkar, Vol. 2*. Ed. by N. B. Utgikar. Poona: Bhandarkar Oriental Research Institute.

Buddha Prakash. 1970. "A Historical Study of the Sanskrit Term Devānāṃpriya." *Vishveshvarananda Indological Journal*, Vol. VIII, pts. i–ii, March and September.

Bollée, W. ed. and tr. 2002. *The Story of Paesi (Paesi-kahāṇayam), Text, translation, notes and glossary*. Beiträge zur Kenntnis südasiatischer Sprachen und Literaturen. Wiesbaden: Harrassowitz Verlag.

Chattopadhyay, B. 1967. *The Age of the Kushanas—A Numismatic Study*. Calcutta: Punthi Pustak.

Chaturvedi, S. P. 1935. "History of an important Historical word in the Pāṇinian school of grammar." In *Proceedings of the All-India Oriental Conference*, Mysore.

Coningham, R. A. E. 1995. "Monks, Caves and Kings: A Reassessment of the Nature of Early Buddhism in Sri Lanka." *World Archaeology*, Vol. 27, No. 2, pp. 222–42.

Cunningham, A. 1877. *Inscriptions of Aśoka*. Corpus Inscriptionum Indicarum, Vol. I. Calcutta: Office of the Superintendent of Government Printing. [reprint Banaras: Indological Book House, 1961]

Deshpande, G. T. 1969. "On the Import of the Term Devānāmpriya." In *Vidarbha Saṃshodhana Maṇḍaḷa Vārshika*. [Reprint Vidarbha Samshodhan Mandal Series No. XXV, Indological Papers (by G. T. Deshpande), Vol. I, 1971, pp. 201–215. Nagpur: Vidarbha Samshodhan Mandal.]

Deshpande, M. M. 2006. "Changing Perspectives in the Sanskrit Grammatical Tradition and the Changing Political Configurations in Ancient India." In *Between the Empires: Society in India 300 BCE to 400 CE*. Ed. J. P. Olivelle, pp. 215–225. New York: Oxford University Press.

———. 1979. *Sociolinguistic Attitudes in India: An Historical Reconstruction*. Linguistica Extranea, Studia, 5. Ann Arbor: Karoma Publishers, Inc.

Dīpavaṃsa. ed. and tr. H. Oldenberg. London: Williams and Norgate, 1879. [reprint Delhi: Asian Educational Services, 1982]

Eggermont, P. H. L. 1956. *The Chronology of the Reign of Asoka Moriya*. Leiden: E. J. Brill.

Evers, H. 1972. *Monks, priests and peasants. A study of Buddhism and social structure in central Ceylon*. Leiden: E. J. Brill.

Filliozat, J. 1949. "Les deva d'Aśoka: dieux ou divines majestés." *Journal Asiatique*, Vol. 237, pp. 255–47.

Gandhi, H. B. ed. and tr. 1938. *Rāyapaseṇiyasutta, First Part*. Surat: Hiralal B. Gandhi.

Glasenapp, H. 1970. *Buddhism, A non-theistic religion* [English translation by I. Schlogel of *Buddhismus und Gottesidee, Die Buddhistischen Lehren von den überweltlichen Wesen und Mächten und ihre religionsgeschichtlichen Parallelen* in Abhandlungen der geistes- und sozialwissenschaftlichen Klasse der Akademie der Wissenschaften und der Literatur in Mainz, 1954, Nr. 8]. London: George Allen and Unwin Ltd.

Gombrich, R. F. 1971. *Precept and Practice: Traditional Buddhism in the Rural Highlands of Ceylon*. London: Oxford University Press.

Hara, M. 1969. "A Note on the Sanskrit Phrase devānāṃ priya." *Indian Linguistics*, Vol. 30. *Katre Felicitation Volume*, Part II. pp. 13–26. Pune: Deccan College, Linguistic Society of India.

Henning, W. B. 1949. "The Aramaic Inscription of Asoka Found in Lampaka." *Bulletin of the School of Oriental and African Studies*, Vol. 13, No. 1, pp. 80–88.

Hettiarachchy, T. 1972. *History of Kingship in Ceylon upto the fourth century A. D.* Colombo: Lake House Investments Ltd. Book Publishers.

Hoernle, A. F. R. ed. 1885–90. *The Uvāsagadasāo, vols. I–II*. [Reprinted in 1989. Calcutta: Asiatic Society.]

Jaina Sutras [*Ācārāṅgasūtra* and *Kalpasūtra*], *Part I*. 1901. tr. H. Jacobi. Sacred Books of the East, Vol. X. American Edition. New York: Charles Scribner's Sons.

Jaini, P. 1977. "Jina Ṛṣabha as an avatāra of Viṣṇu." *Bulletin of the School of Oriental and African Studies*, Vol. 40, Pt. 2, pp. 321–37.

———. 1970. "Śramaṇas: Their Conflict with Brahmanical Society." In *Chapters in Indian Civilization, I*. Ed. J. W. Elder, pp. 40–81. Dubuque, Iowa: Kendall Hunt Publishing Company.

Karandikar, A. J. 1962. *Aśok te Kālidās* [In Marathi: "From Aśoka to Kālidāsa"]. Pune: published by author, distributed by Venus Bookstall.

Karttunen, K. 1997. *India and the Hellenistic World*. Studia Orientalia, no. 83. Helsinki: Finnish Oriental Society.

Kent, R. G. 1950. *Old Persian: Grammar Texts Lexicon*. American Oriental Series, Vol. 33. New Haven: American Oriental Society.

Kern, H. 1896 [reprint 1972]. *Manual of Indian Buddhism*. Grundriss der Indo-Arischen Philologie und Altertumskunde, Band III, Heft 8. Strassburg: K. J. Trübner. [reprint Benaras: Indological Book House, 1972]

Kielhorn, F. 1908. "Bhagavat, Tatrabhavat and Devānāṃpriya." *Journal of the Royal Asiatic Society*, pp. 502–505.

Lévi, S. 1911. "Viyuthena 256." *Journal Asiatique*, 10,7, pp. 119–223.

———. 1891. "Notes de chronologie indienne, devānāṃpriya—Açoka et Kātyāyana." *Journal Asiatique*, Vol. 18, pp. 549–53.

Limaye, V. P. 1974. *Critical Studies on the Mahābhāṣya*. V.I. Series, 49. Hoshiarpur: Vishveshvaranand Vedic Research Institute.

Mahābhārata, *Ādiparvan*, Critical Edition, Vol. I, Pt. I. ed. V. S. Sukthankar. 1933. Pune: Bhandarkar Oriental Research Institute.

Mahāvaṃsa. ed. N. K. Bhagwat. 2nd edition. 1959. Bombay University Publications, Devanāgarī Pālī Text Series, No. 12. Bombay: Bombay University.

Meile, P. 1949. "Misā devehi chez Asoka." *Journal Asiatique*, Vol. 237.

Mookerji, R. K. 1962. *Asoka*. 3rd revised and enlarged edition. [1st edition London: MacMillan, 1928]. Delhi: Motilal Banarsidass.

Murti, S. G. and Krishna Aiyangar. A. N.1951. *Edicts of Aśoka*. 2nd edition. Adyar Library Series, no. 72. Madras: Adyar Library.

Norman, K. R. 2001. *Collected Papers, Vol. VII*. Oxford: Pali Text Society.

———. 1997. *A Philological Approach to Buddhism, The Bukkyō Dendō Kyōkai Lectures 1994*. The Buddhist Forum, Vol. V. London: School of Oriental and African Studies, University of London.

Ovavāiyasutta [*Aupapātikasūtra*]. ed. N. G. Suru. 1931. Pune: Ganesh Printing Press.

Palsule, G. B. 1969. "Devānāṃ-priyaḥ." *Indian Linguistics, Vol. 30, Katre Felicitation Volume*, Pt. II, pp. 134–161. Pune: Deccan College, Indian Linguistic Society.

Paranavitana, S. 1970. "Early Brahmi Inscriptions." In *Inscriptions of Ceylon, I and II.1*. Colombo: Archaeological Survey of Ceylon.

Przyluski, J. 1923. *La Légende de l'empereur Açoka*. Paris: Paul Geuthner.

Raghavan, V. 1946. "The semantics of the expression devānām priya." In *Dhruwa Commemoration Volume*, Pt. III, pp. 197–9. Ahmedabad.

Saddharmapuṇḍarīkasūtra. 1960. Buddhist Sanskrit Texts, no. 6. Ed. P. L. Vaidya. Darbhanga: Mithila Institute.

Samādhirājasūtra. 1961. Buddhist Sanskrit Texts, no. 2. Ed. P. L. Vaidya. Darbhanga: Mithila Institute.

Samantapāsādikā, *Vinayaṭṭhakathā*, by Buddhaghosa. Pt. I. Ed. B. Sharma. 1964. Patna: Nava Nālandā Mahāvihāra.

Scheller, M. 1958. *Vedisch priyá- und die Wortsippe Frei, Freien, Freund, Eine bedeutungsgeschichtliche Studie*. Ergänzungshefte zur Zeitschrift für vergleichende Sprachforschung auf dem Gebiet der indogermanischen Sprachen, Nr. 16. Göttingen: Vandenhoeck and Ruprecht.

Schlingloff, D. 1985. "König Asoka und das Wesen des ältesten Buddhismus." *Saeculum*, Vol. 36, Pt. 4, pp. 326–333.

Schmithausen, L. 1992. "An attempt to estimate the distance in time between Aśoka and the Buddha in terms of doctrinal history." In *The Dating of the Historical Buddha/Die Datierung des historischen Buddha, Part 2*. Ed. H. Bechert, pp. 110–47. Symposien zur Buddhismus-forschung, IV, 2. Göttingen: Vandenhoeck and Ruprecht.

Schopen, G. 1991. "Archaeology and Protestant Presuppositions in the Study of Indian Buddhism." *History of Religions*, 31:1, pp. 1–23.

Seneviratna, A. ed. 1994. *King Aśoka and Buddhism: Historical and Literary Study*. Kandy, Sri Lanka: Buddhist Publication Society.

———. 1994a. "Aśoka and the Emergence of a Sinhala Buddhist State in Sri Lanka." In *Seneviratna* (1994), pp. 111–140.

Sharma, D. 1950. "Devānāṃpriya." *Indian Historical Quarterly*, Vol. XXVI, No. 2, June.

Skandapurāṇa, ascribed to Vyāsa. Gurumaṇḍala Granthamālā, No. 20, Pt. 4. 1961. Calcutta.

Smith, R. M. 1973. *Dates and Dynasties in Earliest India*. Delhi: Motilal Banarsidass.

Smith, V. A. 1901. "Translation of Devānāṃpriya." *Journal of the Royal Asiatic Society*.

———. 1901b. *Asoka: The Buddhist Emperor of India*. Oxford: Clarendon Press.

Strong, J. S. 1983. *The Legend of King Aśoka: A Study and Translation of the Aśokāvadāna*. Princeton: Princeton University Press.

Tārānātha's History of Buddhism in India. Tr. from Tibetan by Lama Chimpa and Alaka Chattopadhyaya. 1970. Simla: Indian Institute of Advanced Study.

Thapar, R. 1994. "Aśoka and Buddhism as reflected in the Aśokan Edicts." In *Seneviratna* (1994), pp. 15–36.

———. 1961. *Aśoka and the Decline of the Mauryas*. London: Oxford University Press.

Vasubandhu, *Abhidharmakośabhāṣya*. Ed. P. Pradhan. Tibetan-Sanskrit Works Series 8. Patna: K. P. Jayaswal Research Institute, 1967.

Vaidya, N. V. ed. 1954. *Śrīmadbhagavatīsūtram, Pañcadaśaṃ Gośālakākhyaṃ Śatakam*. Shri Vijayadevsur Sangh Series, No. 9. Bombay: Shri Vijayadevsur Sangh Gnan Samiti.

Viṣṇupurāṇa, ed. and tr. into Hindi by Munilal Gupta. 1934. Gorakhpur: Gitapress.

Vivāgasuya [*Vipākaśruta*]. Ed. P. L. Vaidya. 1993. Pune.

Vyākaraṇa-Mahābhāṣya, by Patañjali. Originally edited in three volumes (1880, 1883, and 1885) by Franz Kielhorn and published from Bombay: Government of Bombay. Third revised edition by K. V. Abhyankar in three volumes (1962, 1965 and 1972). Pune: Bhandarkar Oriental Research Institute.

Vyākaraṇa-Mahābhāṣya, by Patañjali, with the commentaries *Pradīpa* by Kaiyaṭa and *Uddyota* by Nāgeśa. Ed. S. D. Kuddala. Vol. 2. 1912. Bombay: Nirnayasagara Press.

Weber, E. 2001. "Buddhism: An Atheistic and Anti-Caste Religion? Modern Ideology and Historical Reality of the Ancient Indian Bauddha Dharma." *Journal of Religious Culture/Journal für Religionskultur*. No. 50.

Woolner, A. C. 1924. *Asoka Text and Glossary, Pts. I–II*. Panjab University Oriental Publications. London: Oxford University Press.

Yaśomitra, *Abhidharmakośavyākhyā*. Ed. N. N. Law. Calcutta, 1949.

Aśoka and the 'Epigraphic Habit' in India

Richard Salomon

The history of Indian epigraphy embodies a grand paradox, in that the inscriptions of Aśoka, which are nowadays regarded by many authorities[1] as the earliest Indian inscriptions, are highly untypical. To put the matter another way, the epigraphic tradition in India after Aśoka—what I propose to call India's "epigraphic habit"[2]—derives very little inspiration from Aśoka's model beyond the basic notion of recording proclamations in permanent written form in public places. In terms of format, contents, and tone, there is practically nothing in the later inscriptional corpus of the Indian world that even resembles Aśoka's inscriptions.

To begin with a minor but revealing example, one frequently finds among the Aśokan inscriptions statements formulated in the first person. For example, in the Rūpnāth minor rock edict, we read *sumi pakāsa [sa]k[e]*, "I am openly a Buddhist." Similarly, in major rock edict 6 (Girnār version), Aśoka says, *ta mayā evaṃ kataṃ*, "This has been done by me, as follows." In and of itself, there is nothing strange about this, as the first person address is perfectly suited to the context of his edicts. It only seems strange in comparison with later Indian inscriptions, where instances of first person narration (with the occasional exception of an imbedded first-person quotation within a third-person narrative) are extremely rare; to date, I have only noted two such cases outside of the Aśokan inscriptions.[3]

The inspiration for Aśoka's use of first-person address might be attributed to the trilingual inscriptions of the Achaemenid kings of Iran. We read, for example, in the Old Persian version of the Bīsutūn (Behistun) inscription (ca. 520 BCE) of Darius:

1 See, for example, Falk 1993, esp. pp. 177–218.

2 The term is adaped from MacMullen 1982, "The Epigraphic Habit in the Roman Empire."

3 In the Kharoṣṭhī inscription of Senavarma, King of Oḍi (early first century CE), the king memorialized his reconstruction of a *stūpa* in first person narration, as in, for example, *te ma[ye] seṇavarmeṇa kiḍa hovati*, "Those [*stūpa*s] were made by me, Senavarma"; see von Hinüber 2003: 14–15. In another Kharoṣṭhī inscription of about the same period, the donor, a woman named Ariaśrava, declares *tasa bhagavato dhatu parịthavemi*, "I establish the relics of the Lord" (Sadakata 1996: 309). There are no doubt some other examples of first person narration in inscriptions that have escaped my notice, but I am confident in stating that they are rare.

> I am Darius the Great King, King of Kings, King in Persia, King of countries. . . . Saith Darius the King, By the favor of Ahuramazda I am king; Ahuramazda bestowed the kingdom upon me. Saith Darius the King, These are the countries which came unto me. . . : Persia, Elam, Babylonia, Assyria, Arabia, Egypt. . . .[4]

Of course, this association rests on the widely-held theory that the inscriptions of the Achaemenids were the inspiration for Aśoka's epigraphic project; and although there is no conclusive proof for this, I consider it to be reasonably likely in view of the chronological, geographical, and historical overlap between the Achaemenid and the Mauryan dynasties.

But, however this may be, the similarities between the inscriptions of Darius and Aśoka do not go much deeper than this. There are some resemblances in features of the narrative style, such as the aforementioned use of first person address, and we can also suspect that Aśoka's use of multiple languages for his edicts may have been influenced by the trilingual edicts of the Achaemenids. Aśoka's practice of recording his inscriptions in multiple copies in different parts of India in different local dialects is unparalleled in the later history of Indian epigraphy. Duplicate inscriptions of any sort are elsewhere quite rare, and in any case they are never found distributed across wide geographical spans, nor are they reproduced in different languages or dialects. Nevertheless, the distribution of languages in the Achaemenid inscriptions is not directly comparable to that of the Aśokan inscriptions, in that the former were engraved in trilingual combinations (Old Persian, Akkadian, and Elamite) at each site, whereas in the latter the local languages were used individually in different regions, at least as far as the Aśokan inscriptions in India proper are concerned, although there are a few examples of bilingual (Greek and Aramaic or Indic and Aramaic) Aśokan edicts from Afghanistan.[5] So, even if Aśoka did at all derive his multilingual strategy from the Achaemenid model, he did so only loosely, and with an important innovation.

But when we turn from matters of linguistic policy to a comparison of the content, and more importantly the tone, of the Achaemenid and Aśokan inscriptions, we find that they could hardly be more different.[6] The former abound in what might be characterized as standard royal bluster of a sort which is abundantly attested in the epigraphic records of kingdoms all over the ancient world. For example, to cite again from the Bīsutūn inscription: "These are the kingdoms which came unto me; by the favor of Ahuramazda they were my subjects; they bore tribute to me; what was said unto them either by night or by day, that was done." How different from the words of Aśoka, who, in his famous thirteenth rock edict, speaks of his conquests only in terms of his repentance for the death and devastation which they caused, and who elsewhere claims to make himself available "at any time, anywhere" (*savraṃ kalaṃ. . . savatra*; rock edict 6-D [Shābāzgaṛhī, line 14; Hultzsch 1925: 57]), not in order to give commands to his subjects, but rather to be

4 §§1,5–6; translation by Kent (1953: 119).

5 See Falk 2006: 241.

6 This contrast has been remarked on by many historians, for example Kosambi (1975: 198), Salomon (2007a: 55–56) and Thapar (1973: 127–8).

approached by his officers with regard to "the affairs of my people" (*aṭhe me janasa*, 6-C [Girnār, line 4; Hultzsch 1925: 11]). So, even if it is true that Aśoka's inspiration for recording public inscriptions was the Achaemenid model, he adopted at most only some of its superficial characteristics, and virtually nothing of its content.

This in itself is not so strange, since by the time in question Iran and India had developed into very different cultural regions with distinct religious, moral, and cultural values. What is however quite strange is that Aśoka's model of a direct and personal, even confessional address to his subjects has no more parallel in the later Indian world than it does in Iran. Nowhere in post-Aśokan epigraphy is there anything even remotely similar to the content and flavor of his edicts; it is almost as if they never existed. Instead, what we do find, in vast profusion, is royal bluster very much like that of the Achaemenids, and as different as it could be from Aśoka's rhetoric.

By way of illustrating this contrast, I cite here a classic example of a royal epigraphic proclamation from post-Aśokan India, namely the Junāgaṛh inscription of the Western Satrap ruler Rudradāman. I cite this inscription, among other reasons, because it is one of the earliest specimens, dating from about 150 CE, of the classical epigraphical panegyric genre, or *praśasti*. Here is part of its description (line 9) of the king:

> . . . he who, because from the womb he was distinguished by the possession of undisturbed consummate Royal Fortune, was resorted to by all castes and chosen their lord to protect them. . . not failing to deal blows to equal antagonists meeting him face to face. . . who is the lord of the whole of eastern and western Ākarāvantī, the Anūpa country, Ānarta, Surāṣṭra, Śvabhru, Maru, Kaccha. . . and other territories gained by his own valour. . .[7]

And so on. The words of Rudradāman's panegyrist are strikingly like those of Darius: substitute Ahuramazda for "Royal Fortune" (*Rājalakṣmī*), substitute Persia, Elam, Babylonia, Assyria, Arabia, Egypt, etc., for Ākarāvantī, Anūpa, Ānarta, Surāṣṭra, Śvabhru, Maru, etc., and we are, *mutatis mutandis*, in very much the same rhetorical realm. Here in the Junāgaṛh inscription we hear, not the voice of the king himself expressing heartfelt pleas for righteousness and the agonies of his own self-doubts, but rather that of a court panegyrist, singing his master's praises without limit or restraint. We can almost picture the king basking in the delicious verbal massage of his massive ego; quite different stuff from what Aśoka seems to have been made of.

But there is also another reason that I have chosen the Junāgaṛh *praśasti* as a counterpoint to Aśoka's edicts. This inscription is one of extremely few Indian inscriptions (other than those of Aśoka himself, of course) which refer to Aśoka, and moreover it is, to my knowledge, the only non-Buddhist inscription to do so.[8] The

7 Translation by Kielhorn (1905: 47).

8 For a rare example of an Indian Buddhist inscription referring to Aśoka, see the "Aśo-raya" inscription (Bailey 1982), referring to a *stūpa* founded by King Aśo[ka] (. . .

principal—or perhaps rather the ostensible—purpose of Rudradāman's proclamation was to record the reconstruction of Lake Sudarśana, and in the course of describing previous public works projects on this lake the panegyrist refers to its having been "adorned with conduits for Aśoka the Maurya by the Yavana king Tuṣaspha while he was governing [there]" (lines 8–9, *aśokasya mauryasya <*kṛ>te yavanarājena tuṣ[ā]sphenādhiṣṭhāya praṇāḷibhir ala[ṃ]kṛta[ṃ]*). This tells us that the historical memory of Aśoka was still alive during Rudradāman's reign, some four centuries after his lifetime, although, unfortunately, we have no way to know exactly what Rudradāman and his contemporaries knew and thought about Aśoka.

This tantalizing connection between Aśoka and Rudradāman becomes all the more intriguing when we recall that Rudradāman's inscription is engraved on the very same boulder on which, almost exactly four hundred years earlier, a complete set of Aśoka's major rock edicts (the so-called Girnar version) was inscribed. So, the reference to Aśoka in the later record is not merely casual; a historical linkage and some sort of association between the two great kings is clearly intended.[9] It can, moreover, be assumed that at this point—that is, in the second century CE—the Aśokan inscriptions were still at least partially legible and comprehensible (although we know that in later periods of Indian history the early forms of Brāhmī script had been forgotten and the Aśokan inscriptions had become an impenetrable mystery).[10] So, the reason that the composers of the later inscription didn't copy or imitate Aśoka's model was not that they couldn't understand it. But it is harder to say what the reason was; I will return to this question later.

First, though, we must return to Aśoka's time in order to see what else we can find there, or thereabouts, to help us understand the curious progress of Indian epigraphic rhetoric. As mentioned at the outset, it is now believed by several authoritative experts that Indian epigraphy essentially began with Aśoka, and that the handful of inscriptions which had been considered by earlier scholars as pre-Aśokan are probably actually more or less contemporary with him. Among these, the Sohgaurā copper plaque, from Gorakhpur District, Uttar Pradesh, is generally agreed to be one of the very earliest Indian inscriptions other than those of Aśoka; it may well date from the time of Aśoka's reign, or possible even somewhat earlier.[11] Like the Aśokan inscriptions, it is in several important respects entirely untypical of later Indian inscriptions. First, in terms of physical format, it is cast in copper. This is surprising in that the later Indian inscriptions on copper plates, which are exceedingly numerous, are engraved into hammered sheets rather than cast as a unit. Also, the object is remarkably small, measuring (according to Fleet 1907: 509) about 2½" by 1⅞", again unlike later inscriptions on copper and other materials, which are typically much larger than this. These features led Fleet (ibid., p. 527) to

dhamaraïaṃmi aśoraya-praïstavidami. . . "in the Dharmarājika [*stūpa*] established by King Aśo[ka]"). (This inscription is re-edited in Salomon 2007b: 283.)

9 This historical continuity is further extended by the third inscription on the same rock, recorded by Skandagupta some four hundred years after the time of Rudradāman, although this inscription does not explicitly refer to Aśoka or other ancient kings.

10 See Salomon 1998: 199.

11 Compare Falk 1993: 180: "Die Platte als solche kann aus sich heraus mit absoluter Sicherheit weder vor noch nach Aśoka datiert werden."

propose, quite plausibly, that the surviving inscription was one of multiple copies, each to be posted at various storehouses. If Fleet's hypothesis is correct, this is yet another pattern which is not repeated, to my knowledge, among later Indian inscriptions, though it does resemble to some extent the pattern of the Aśokan inscriptions, which were also erected in multiple copies in different locations.

Second, in terms of its content the Sohgaurā inscription is again highly anomalous. Here it must be conceded that the text still remains quite obscure and has never been completely or convincingly interpreted. But despite many problems of detail, it is agreed by all that the subject matter is an official order concerning the storage of provisions as a safeguard against scarcity or famine. Once again, one is hard put to find even approximate parallels to this among later Indian inscriptions. Although there are ample specimens of inscriptions recording public works projects such as wells, tanks, and especially temples and other religious institutions or endowments, I know of none which concerns the administration of storehouses or granaries.

Moreover, there is yet another, and more important difference. In later inscriptions recording public works, the sponsor, whether a king or private individual, always figures prominently, and indeed the primary purpose of such inscriptions is to honor the donor. In other words, the later inscriptions are, virtually without exception, essentially donative or celebratory in character and purpose; this, in contrast to Sohgaurā, which is purely administrative.

Thus the content as well as the format of the Sohgaurā inscription is virtually unique, and the same, *mutatis mutandis*, goes for the Mahāsthān stone inscription, written on a small stone disk found in Bogra District of modern Bangladesh. The text is even more fragmentary, obscure, and controversial than that of Sohgaurā, but also seems to concern the storage and transfer of foodstuffs in public granaries.

The only other inscriptions which can be fairly securely dated to the Aśokan or Mauryan period, besides those of Aśoka and his successor Daśaratha, are the Jogīmārā and Sītābeṅgā cave inscriptions from the Rāmgaṛh Hill in Surguja District, Madhya Pradesh. These two inscriptions are as different as they could be from the Sohgaurā and Mahāsthān records; but one thing that they do have in common with them is that they too represent a type which is virtually unduplicated in the many thousands of later Indian inscriptions. The Jogīmārā and Sītābeṅgā inscriptions can be characterized as lyrical; each consists of a single verse, the one (following the most recent interpretation, presented in Falk 1991) celebrating the spring festival, and the other, the love of one Devadina for a *devadāsī* called Śutanukā. Whereas this might seem to be the stuff of casual graffiti, the format of the inscriptions suggests something quite different; they are written in large, deeply engraved characters, with the look of a formal record. According to the generally accepted interpretation, the site in question was a theater, so that the inscriptions can be understood as a sort of mood-setting decoration.

But if this is correct, we have here, yet again, something virtually without parallel in later Indian epigraphy. Although there are specimens, from a much later period, of formal inscriptional records of complete literary works, including both *mahākāvya*s and *nāṭaka*s (Salomon 1998: 123), they are quite different in character from these isolated verses. Thus the Jogīmārā and Sītābeṅgā cave inscriptions, like the other contemporary inscriptions of the Mauryan period, stand out as anomalous in comparison to the later epigraphic traditions. The Jogīmāra inscription is additionally unusual in being composed in Māgadhī Prakrit, which is otherwise unattested in Indian inscriptions except for the aforementioned late (twelfth century CE) inscriptions of *nāṭakas* in which certain characters speak this dialect (Kielhorn 1901). Jogīmāra is therefore the only known inscription composed entirely in Māgadhī.

Thus among the few surviving inscriptions of the Mauryan period other than those of Aśoka, we find nothing that resembles the format, tone, and content of his records. In this way, the Aśokan inscriptions are unique, not only in comparison with later epigraphy, but even in their own time. But it must be equally stressed that the other Mauryan period inscriptions are similarly anomalous in comparison with what follows them, so that, in the perspective of the overall history of Indian epigraphy, the inscriptions of the Mauryan period as a whole seem to constitute a set of experimental probes which failed to set the pattern for the later epigraphic genres, or at best only left the slightest impression on them.

As for Aśoka's inscriptions, they could be considered, in a very broad sense, the predecessors of the abundant royal *praśasti* inscriptions of later centuries, if only in that they present royal proclamations in epigraphic form. But as has already been seen above by a comparison with an early *praśasti* of the second century CE, Aśoka's edicts are very much unlike the later *praśasti*s in tone and content. Some further hints about the early development of the *praśasti* genre, which is unfortunately not well documented, can be gleaned from the oldest surviving example of something approaching a classical *praśasti*, namely the Hāthigumphā inscription of Khāravela, which dates from about the late second or early first century BCE. In terms of tone and content it is fairly close to later *praśasti*s, insofar as it relates Khāravela's conquests and good works in the form of a third person narrative. In particular, it resembles Rudradāman's Junāgaṛh inscription, the earliest surviving high classical *praśasti*, in that the narrative is in ornate prose, rather than in verse like most classical specimens of the genre. But it also untypical in that it presents a year-by-year biography of the king from his childhood through his thirteenth regnal year, a format that, as far as I am aware, is nowhere repeated in any later inscriptions.

Thus Khāravela's eulogy, in broad terms, prefigures the classical forms of the *praśasti* genre, even while it differs from them in several respects. But the same can hardly be said for Aśoka's inscriptions, which still stand alone and unique. When we look at the overall picture of the development of inscriptional genres in India, the records of the Mauryan period in general and those of Aśoka in particular seem like a false start. Virtually the only thing that continues from this earliest period is the notion of leaving inscriptions itself; as far as the actual form of the later inscriptions is concerned, it seems as if their composers started over from step one after the fall of the Mauryan empire. The inscriptions of the succeeding period, that is, of the last two centuries of the pre-Christian era, are much more distinctly the forerunners of the classical forms of inscriptions, as manifested, for example, in the proto-*praśasti* of Khāravela, and in the Buddhist donative records of the great *stūpa* sites such as Bharhut and Sanchi.[12]

Exactly why this is the case is anybody's guess, as the inscriptional record of these early centuries is simply too sparse to provide a clear answer. Those who view early Indian history as involving a post-Mauryan counter-revolution or restoration of Brahmanical orthodoxy might take some aid and comfort from the epigraphical record, which seems to present us with a surprisingly abrupt break, as if there were a conscious effort to erase all traces of the Mauryan worldview. Then again, those who consider the driving force of history to be the force of personality of certain "Great Men" might be inclined to hold that the uniqueness of Aśoka's inscriptions reflect the uniqueness of his personality, and could claim that the reason they were never duplicated is that no other king matched the combination of political skill, strength of will, and philosophical self-reflectivity which allowed Aśoka to bare his soul in public and, apparently, get away with it. There is something to be said for this argument, and in any case it can hardly be denied that Aśoka stands as a unique figure in Indian, and indeed in world history. And if so, why shouldn't his inscriptions be unique?

12 It is true, however, that donative records of this type are partially prefigured by the Barābar cave inscriptions of Aśoka and the Nāgārjunī cave inscriptions of his successor Daśaratha. Here, contrary to the general pattern, we have among this special subset of Mauryan inscriptions a few specimens which anticipate an epigraphic genre that becomes very common in later times.

Bibliography

Bailey, H. W. 1982. "Two Kharoṣṭhī Inscriptions." *Journal of the Royal Asiatic Society of Great Britain and Ireland* 1982: 141–55.

Falk, H. 1991. "Kunstdichtung in den Höhlen von Rāmgarh." *Asiatische Studien/Études Asiatiques* 45: 257–76.

———. 1993. *Schrift im alten Indien. Ein Forschungsbericht mit Anmerkungen.* ScriptOralia. Tübingen: Gunter Narr Verlag.

———. 2006. *Aśokan Sites and Artefacts: A Source-Book with Bibliography.* Monographien zur indischen Archäeologie, Kunst und Philologie. Mainz am Rhein: Philipp von Zabern.

Fleet, J. F. 1907. "The Inscription on the Sohgaura Plate." *Journal of the Royal Asiatic Society of Great Britain and Ireland* 1907: 509–32.

Hinüber, O. von. 2003. *Beiträge zur Erklärung der Senavarma-Inschrift.* Akademie der Wissenschaften und der Literatur, Abhandlungen der geistes- und sozialwissenschaftlichen Klasse, 2003 no. 1. Mainz: Akademie der Wissenschaften und der Literatur/Stuttgart: Franz Steiner Verlag.

Hulzsch, E. 1925. *Inscriptions of Aśoka. New Edition.* Corpus Inscriptionum Indicarum 1. Oxford: Clarendon Press.

Kent, R. 1953. *Old Persian.* American Oriental Series 33. New Haven: American Oriental Society.

Kielhorn, F. 1901. *Bruchstücke indischer Schauspiele in Inschriften zu Ajmere.* In *Festschrift zur Feier des hundertfünfzigjährigen Bestehens der Königlichen Gesellschaft der Wissenschaften zu Göttingen* (Abhandlungen der philologisch-historischen Klasse). Berlin: Weidmannsche Buchhandlung.

———. 1905. "Junagadh Rock Inscription of Rudradaman; the Year 72." *Epigraphia Indica* 8: 36–49.

Kosambi, D. D. 1975. *An Introduction to the Study of Indian History.* 2nd ed. Bombay: Popular Prakashan.

MacMullen, R. 1982. "The Epigraphic Habit in the Roman Empire." *The American Journal of Philology* 103: 233–46.

Sadakata, A. 1996. "Inscriptions kharoṣṭhī provenant du marché aux antiquités de Peshawar." *Journal Asiatique* 284: 301–24.

Salomon, R. 1998. *Indian Epigraphy: A Guide to the Study of Inscriptions in Sanskrit, Prakrit, and the Other Indo-Aryan Languages.* South Asia Research Series. New York: Oxford University Press.

———. 2007a. "Ancient India: Peace Within and War Without." In *War and Peace in the Ancient World.* Ed. K. Raaflaub, pp. 53–65. The Ancient World: Comparative Histories. Malden MA: Blackwell.

———. 2007b. "Dynastic and Institutional Connections in the Pre- and Early Kuṣāṇa Period: New Manuscript and Epigraphic Evidence." In *On the Cusp of an Era: Art in the Pre-Kuṣāṇa World.* Ed. D. Srinivasan, pp. 267–86. Brill's Inner Asian Library. Leiden: E. J. Brill.

Thapar, R. 1973. *Aśoka and the Decline of the Mauryas.* 2nd ed. Delhi: Oxford University Press.

Assessing Evidence of Aśokan-Period Art

JANICE LEOSHKO

Artistic developments in the Maurya period, especially during the reign of Aśoka in the third century BCE, are important concerns since many new things seem to have happened. The problem remains that we are not sure of what these are exactly, for the body of visual evidence is so incomplete. Nonetheless, the Aśokan pillars have led to a certainty that this period must have witnessed other amazing artistic achievements besides these skillfully worked monoliths. A better view will no doubt emerge from more and fuller archaeological investigations, but further reflection on what we think we already know may also lead us to new understanding. This seems especially promising given that most discussions of the art associated with Aśoka continue to be framed by questions of an earlier age.[1] In an attempt to develop additional perspective for this visual evidence, I focus here on what are best known and thus perhaps hardest pressed into various lines of interpretation and significance. These are works made of stone.

It seems that the Maurya period if not specifically Aśoka's reign is when shaping and sculpting stone on a large scale began in India. This is at least when the earliest substantial evidence survives of the skills that in subsequent centuries would create India's many astonishing monuments and sculptures. Since the role of this king looms so large in the story of the support and spread of Buddhism, one might at least expect some recent reassessment of how Aśokan material affects the larger narrative concerning the development of Buddhist art. Even this has, however, not yet happened. By focusing upon certain aspects of the pillars and their capitals, the limits of the way in which they and the few anthropomorphic figures usually associated with them are treated may become clearer. We may then be able to see what has not yet been asked and, as importantly, what has been too easily assumed.

More often than not the capitals of the Aśokan pillars do not survive—only seven complete ones are known—but even the scale and craftsmanship of the extant

1 See, for example, Allchin 1995: 251–256. There have been new and intriguing approaches in recent discussions, but these are usually for other types of evidence. Examples include the exploration of differing strands of Aśoka's life emphasized in later Buddhist texts (Strong 1994), nuanced study of the importance of Aśoka for the development of Buddhist devotion (Walters 1997) and further focused treatments of the contents of Aśokan inscriptions (Tieken 2000).

columns demonstrate astonishing technical skill of now unknown artisans. This can be appreciated in early photographs such as this one from the nineteenth century of the remains of an Aśokan pillar at Rummindei, the modern name for the Buddhist site of Lumbinī (fig.1). The pillars garnered attention through many centuries so that we know more about their effect upon later viewers, both inhabitants of the subcontinent and visitors, than those of Aśoka's time. Evidence of the continued regard for these monumental pillars ranges from various inscriptions added centuries after Aśoka's reign to notices published by British officials as they participated in the conquest of India throughout the nineteenth century.

An interest in recording the appearance of the various monuments that seemingly reflected India's past was part of the earliest British explorations of the subcontinent. This led to the creation of many paintings by Indian artists such as this work from 1820 (fig. 2). Inscribed "Firoz Shah's pillar," which translates the Persian inscription on this painting for this new group of patrons, the depiction shows an Aśokan pillar standing amidst various structures built by the Tugluq ruler, Firuz Shah (r. 1351–88).[2]

Western interest was not the beginning of wonder for these impressive monoliths, as this painting actually demonstrates; for it depicts a relocated pillar, brought from its original site some one hundred miles away in the fourteenth century. Firuz Shah's interest in these pillars led to laborious operations to move and re-erect two Aśokan pillars at his new capital in Delhi, which is detailed in a surviving account by one of his court historians.[3] This relocation may have served more than a desire to demonstrate Tugluq control of others as Firuz Shah seems to have viewed the pillars as suitable enhancements to his large and ambitious architectural program that proclaimed the assumption of India's grand past into its even grander present.

Although we have no contemporaneous accounts of the creation of the pillars other than Aśoka's statements that are inscribed upon them, surely they garnered attention during the reign of Aśoka as well as afterward.[4] It is not difficult to imagine that the operations involved in their completion and installation were astonishing events to witness, and continued attention to Aśokan pillars even when their edicts could not be read signals an especial regard that may be hard for us to appreciate fully from our position of knowing their historical importance.[5] The

2 These depictions, painted by Indian artists, demonstrate how they adapted to both new interest and taste—hence the Western style—of British patrons. Long ignored, there are now various studies of such works.

3 Firuz Shah's personal role in creating buildings as well as repairing old monuments is also recorded in this account. Because Firuz Shah's mother was Hindu, his general interest in the past is intriguing; for discussion of his architectural patronage see Welch 1993.

4 It is useful to remember how often the pillars or other surfaces on which Aśoka's inscriptions appear have added inscriptions, sometimes royal, sometimes pilgrims, sometimes wandering British agents. The likelihood that many of these later inscriptions were added to the Aśokan ones without the ability to read them is clear testimony to the powers of images of texts rather than simply the contents of the texts.

5 While such attention may imply that there is a long history of excavation of sites attached to Aśokan-period activity, in fact, this is not the case. (Topra and Meerut, for instance, from which Firuz Shah removed the Aśokan pillars, have yet to be excavated or yet

problem is that the modern importance accorded the content of the inscribed texts has partially obscured the materiality of the pillars and the commanding presence this conveys. As Thomas Trautmann and Carla Sinopoli recently note, archaeological study of India has been a practice so guided by literary sources that material evidence is often valued for how it lends tangible substantiation to textually attested events and places (Trautmann and Sinopoli 2002). It is an interesting perspective for considering the many studies of Aśokan pillars.

These scholars argue that we must be vigilant to recognize the full effects of a subordination of material culture by textual evidence. This they posit arose in the late eighteenth century, paralleled by a new and superior status accorded those with knowledge of Oriental languages over sources whose authority derived from having directly seen something (Trautmann and Sinopoli 2002: 495). Thus information that could be found in texts by those who could read texts was believed to be more authoritative than actual remains (and by extension, the knowledge of actual inhabitants). It is ironic that this occurs just when Westerners gain greater direct access to material remains in India, becoming a widely held view that affected even those who primarily study visual works.

There is so little concrete footprint of Aśoka's empire known from surviving material that, as Trautmann and Sinopoli point out, most of what we think we know actually comes from textual evidence of different kinds.[6] For instance, the well known account of Megasthenes, the Seleucid ambassador to the Maurya capital Pāṭaliputra during the time of Aśoka's grandfather, Candragupta, relays far more about how Pāṭaliputra—present-day Patna—looked than does material from the few excavations and chance finds from the site. Combining such textual evidence with actual material is still a frequent approach when Aśokan sites are discussed. For example, Raymond Allchin notes in his recent survey of early historic South Asia how seeming correspondences among Megasthenes' account and other texts, such as the *Arthaśāstra*, assumed by Allchin to be composed during the reign of Candragupta, with known remains suggest the usefulness of this approach (Allchin 1995). But it is disconcerting to find conjectural drawings based on the *Arthaśāstra* interspersed with actual plans and excavation photographs in his discussion of Maurya architecture.[7]

Textual descriptions do not alter the fact that we have very little real idea of architectural forms and decoration. Despite the widely assumed replication at Pāṭaliputra of a pillared hall similar to the audience hall at Persepolis, actual evidence is quite limited. The same is true for specific details and motifs, largely

given much serious surface study.) Although surveys and reports were made in the nineteenth century after the initial discoveries of many sites having Aśokan inscriptions, these were not always followed by more thorough and careful operations.

6 There are various bodies of evidence such as BPW pottery and many terracotta figurines, but we do not know the connections of such evidence to Aśoka.

7 Given the continued occupation of the site and the early date of the Maurya period, it is not surprising that knowledge about Aśoka's capital is incomplete, but it is surprising that Pāṭaliputra has garnered so little archaeological effort. Although not recent, a survey of studies of sites in Bihar remains a relatively thorough guide to the accumulated knowledge about archaeological notices in the region of Patna (Patil 1963).

based on isolated finds such as the stone capital now in the Patna Museum. Motifs in this capital—palmettes, rosettes and the volute forms—do correspond to Persian examples, but what can we really say about this phenomenon when we have no other knowledge about the object? Even its date is not certain as it is often thought to have been made some time after the third century BCE.

Insufficient physical corroboration for textual descriptions of the Aśokan empire means that we literally have to take an early author's word(s) for it. The fact that the accuracy of Megasthenes' account is still not always questioned—even though it is only partially preserved in paraphrased form within records of other ancient writers—reflects an unproblematic regard often given textual evidence. As Romila Thapar has cautioned, Megasthenes was writing within a Greek or Hellenistic view that needs to be taken into account when using his descriptions of Pāṭaliputra and India (Thapar 1997: 296). It may seem appropriate to rely on these remarkably surviving and known sources, such as that of Megasthenes, the various accounts of later Buddhists texts and most importantly the thoughts of Aśoka in the surviving edicts, in order to understand an important period of India's past. But these texts are also evidence about their particular authors, and while the viewpoints they reflect are as valid as the actual evidence they may offer about the Aśokan period, the two are not necessarily identical. Without recognition of these difficulties, combining textual evidence of different periods can create false images and so too can an uncritical use of material evidence in combination with that of texts. Perhaps the most dangerous result is the impression that we have more than we really do.[8] Confronting the fragmentary nature of the evidence as well as the way in which textual evidence both impedes and helps our understanding seems critical for moving beyond established views. Romila Thapar as well as others have pointed out the continued consequences of past studies upon new investigations of India's history. (Thapar 1989: 231). In a similar manner careful consideration of how visual evidence has been studied also remains a significant component of further explorations.

Looking Back to Move Forward

The pillars still standing in the nineteenth century especially attracted attention; Brian Hodgson prepared an account of two in northern Bihar at Lauriya Araraj and Lauriya Nandangarh and sent it to James Prinsep and the Asiatic Society of Bengal in 1836. Striking images were made of these (figs. 3 and 4), and the pillar at Lauriya Nandangarh became particularly famous since it was the only inscribed standing pillar with its capital intact. Photographs taken by Sir Benjamin Simpson in the 1860s are still reproduced today; illustrated here is one of his less frequently used views. Even before photography was invented in 1839, the appearance of this pillar was noteworthy as demonstrated by the interesting notebook of James Rind from

8 This is the caution I would give recent studies such as Harry Falk's essay, "The Tidal Waves of Indian History" (2006), which remain nonetheless quite valuable.

1797 containing his transcription of the edict as well as details that record the pillar's form and dimensions now in the British Museum.

The nineteenth-century photograph of the pillar at the site of the Buddha's birthplace at Rummindei (see fig. 1) reflects British interest with the large monoliths as part of their pursuit of uncovering the Buddhist past in the second half of the nineteenth century (Leoshko 2003). This photograph was taken in 1896 during excavation operations at Rummindei to verify that it was Lumbinī, the site long believed to be the birthplace of the Buddha. By the end of the century, Aśoka's image as an early supporter of Buddhism was well established, and Aśokan pillars were expected at Buddhist sites. The Śaiva ascetic also pictured in this photograph, however, is a reminder of how objects accrue further meanings in later times, sometimes taking on additional lives, a concept so usefully examined in the Indian context by Richard Davis (Davis 1997).

The ascetic's presence for us today may document contemporary worship of the monolith, ongoing but different religious practice and the appropriation and reinterpretation of a work from an earlier time. We might contrast that with the controlled activities given to Indians by the British as illustrated by the second person in the photograph who serves as a gauge of the pillar's size in the photograph and perhaps assists with other tasks during the British exploration of the site. For nineteenth-century British viewers of the album of which this photograph was once a part, however, the image might seem to contrast the greater glory of India's past with its current unsophisticated nature. What else could a practitioner of an enlightened and civilized religion (i.e., Anglican Christianity) think of those whose religion (i.e., Hinduism) condoned the worship of objects and ascetic practice? And likewise we might wonder about the nineteenth-century need to make Aśoka, a past ruler of South Asia, a significant supporter of a seemingly more reasonable religion that was no longer practiced in its place of origin. In this regard it is useful to remember Gregory Schopen's observation that a Protestant bias for textual evidence and an aversion to ritual significantly shaped the study of Buddhism in the nineteenth century (Schopen 1991). Ironically, this also created a certain perspective on the artistic value of the visual material, limiting how Aśokan-period material was studied.

The edict on the Rummindei pillar is important to scholars interested in particular evidence of history and religion since it records Aśoka's journey to the site of Buddha's birthplace and his exemption of the village from normal tax obligations. Different from other pillars that repeat edicts found elsewhere or are less specific with reference to Buddhism, this inscription seems contemporary and explicit confirmation of Aśoka's interest in the Buddha. It is especially important since so much of the evidence of Aśoka's specific embrace of Buddhism actually comes from Buddhist texts dating much later than his reign (Strong 1983). As scholars now frequently note, the Buddhist Aśoka is perhaps best studied in the much later Buddhist texts (e.g., the Sri Lankan chronicles) or in the partisan accounts of individuals such as Xuanzang. Aśoka, for many living before the recent past, was not known through his edicts but from various stories in Buddhist sources that emphasized his spectacular support of Buddhism.[9]

Although frequently cited as evidence of Aśoka's support of Buddhism, the pillar at Rummindei, is rarely illustrated in scholarly discussions of Aśokan-period art, probably because its capital was never found, but such monumental yet finely finished shafts deserve more attention in terms of the artistic skills they document. Most discussion of artistic issues, however, focuses on whether the much fewer surviving capitals are evidence of an indigenous style or foreign influence. Most often foreign influence is posited in terms of reflecting Persian traditions as can be encountered in the surviving monumental pillars once part of the palace complex at Persepolis. While there are indeed similarities, there are also differences. Such Persian pillars were originally part of structural supports so their capitals bore roof timbers upon their backs; the Indian examples crowned their shafts. The Persian pillars were fluted rather than smooth, and importantly, they did not bear edicts of a king. This question of seeming influence, however, dominates much discussion of the pillars even though scholars such as Niharranjan Ray highlight these other concerns (Ray 1975). The assumption that the capitals especially demonstrate outside influence was first fully expressed by Vincent Smith in 1911, who felt after considerable study that this could be the only explanation for works of such high caliber found in India (Smith 1911). This as well as the fact that it is an element in fierce debates about true creativity in other periods of Indian art should cause reflection on what lies beneath such limiting perspectives. Indeed, assumptions about foreign influence in the Maurya period eerily reverberate in controversies over the development of the Buddha image.

When considering how the capitals have been discussed, it is useful to realize the gradual way in which they were encountered. Besides the lion atop the still standing pillar at Lauriya Nandangarh and a similar one at the site of Vaishali, the capital of an Aśokan pillar at Sanchi was also known in the first half of the nineteenth century although it was not found on its pillar (Fell 1834). It was noticed lying amidst the fallen remains of the southern gateway; the remains of the shaft were found later (fig. 5). The Sanchi capital presents four conjoined lions, whose heads are unfortunately quite damaged (fig. 6); this form is like the more famous Sarnath capital and significantly, the Sanchi pillar also bore the same edict. Discovered in 1862, it was the first capital to be encountered not depicting a lion subject. Depicting an elephant, it is still located at its findspot, Sankasya. (fig. 7). No inscription, however, was ever found. The only other known capital not depicting a lion subject is the much more famous and often illustrated Rampurva bull; it was not discovered, however, until the first decade of the twentieth century along with a the capital of the second pillar there, one presenting a single lion.[10] In the nineteenth century attention to the capitals was minimal; they were simply seen

9 Prinsep's use of Sri Lankan texts, the *Dīpavaṃsa* and the *Mahāvaṃsa*, in his identification of Aśoka exacerbates this as their unbiased nature was long assumed (Kejariwal 1988: 215).

10 Although well known through frequently published illustrations, the bull capital cannot actually be seen easily today as it is now in the Rashtrapati Bhavan. The complete shaft of the pillar was recovered (still at Rampurva), but interestingly, it lacks any inscription.

as part of an Aśokan monument of which the inscribed edicts were far more important. Thus they served as general, but largely unexamined evidence of Aśokan-period achievements. Today they largely function as vague background setting for what is often regarded as the jewel of Aśokan material, the capital found at Sarnath.

The Sarnath pillar and its capital were only discovered in excavations conducted there in 1905. Unknown in the nineteenth century, they were thus not part of the initial re-discovery of Aśoka although Sarnath had long been important. It was a crucial site for the British realization of Buddhism's past importance in India. The Dhamekh *stūpa*, which was a prominent ruin at Sarnath, was easily studied (i.e., dug into) by British officers working in nearby Varanasi (Leoshko 2003). Alexander Cunningham also excavated there later in the nineteenth century, but the most extensive work occurred in the early twentieth century. Photographs taken at the time of its discovery show the fragmented pillar with its inscription and the now famous capital (fig. 8). F. O. Oertel, who unearthed this Aśoka pillar at Sarnath, was most struck by this discovery, even though the same season's work yielded what has become perhaps the most famous Buddha image, the Gupta-period sculpture of the Buddha making the gesture of teaching (*dharmacakra).* The Sarnath capital now reigns over this and many other Buddhist works in the Sarnath site museum, and its status as the emblem of India ensures its fame.[11]

Seemingly, the most significant aspect of Sarnath was as the place of Śakyamuni's first sermon, what comes to be represented in Buddhist art by the *cakra* or a figure of the Buddha making the *dharmacakramudrā*. This important site was visited in succeeding centuries by pilgrims, some of them from outside of India such as Xuanzang. His seventh-century Chinese account of travels through India was translated in the nineteenth century. It then became a valuable source for various explorers who wished to locate and investigate Buddhist sites such as in the case of Lumbinī. In particular, Alexander Cunningham, who prodded the Indian government into establishing the Archaeological Survey, wrote frequently about his extensive use of the account by Xuanzang to guide his explorations (Leoshko 2003). Although he knew of this Chinese description of an Aśokan pillar at Sarnath, Cunningham died before it was discovered.

As the Aśokan capital from Sarnath is one of the earliest sculptures that can be discussed within the tradition of Buddhist art, its imagery is regularly pressed into various symbolic interpretations. This occurs in part because of the significance accorded much later texts, such as the pilgrim record of Xuanzang that dates some eight hundred years after the reign of Aśoka. Since Xuanzang, who describes an Aśokan pillar at Sarnath, lauds the monarch's devotion to Buddhism, the assumption has long been made that elements of this capital can be read as Buddhist symbols. This approach, begun with Vincent Smith continues today in many discussions of the Sarnath capital (e.g., Allchin 1995: 215). Given its Buddhist location and the seeming Buddhist content of its edict, it has not seemed an

11 Its iconic status today as the emblem of the nation of India omits a direct Buddhist meaning and changes the original form; perhaps most interestingly, the pillar which it once topped is omitted.

unreasonable approach. The Sarnath capital's four addorsed lions are thus often described as symbolizing the spread of the Buddha's *dharma* which itself is thought to be symbolized by the large *cakra* that once surmounted the heads of the lions and the four *cakras* appearing on the abacus beneath each lion's feet (fig. 9).

While indeed the *cakra* and the gesture of *dharmacakra* are clearly used later to symbolize Śākyamuni preaching and/or the place where this began (i.e., Sarnath), such use of the *cakra* as this specific Buddhist symbol is otherwise unknown in the Aśokan period. We may be looking then at one of the early surviving examples of this as a Buddhist symbol. Given the fact that it is part of an Aśokan message, the use of this imagery may represent a truly creative moment, perhaps paralleling Aśoka's appropriation of the concept of *dharma* as recently suggested by Patrick Olivelle (2005: 491–511). Can we consider the Sarnath capital as evidence of the appropriation of the *cakra* as a symbol for the concept of *dharma* rather than seeing it only as an expected use of a Buddhist form? The very reasonableness of its use in a Buddhist context masks the fact that its appearance here may be near the beginning if not the beginning of distinctly Buddhist imagery.

The various lives an object accrues may not always be in addition to some earlier one; the multivalency of a symbol may not always have existed. We must not forget how easy it is to project meaning backward from our position of knowing later developments. Attaching a Buddhist meaning for the imagery of the Sarnath pillar might exemplify this. The use of the *cakra* in the Sarnth pillar may symbolize in some way the Buddha's teaching at the time that it was carved, but this interpretation arises from later material where the *cakra* is clearly used as a symbol of teaching and sometimes specifically as a symbol of the Buddha's first teaching at Sarnath. We do not know, however, when it began to have this meaning and when it began to be so depicted. The use of later Buddhist imagery to interpret earlier evidence assumes that meanings are stable with respect to particular symbols. But it is an assumption that must be scrutinized; we simply cannot assert a symbol's meaning because later it was used this way.[12]

In terms of artistic achievement, the Sarnath capital is emphasized for its seeming high caliber and how that reflects Aśoka's greatness, an interesting evaluation given the fact that there is still really little serious consideration of its forms. The sculpting of the Sarnath lions or the Sanchi lions as well as that of capitals with a single lion like that found at Rampurva and now in the Indian Museum (fig. 10) is usually defined in terms of artistic elements presumably found in Persian works. But there are differences among these Indian capitals as well as differences with Persian works.[13] Capitals from Persepolis such as the one now in the Musée Guimet depicting a bull are frequently invoked as evidence of likely influence (fig. 11).

12 With respect to the meaning of depictions of the *cakra*, an exploration that incorporates the perspective of Patrick Olivelle's study of the semantic development of *dharma* in its adoption and adaptation by Buddhism could be quite illuminating. See Olivelle 2004.

13 Lions in the capitals other than the Sarnath one extend their tongues; such details as well as some clumsy sculpting as in the area of the mouths of the Sarnath lions (unfortunately not visible in available photographs) as well as differences in the lion bodies suggest the need for further stylistic study.

There is certainly a similar demarcation in sculpting stone surfaces, what we might call a hard-edged treatment of forms, but this seems hardly enough to infer specific ties, and, as another example now in the University of Chicago Museum demonstrates, there are also many differences (fig. 12). Persian examples differ among themselves, and various styles may have been consciously employed to reflect the cosmopolitan taste of ruling Persian elites. One Near Eastern scholar wrote some time ago about evidence of Greek sculptors working at Persepolis in the creation of animal sculptures. The complexities of such cultural interaction should surely be considered when looking at the Aśokan-period material (Kawani 1986). James Harle, in his survey of Indian art, gave a valuable caution to the frequent assertion of foreign influence, writing:

> A great many misguided judgments have been made about the purpose and style of these pillars and their capitals, due in part to a grossly uninformed drawing of Iranian parallels, due in part to the absence of any surviving progenitors of the pillars in India, and in part to a failure to disentangle the complex relationship between the physical and historical reality of a work of art and all that it embodies (Harle 1985: 24).

In many ways Aśokan pillars may be closer to Near Eastern steles or Egyptian obelisks that were created for particular rulers. I do not raise this in order to pursue further the role of vague outside influence but to suggest there are comparisons that may be more meaningful. It is these different Near Eastern or Egyptian works that allow us to think further about the patron and the intended audience as Aśokan pillars had a distinct intention that was much more than being parts, albeit impressive ones, of a building. Royal obelisks in Egypt celebrated a particular king and often contained references to historical events as well as proclamations of the king. Moreover these impressive lithic forms mixed inscriptions with visual depictions. Creating such markers of imperial grandeur was a long-lived tradition with many examples throughout the second millenia BCE, and it received especial focus in Egypt in the second half of the first millennium BCE. Thinking about the Aśokan pillars and capitals from this perspective allows us to consider issues of agency that are increasingly featured in studies of this monarch. We might consider how the Aśokan pillars reflect the crafting of identity, an issue that relates to ideas of Near Eastern kingship and an issue that might have especially mattered in the environment of greater Greek presence in South Asia after the time of Alexander the Great.

Since lions seem to have no place in indigenous forms, the lion capitals of the Aśokan pillars—accounting for five of the total seven that survive—are often construed as evidence of outside influence, couched in terms that suggest the adoption of greater traditions by lesser ones. This is not, however, the only interpretation to be made of such possible influence. The proud way in which Achaemenid rulers at Persepolis proclaimed their ability to draw accomplished craftsmen from many parts of their empire for the creation of their monuments should cause us to reflect on an insistence for defining purely indigenous elements in Aśokan material. The identification of indigenous elements seems really more our issue, reflecting a value for "authentic" that was not necessarily held in the past. Why is influence perceived in a manner that implies subordination? When elements are borrowed or adapted, why is this not seen as a creative manipulation of existing forms? Viewed in this manner, do the capitals offer intriguing evidence of Aśoka's engagement with international definitions of kingship that in turn distinguish him amongst ruling elites in the subcontinent?

To move the question of influence beyond matching general types like pillars or simply a similar subject is to be concerned about what is reflected in the choices that were made to adopt and/or adapt certain symbols. In the case of the lion subject, moving beyond a simple comparison raises some intriguing ideas as lion imagery in the Near East signaled complex concepts of royalty and power. Conversely, bulls were also an important symbol in the Near East, but when they appear in Indian art, this fact is never invoked, assumed to be wholly indigenous symbols. Lions appear in Near Eastern art in many ways, examples at Persepolis beyond the lion capitals include reliefs of lions attacking bulls as well as kings fighting with lions. These Persian images continue earlier Assyrian depictions, the most elaborate of which are the well-known reliefs of kings hunting lions that line the walls of Assyrian palaces. In fact, Persian kings follow the greater emphasis on portraying royal power first instituted by the Assyrians. It is useful to contemplate how this echoes through emphatic presentations of combat or potential combat in various ways. Interesting forms found at Persepolis that are also adopted from Assyrian examples include well-muscled guardian figures known as *lamassu*. These mythical creatures are winged lions or bulls with human heads. As protective deities they served as guardians and heralds of power, often figured at royal portals. These mythical creatures also appear in sophisticated luxury goods such as a gold rhyton (drinking cup) shaped like a winged lion now in the British Museum; although there are not many surviving examples, likely there were once more.[14]

The limited nature of the question of influence has certainly prevented more interesting discussions of relationships to foreign forms. We might ask why this issue still devolves so regularly into polarized views instead of leading to closer studies of forms even when scholars such as Niharranjan Ray advocated focusing on other questions? They were interested in how Aśokan-period material might be discussed as evidence of the developing skills of Indian artists, and they were not simply trying to recover credit for Indian artists from those who want to see the Aśokan monuments as dominated by foreign intervention. There seem to be so many possible questions, one might wonder why so few have been asked. Considering how the pillars give form to the speech of the king, do the capitals give animate presence to the body of the king's words? Does the lack of anthropomorphic representations reflect particular choices to distinguish this Indian imagery? What are the further meanings perhaps conveyed by the particular forms and styles of lion capitals? How, for instance, in the case of the Sarnath pillar does the distinctive treatment of the four addorsed lions from the naturalistic animals figured below suggest a rhetorical meaning for different visual forms? Rather than see this

14 The gold rhyton shaped as a winged lion is dated to the 3rd century BCE.

difference solely in terms of outside versus indigenous forms as has been the usual approach, does visual difference reflect a strategy for defining but not actually depicting royal power?[15] Finally, how is the independent nature of the Aśokan pillars an important feature? Is it profitable to compare them to obelisks as well as Indian traditions of independent pillars? Should the initial attempts by John Irwin to place Aśokan pillars within the larger context of independent pillars in India be further developed?

In his long-term study, John Irwin, the former keeper at the Victoria and Albert Museum, attempted to change the limited perspective that has for so long dominated the discussion of Aśokan pillars. In a series of articles, he literally tried to reassess all aspects of the evidence that the pillars and capitals offered, but his admirable efforts were constrained by his own concerns to uncover links to what he vaguely describes as a religion of axis mundi (Irwin 1973–76). His studies reveal this over-riding concern for demonstrating the true meaning of many pillars as symbols of a cosmic axis, and he falls into the trap of using different kinds of visual evidence in an ahistorical manner (e.g., Irwin 1987). Harry Falk is thus likely right when he notes that aspects of Irwin's work such as a disregard of the Aśokan edicts and a belief that some of the pillars were pre-Aśokan in date have reduced the impact of these studies (Falk 2006: 154).

Irwin's attention to the details of the pillars' edicts and capitals in terms of their actual production nonetheless raises a wealth of points to consider, and greater concern is now given at least to the process of engraving Aśokan inscriptions. Irwin had noticed that the edicts appear in various formats, and he linked these differences to whether or not the pillar was already standing when engraved. It is unfortunate that his reassessment was so oriented towards proving some indigenous pillar cult for he arrives at conclusions that seem extremely speculative, undermining his progress towards opening up the nature of the evidence provided by the pillars. This may be why the lines of inquiry have settled so well back into issues of invention and influence.

In his initial article, Irwin nicely summarized the earlier stages of study, first Prinsep's amazing decipherment and then the publication of Chinese travel accounts that enormously helped investigators to rediscover long abandoned Buddhist sites. Irwin notes that Vincent Smith's claim of the foreign style of the capitals was reinforced by D. B. Spooner's excavation of Maurya sites at Patna, concluding that they largely replicated Persian forms. This emphasis on foreign influence was to be repeated by later scholars who presented it in terms of a demonstration of India simply adopting a greater tradition. Sadly, this simple construction still resonates today, tied to assumptions about the limited role of Indian creativity in the creation of some of their most famous monuments. Again, most authors still feel the need to address the possibility of foreign influence in the pillars and especially in the capitals, but these remain largely discussions of "did it or did it not happen." Proponents feel it is enough to point out some similar motif or stylistic comparison

15 Such distinctions in style for rhetorical purposes are recognized and discussed in other early but non-Indian traditions of writing and art (e.g., Keightley 1996). And such differences have been noted in various styles used in Near Eastern art (Kawani 1986).

to prove their case, while those seeking to defend the independence of Indian artistic creativity understandably bristle from the lack of real evidence.

This ongoing concern about influence is fueled by an assumption of the power of foreign traditions. It is an assertion made about other aspects of Indian art beyond that of Aśokan date, most relevant here being those of Buddhist traditions. Finding foreign influence in the Mauryan period innocently but insidiously establishes an Indian penchant for adopting others' good ideas at an early time. What the Aśokan capitals need for the consideration of such influence is further examination of their forms, from more detailed examination and further measurement of their sculpted surfaces; so far analysis has largely rested on the identification of motifs: only what and not how. Such further study will provide a firmer basis on which to develop views about the actual creation and production of these works, perhaps even resulting in a relative sequence for the creation of the capitals. It is only then that a serious discussion of the possible presence of an international workforce can be had (as witnessed, for example, by such things as certain systems of masons' marks or similar proportional systems or cutting techniques). Recently a team of scholars has investigated the quarry where the monoliths may have originated (Jayaswal 1998). It is sobering that despite the seeming importance of these Aśokan works, questions about how the stone was initially cut, dressed and made ready for transport and how capitals might have been similarly treated are not yet resolved.

One aspect of Irwin's work that helps move us to questions not yet asked results from his changing view of the Sarnath pillar. In his first article Irwin followed the accepted wisdom that it represents the high point of Aśokan production, but he later reverses his opinion, concluding that the Sarnath pillar must be one of the earliest as it exhibits nothing but foreign forms (Irwin 1983). There is indeed some reason to see this particular pillar as distinct in its style, and viewed in this way, it raises interesting questions about the exact mechanics of the production of these sculptures. If it is one of the earliest (and with such a limited number we must be extremely cautious with such assertions), it may reflect a conscious appropriation that is much more than the passive acceptance of more brilliant, stronger traditions. Indeed, this is not a matter of splitting hairs as it might seem. What I am suggesting is that we cease dwelling on the question of whether or not foreign intervention was needed to carve stone and consider instead the implications of the decision to do so (or more appropriately to have others do so). In such light, the commitment of considerable resources to create a series of massive pillars seems a decision with wide implications in terms of the construction of royal identity. Was this a move by Aśoka to place himself on par with other great rulers and other great kingdoms to the West?[16] At the same time this decision creates an identity that could make this monarch and his kingdom distinct from those surrounding him and with whom he more intimately interacted. The intriguing study by Patrick Olivelle (2005) suggests that later developments in *Dharmaśāstra* literature may be evidence of Aśoka's success (seen as a response and adjustment by the Brahman community which had before this time enjoyed a privileged relationship with Indian rulers,

16 Constructing pillars is then a related but different act than inscribing edicts whether on pillars or other types of stone surfaces.

upset by Aśoka's identity as a ruler who supported Buddhism). Here then in the Sarnath pillar, the use of symbols and forms that mix foreign and Indian might well be evidence of a specific desire for distinctive presence for visual works associated with Aśoka.

Some Further Implications

Purāṇic sources note that Aśoka came from a family of low status, but he and the other rulers of his dynasty nonetheless operated in a Brahmanical world. It was, however, a world undergoing many changes from increasing urbanization to changing world views prompted by the alternative systems of emerging heterodox practices (which included Buddhism). The distinct possibility that stone was used for these pillars (Asher 2006: 57), but not other types of works might be seen to parallel the way in which writing on stone is saved for the voice of the king (also paralleling suggestions that earlier writing was used for commercial reasons but not for religious or legal ones). The question of whether stone was used in this early period for creating large anthropomorphic figures has only recently been raised; scholars for a very long time have simply assumed that it was so. The seeming high quality of the Sarnath capital has long been linked to the striking sculpture with a similarly polished surface known as the Didarganj chauri-bearer so that this sculpture is often attributed to the period of Aśoka (fig. 13). Since its accidental discovery by villagers in the early twentieth century, the life-sized image has been heralded as a masterpiece (Guha-Thakurta 2004). But the date remains controversial for major Indian scholars as well as some Western ones have placed it later (e.g., Ray, Auboyer 1948). Many more, however, have steadfastly maintained its Mauryan pedigree. Allchin's approach is a common one; while stating that he is not arguing that it must be Mauryan, he includes it nonetheless in his discussion of Maurya-period works (1995). The reluctance to remove it at least visually from the Maurya period even if the accompanying textual discussions equivocate reveals an interesting belief that there must have been ongoing image-making even if there is no real surviving evidence, at least created on a large scale.

A most useful intervention in the tyranny of this view occurs in a recent article by the art historians Frederick Asher and Walter Spink (Asher and Spink 1989). They confront the long held controversy over the date of the Didarganj sculpture with recently found female images that, despite their polished surface, clearly fall outside of the range of the Maurya period due to stylistic features. Thus Asher and Spink propose that the polish technique, which had long been accepted as incontrovertible evidence of Maurya-period manufacture, is better seen as a regional rather than a chronological marker. Begun during the Maurya period, they posit that this technique continued to be employed beyond the Maurya period at least in certain regions, and such continuity could certainly be expected in the region of the Maurya capital. While others expressed doubt over the reputed early date of the Didarganj sculpture, Asher and Spink have engaged the issue most fully. They find various stylistic similarities between the Didarganj work and Kushan-period sculptures, giving the stalled controversy some much needed serious reflection.

It is interesting how long lived the belief in this date has been when we consider that proponents have only the polish and the findspot (in the region of the Maurya capital) as major evidence. If the Didarganj work is removed from the Maurya period, the few other large anthropomorphic sculptures related to it in style and similarly polished might also date later. But there are some benefits to this shifted view, as, for example, with the two nude male fragmentary figures from Lohanipur that no longer need to stand alone for centuries, separate from the evidence of production of other Jina sculptures (fig. 14). As works from the first or second centuries, they can instead challenge Mathurā as the most important center in north India for the production of images when anthropomorphic forms are adopted for the Jain, the Buddhist and finally the Brahmanical religions around the beginning of the Common Era.[17] This view also usefully illuminates the narrow concern for such figures as there is scarcely any consideration of how the Lohanipur fragments or the other figures functioned.

As Asher and Spink note, it is significant that so many are loath to reduce the achievements of the Aśokan age. They feel the reluctance to remove these few anthropomorphic sculptures from the Maurya period reflects the desire to let the Aśokan period be as grand as possible. Perhaps, but the effect is more wide-ranging for it also bears on other issues, including the seeming reluctance to make images of the Buddha even though other kinds of divine figures are made (and thus we are to assume worshipped). In other words the existence of Maurya-period anthropomorphic figures removes the question of when such figures began to be fashioned and thus worshipped. And in turn since Buddha images don't appear until centuries later, the questions that do arise are: Why are they not made? And when they are, and why are they? Again, notions of Western influence have been assumed to answer these questions, while at the same time fitting into a general belief in the degradation of religion which at first did not condone or use images (reverberation again perhaps of Anglican views of the inferior nature of other religions).

The view that large scaled anthropomorphic figures were made as early as the Maurya period seemed natural, reflecting the assumption, widely held but unproven, that image worship was already well in place in India (thought of as an essentially timeless practice in the nineteenth century). Until the end of the twentieth century, the introduction of anthropomorphic Buddha images into Buddhist devotion was often viewed as an issue of Buddhism catching up to other long-existent religious practices. In this perspective we can perhaps understand better the creation of the explanation that this development was driven by lay rather than monastic practitioners as proposed by various early scholars such as Ananda Coomaraswamy. It is an assumption, however, Gregory Schopen decisively undermined with his study of inscriptions on early and massive Buddha images such as that from Sarnath dated in the third year of Kanishka (fig. 15). This early second century sculpture's inscription clearly identifies its donor as a learned monastic and other similarly inscribed images demonstrate that this was not purely a lay concern (Schopen 1989).

17 Scholars have begun to find that long held assumptions about the beginning of anthropomorphic images have serious problems. See, for example, Linrothe 1993.

Clinging to an Aśokan date for the Didarganj and other Patna area sculptures obscures a full consideration of the adoption of Buddha imagery by Buddhist devotees, and it prevents other considerations as well such as the remarkable possibility that the popularity of creating images of *yakṣas* and *yakṣīs* may well emerge after the rise of Buddhism rather than before it. Recent research around the area of Sanchi regarding both aspects of ancient irrigation and *nāga* figures has begun to illuminate the development and intertwined nature of such evidence (Shaw 2004). Rather than timeless and peripheral figures, these figures of protection and fertility are likely immensely more important than is often realized.[18]

Later evidence of the importance of the Aśokan pillars, as documented by the Chinese visitors such as Faxian and Xuanzang, is useful when we want to think about the regard for the past held by later Buddhist devotees. We also have some evidence of this in visual works beyond the depiction of Aśoka-style pillars in later Buddhist reliefs. For example, the fact that an Aśokan pillar was referenced in the later construction of the southern gateway of the Great *Stūpa* at Sanchi is decidedly interesting. As mentioned earlier, remnants of the Aśokan pillar and the capital were lying along with surviving parts of the fallen gateway in the middle of the nineteenth century (see fig. 5). In the 1880s, the southern gateway and the western one were re-erected and other parts of the *stūpa* were restored (figs. 16 and 17).

The capital which once topped the Aśokan pillar was removed to the museum at the site where it remains today (see fig. 6). For those visiting Sanchi after the enlargement of this Aśokan *stūpa* and the addition of the surrounding railing and four monumental gateways, a connection with the older monument was certainly made by the southern gateway's quadrapartite lions that repeat the form of the earlier pillar's capital also then still standing on the south side. Today sadly only a stump of the pillar's shaft remains for modern viewers, so that the remarkable conversation created by the additions to the *stūpa* some two thousand years ago is rarely noticed. We do not know what Buddhist devotees knew of Aśoka at the time that these additions were made to the Sanchi monument, but clearly the Aśokan pillar proclaimed that serious attention had been given to this site at an earlier time. This is one of the simpler messages given by surviving artifacts. It is interesting to consider how the lions on the southern gate may be a visual demonstration of the power of the Aśokan legend, more clearly preserved in textual sources.

Other pillars from even later centuries suggest a continued regard for the early pillar at Sanchi; two later copies of the quadripartite capital at Sanchi, survive at the site. Even more intriguing is another capital discovered in the early twentieth century at nearby Udayagiri. Unlike the Sanchi copies that are decidedly different in scale and execution, this one, now in the Gwalior Fort Museum, has caused one noted art historian to consider seriously whether it is in fact a recut Aśokan capital (fig. 18). In an article where she explores this possibility in detail, Joanna Williams offers some careful observations that suggest this capital is not a copy but that

18 While this is not exactly the view of Robert De Caroli, his discussion of the challenging powers of these spirits indeed is quite useful in changing the way we think about early *stupa* imagery (De Caroli 2004).

instead only its abacus has been recut to depict figures of the *ādityas* (Williams 1973). I have not seen this capital myself, but I find Williams arguments interesting, and they certainly warrant serious consideration. The similar size and presence of polish as well as details of cutting make this seem possible, but in either case, it is an interesting work. Reused or carefully copied, this capital shows a distinctly careful attitude towards looking back, a concept that we do not normally consider with respect to early Indian art. It underscores a sense of importance accorded such sculptures—as perhaps potent or magical—that goes beyond just being part of pillars bearing inscriptions.

Romila Thapar seems quite right when she wrote in 1960 that the cult of Aśoka was important for the twentieth century, but it was also important earlier. Clearly in various ways, his remarkable achievements and the perceptions of them have affected those who lived after his reign in many different ways. Many questions arise when considering these gigantic pillars that allowed unprecedented acts of inscribing edicts and sculpting capitals. Questions of foreign influences raise possibilities of acts of deliberate presentation when we consider them in a larger context. Do the animal capitals parallel the powers accorded animal imagery in adjacent parts of the ancient world? Can we see the inscriptions on the Aśokan pillars as an amazing intervention in the common practices of using words? Do they allow us to contemplate the place of writing versus the place of reciting texts in early India more fully? What does this signify about the status of those who pronounce the content of these inscriptions during the Aśokan period (and conversely those who previously had been privileged by their use of Sanskrit)? Does the power of ritual in which the words are performed parallel the power of non-anthropomorphic forms created in stone?

To conclude, I would like to note that when the pillars are visually considered along with the rock formations that also bear Aśoka's edicts, the pillars and their capitals become part of a larger system although nonetheless a distinct part. For instance, if we look at a late nineteenth-century photograph of Dhauli in Orissa, we see on the north side of a range of rock a section some ten feet by fifteen feet that has been planed and polished and inscribed with an Aśokan edict that was first noticed by Markham Kittoe in 1838 (fig. 19). This monument presents a further way to consider the richness of activity in the Aśoka period as another late nineteenth-century photograph shows this rock formation sculpted with the forepart of an elephant emerging from it (fig. 20). The view today that is used most often for the site, however, focuses totally on the elephant so that there is little sense of its truly remarkable character as emerging from the rock (fig. 21). Although the high quality of sculpting evident in this figure of an elephant, believed to be Aśokan in date, may be acknowledged in such photographs and by modern scholars, the full power of the monument—the integration of natural forms, sculpted forms and inscribed forms—is not conveyed by the scholarly discussions. This is an interesting reversal of a common practice where inscriptions are illustrated but not the sculptures to which they are attached. The sculpted form is an amazing achievement as the elephant emerges yet remains part of the large rock formation which bears the major rock edict of Aśoka. In flights of fancy one might wish to draw connections to the way it functions like the capitals on the pillars with Aśoka's edicts and how at the same time it highlights the power inherent in the rock. But all I really mean to underscore is the impoverished way in which such visual evidence has often been treated in the hope that further reflection may be given to determining what might still be said about the artistic achievements of the Aśokan period.

Figures

Figure 1: 19th-century photograph of Aśokan pillar at Rummindei (Lumbinī), Courtesy of The British Library

Figure 2: 19th-century painting of Firoz Shah pillar in Firozabad, Courtesy of The British Museum

Figure 3: 19th-century photograph of Aśokan pillar at Lauriya Araraj, Courtesy of The British Library

Figure 4: 19th-century photograph of Aśokan pillar at Lauriya Nandangarh, taken in 1865 by Sir Benjamin Simpson, Courtesy of The British Library

Figure 5: 19th-century photograph of scattered sculptural fragments, south side of Great Stūpa, Sanchi, Photograph courtesy of The British Library

Figure 6: Aśoka lion capital, Sanchi, Sanchi Site Museum, Photograph courtesy of AIIS, Center of Art and Archaeology Archive

Figure 7: 19th-century photograph of Aśokan elephant capital at Sankasya, Photograph courtesy of The British Library

Figure 8: Photograph of Aśokan pillar and capital at Sarnath excavation, 1904–05, Photograph courtesy of The British Library

Figure 9: Aśokan capital, Sarnath Site Museum, Photograph courtesy of AIIS, Center of Art and Archaeology Archive

Figure 10: Lion Capital from Rampurva, now in the Indian Museum, Calcutta, Photograph courtesy of AIIS, Center of Art and Archaeology Archive

Figure 11: Bull capital from Persepolis, Musée Guimet

Figure 12: Horse capital and part of pillar from Persepolis, University of Chicago

Figure 13: Didarganj chauribearer, Photograph courtesy of AIIS, Center of Art and Archaeology Archive

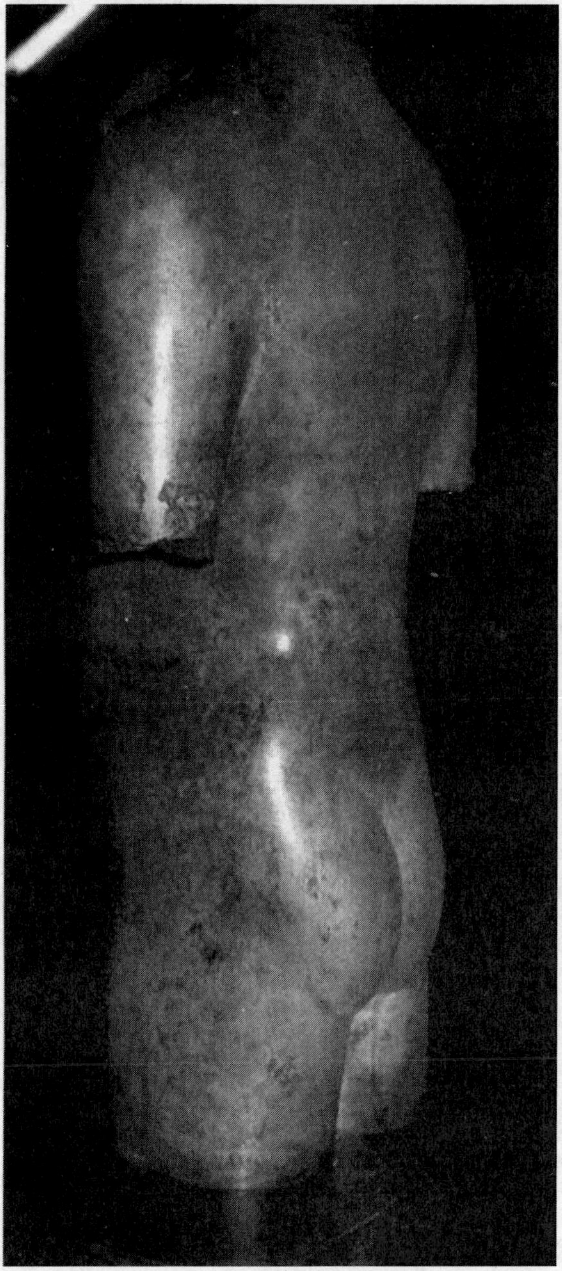

Figure 14: Back view of torso from Lohanipur, c. 3rd century BCE? 1st century CE? Patna Museum

Figure 15: Sarnath sculpture of the Buddha, inscribed Bodhisattva of Bhikṣu Bala, year 3 of Kanishka, Photograph courtesy of AIIS, Center of Art and Archaeology Archive, Sarnath Site Museum

Figure 16: 19th-century photograph of in progress restoration of Great Stūpa, Sanchi, view of re-erected south gateway, Photography courtesy of The British Library

Figure 17: Great Stūpa, Sanchi, photograph from south, author's photograph, 1985

Figure 18: Quadrapartite Lion Capital from Udayagiri, recut abacus? Gupta period? Aśokan period?, Gwalior Fort Museum, Photograph courtesy of AIIS, Center of Art and Archaeology Archive

Figure 19: 19th-century photograph of Dhauli inscription. Photography courtesy of The British Library

Figure 20: 19th-century photograph of Dhauli elephant, Photography courtesy of The British Library

Figure 21: Dhauli elephant, Photograph courtesy of Foster Forman

Bibliography

Allchin, F. R. 1995. *The Archaeology of Early Historic South Asia: The Emergence of Cities and States*. Cambridge: Cambridge University Press.

Anderson, P. K. 1991. "Notes on the Engraving Procedures for the Erragudi Version of Aśoka's Minor Rock Edict." *Indo-Iranian Journal* 34: 267–276.

Asher, F. M. 2006. "Early India Art Reconsidered," In *Between the Empires, Society in India 300 BCE to 400 CE*. Ed. P. Olivelle, pp. 51–66. New York: Oxford University Press.

Asher, F. M. and W. Spink. 1989. "Maurya Figural Sculpture Reconsidered." *Ars Orientalis* 19: 3–24.

Auboyer, J. 1948. "Indian Sculpture at Burlington House." *The Burlington Magazine* 90: 32–41.

Chakrabarti, D. K. 1995. "Budddhist sites across South Asia as influenced by political and economic forces." *World Archaeology* 27: 185–202.

Davis, R. 1997. *Lives of Indian Images*. Princeton: Princeton University Press.

De Caroli, R. 2004. *Haunting the Buddha, Indian Popular Religions and the Formation of Buddhism*. New York: Oxford University Press.

Falk, H. 2006. "The Tidal Waves of Indian History: Between the Empires and Beyond." In *Between the Empires, Society in India 300 BCE to 400 CE*. Ed. P. Olivelle, pp. 145–168. New York: Oxford University Press.

Fell, E. 1834. "Description of an ancient and remarkable monument near Bhilsa." Reprinted by James Prinsep with his own notes in the *Journal of the Asiatic Society of Bengal* 3: 488–94.

Guha-Thakurta, T. 2002. "The Endangered Yakshi: Careers of an Ancient Art Object in Modern India." In *History and the Present*. Ed. P. Charterjee and A. Ghosh, pp. 71–107. Delhi: Permanent Black.

Gupta, S. P. 1990. *Les Racines de l'art indien: epoque de formation de l'art et de l'architecture de l'Inde maurya et post-maurya* (3e et 2e siecles av. J.). Paris: Editions du Centre nationale de la recherché scientifique.

Harle, J. C. 1986. *The Art and Architecture of the Indian Subcontinent*. New Haven: Yale University Press.

Irwin, J. 1973. "Aśokan Pillars: A Reassessment of the Evidence." *The Burlington Magazine* 115: 706–720.

———. 1974. "Aśokan Pillars: A Reassessment of the Evidence—II: Structure." *The Burlington Magazine* 116: 712–727.

———. 1975. "Aśokan Pillars: A Reassessment of the Evidence—III: Capitals." *The Burlington Magazine* 117: 631–643.

———. 1976. "Aśokan Pillars: A Reassessment of the Evidence—IV: Symbolism." *The Burlington Magazine* 118: 734–753

———. 1983. "The True Chronology of Aśokan Pillars." *Artibus Asiae* 44: 247–265.

Jayaswal, V. 1998. *From Stone Quarry to Sculpturing Workshop, a Report on the Archaeological Investigations around Chunar, Varansai and Sarnath*. Delhi: Agam Kala Prakashan.

Kawani, T. S. 1989. "Greek Art and Persian Taste: Some Animal Sculptures from Persepolis." *American Journal of Archaeology* 90: 259–268.

Kejariwal, O. P. 1988. *The Asiatic Society of Bengal and the Discovery of India's Past, 1784–1838*. Delhi: Oxford University Press.

Keightley, D. N. 1996. "Art Ancestors, and the Origins of Writing in China." *Representations* 56: 68–95.

Leoshko, J. 2003. *Sacred Traces, Buddhist Explorations of Buddhism in South Asia*. Aldershot, England: Ashgate.

Linrothe, R. 1993. "Inquiries into the Origin of the Buddha Image: A Review." *East and West* 43: 241–256.

Morrison, K. D. 1997. "Commerce and Culture in South Asia: Perspectives from Archaeology and History." *Annual Review of Anthropology* 26: 87–108.

Oertel, F. O. 1904–05. "Excavations at Sarnath." *Archaeological Survey of India, Annual Reports*: 59–104.

Olivelle, P. 2005. "The Semantic History of Dharma: the Middle and Late Vedic periods." *Journal of Indian Philosophy* 32: 491–511.

Pandey, C. B. 1982. *Mauryan Art*. Delhi: Bharatiya Vidya Prakashan.

Patil, D. R. 1963. *The Antiquarian Remains in Bihar*. Patna: Kashi Prasad Jayaswal Research Institute.

Ray, H. 1994. *The Winds of Change, Buddhism and the Maritime Links of Early South Asia*. Delhi: Oxford University Press.

———. 2006. "Inscribed Pots, Emerging Identities." In *Between the Empires, Society in India 300 BCE to 400 CE*. Ed. P. Olivelle, pp. 113–143. New York: Oxford University Press.

Ray, N. 1975. *Maurya and Post-Maurya Art: A Study in Social and Formal Contrasts*. Delhi: Indian Council of Historcal Research.

Schopen, G. 1989. "On Monks, Nuns and 'Vulgar' Practices: The Introduction of the Image Cult into Indian Buddhism." *Artibus Asiae* 49: 153–168.

———. 1991. "Archaeology and the Protestant Presuppositions in the Study of Indian Buddhism." *History of Religions* 31: 1–23.

Shaw, J. 2004. "Naga Sculptures in Sanchi's Archaeological Landscape: Buddhism, Vaishnavism, and Local Agricultural Cults in Central India, First Century BCE to Fifth Century CE." *Artibus Asiae* 64: 5–59.

Sinha, B. P. and L. A. Narain. 1970. *Pataliputra Excavation:* 1955–1956. Patna: Directorate of Archaeology and Museums.

Smith, V. 1911. "The Monolithic Pillars or Columns of Aśoka." *Zeitschrift der Deutschen Morgenlandischen Gesellschaft* 65: 221–33.

Strong, J. 1983. *Legend of King Aśoka*. Princeton: Princeton University Press.

———. 1994. "Images of Aśoka: Some Indian and Sri Lankan Legends." In *King Aśoka and Buddhism, Historical and Literary Studies*. Ed. A. Seneviratna, pp. 99–126. Kandy (Sri Lanka): Buddhist Publication Society.

Thapar, R. 1960. "Asoka and Buddhism." *Past and Present* 18: 43–53.

———. 1989. "Imagined Religious Communities? Ancient History and the Modern Search for a Hindu Identity." *Modern Asian Studies* 23: 209–231.

———. 1997. *Asoka and the Decline of the Mauryas*. Rev. ed. Delhi: Oxford University Press.

Tieken, H. 2000. "Aśoka and the Buddhist Sangha: a Study of Aśoka's Schism Edict and Minor Rock Edict I." *School of Oriental and African Studies* 63: 1–30.

Trautmann, T. R. and C. M. Sinopoli. 2002. "In the Beginning Was the Word: Excavating the Relations Between History and Archaeology in South Asia." *Journal of the Economic and Social History of the Orient* 45: 492–523.

Walters, J. 1997. "Stupa, Story and Empire: Constructions of the Buddha Biography on Early Post-Aśokan India." In *Sacred Biography in the Early Buddhist Traditions of South and Southeast Asia*. Ed. J. Schober, pp. 160–92. Honolulu: Honolulu University Press.

Welch, A. 1993. "Architectural Patronage and the Past: The Tughluq Sultans of India." *Muqarnas (Essays in Honor of Oleg Grabar)* 10: 311–322.

White, H. 1980. "The Value of Narrativity in the Representation of Reality." *Critical Inquiry* 7: 5–25.

Williams, J. 1973. "A Recut Aśokan Capital and the Gupta Attitude Towards the Past." *Artibus Asiae* 35: 225–240.

Aśoka and the Lotus Sūtra

JOHN STRONG

Over the years, a number of scholars have been interested in possible overlaps between the legends and the edicts of Aśoka, looking to the latter for potential roots of the former and to the former for potential elucidations of the latter (see, e.g., Thapar 1994; and Guruge 1994). Fewer have been concerned with the overlaps in literary themes that occur between the Aśoka legends, the edicts, and other Buddhist texts. In this paper, I would like to look at two literary topoi that are central to the Aśoka story—the gift of dirt or dust (*pāṃśu*), and the tradition of the 84,000 stūpas—and highlight their appearance in the *Lotus Sūtra,* a text that is more or less contemporaneous with (if not a bit earlier than) the Sanskrit recension of the *Aśokāvadāna*.

The Gift of Dirt

I need only briefly recount here the story of Aśoka's gift of dirt to the Buddha in a previous lifetime. Once, we are told, when the Blessed One was in Rājagṛha, he met two little boys (*bāladāraka*) named Jaya and Vijaya who were playing at building houses of dirt in the road. Seeing the Buddha, Jaya was inspired to put a handful of dirt into the Buddha's bowl, thinking of it as grain, and to make a resolute wish (*praṇidhāna*) that, in the future, he would become a great king and pay homage to the Buddha—thereby karmically setting up his rebirth as Aśoka and his construction of the 84,000 stūpas (Strong 1983: 200). As the Buddha puts it in confirming his vow:

> After I die there will be an emperor;
> his name will be Aśoka and his fame widespread
> He will adorn Jambudvīpa with my reliquaries
> and cause them to be honored by gods and men
> His meritorious gift was just this:
> He threw a handful of dirt into the Tathāgata's bowl (Mukhopahyaya 1963: 34 = Strong 1983: 204).

It was not long after I read this story, years ago, that I came across, in Hendrik Kern's translation of the *Lotus Sūtra*, in the chapter on skillful means, the following verse: "The little boys even, who in playing erected here and there heaps of sand with the intention of dedicating them as *stūpas* to the Jinas, they have all of them reached enlightenment" (Kern 1884: 50; see also Burnouf 1852: 32 and Watson 1993: 38–39). The "sand" with which these boys are playing here is not "*pāṃśu*" but "*sikatā*," but the "*pāṃśu*" appears in the immediately preceding verse, which speaks of dedicating piles of *pāṃśu* as *stūpas* for the Buddhas, in forests and uncultivated grounds (*Saddharmapuṇḍarīka*, ch. 2 vs. 82–83).

There is nothing unusual about little boys playing in dirt. Indeed, in the Pali canon and commentaries, the term "[*saha*]*pansukīḷita*" is used to denote "childhood companions" or as Woodward(1932–36, 2: 187) puts it in his translation of *Aṅguttara Nikāya* 2: 187, "playmates who used to play at mud-pies." Similarly, in the "*Kālakaṇṇī-jātaka*" (*Jātaka* 1: 364 = Cowell 1895–1907, 1: 209), Anāthapiṇḍika and Kālakaṇṇī enjoy a special relationship because, as boys, they used to play in the dirt together and had gone to the same school (See also Ba Kyaw 1980: 32; *Mahāvastu*, p. 451 = Jones 1949–56, 3: 451; *Jātaka* 5:249 = Cowell 1895–1907, 5: 128).

What is different in the texts we are considering here is the use of dirt (*pāṃśu*) for making offerings or pretend-offerings to the Buddha or Buddhas. Besides the *Lotus Sūtra* and the *Aśokāvadāna* I know of only one other place in which this is featured, that is in chapter 3 of the *Jātakamālā* (p. 19 = Khoroche 1989: 21) where, in a long elegy on giving we are told that "a gift of dirt made by those of childlike wisdom is a good gift" (*bālyaprajñaiḥ pāṃsudānaṃ sudānam*).[1]

We thus have three variations on a theme here: the *Jātakamālā*'s unspecified gift of dirt by boys, which is nonetheless labeled a "good gift"; the youths (*kumāraka*) of the *Lotus Sūtra* who use dirt to make piles that are likened to a gift of *stūpas*;[2] and the *Aśokāvadāna*'s gift of dirt, which the boy Jaya pretends is grain and puts in the Buddha's bowl but which the Buddha's prediction then connects karmically to his building of the 84,000 *dharmarājikās* (*stūpas*) (Mukhopadhyaya 1963: 34 = Strong 1983: 203–04).

The dating of these various texts is a complicated business. Hirakawa (1990: 283) places the verse portions of chapter 2 of the *Lotus Sūtra* in which this passage occurs in the latter part of the first century CE, but others have argued that this particular portion of the text is part of a slightly later interpolation (see Pye 1978: 28 and Fuss 1991: 142). Mukhopadhyaya (1963: lx) fixes the date of the *Aśokāvadāna* as the second century CE. The compilation of the *Jātakamāla* is usually placed in the fourth century (Khoroche 1989: xiii), but, again, there is no way of knowing the original date of this particular trope of the gift of dirt.

Rather than look for influences of one story on another, I would prefer to note thematic parallels and differences. In both the *Lotus Sūtra* and the *Aśokāvadāna*, the gift of dirt is connected to future attainments by its profferer: Buddhahood in the one case, and kingship in the other. This parallelism may be significant. In the

1 Speyer (1895: 24–25) wrongly assumes that "*pāṃśudāna*" here means "*pāṃśukūla-dāna*" ("the gift of rag-robes"), and translates "even rags for dress, given away by the simple-minded, are a well-bestowed gift."

2 This would seem to be an early instance of the common practice of making *stūpas* out of sand, on which see Gabaude 1979.

Aśokāvadāna, the Buddha responds to the gift of dirt by smiling a smile which sends out rays of light that illuminate the cosmos from the highest heaven to the deepest hell. These rays of light then circle back and reenter the Buddha's body at a point that is calibrated to correspond to the future attainment of the merit maker in question. In the case of Aśoka, they enter into the Buddha's left palm that corresponds to the attainment of a *balacakravartin*. In the same passage, we are told that if the Buddha had wanted to predict the attainment of a future deity, they would have entered into his navel, of future *arhat*-ship, they would have entered into his mouth, of future Pratyekabuddhahood, into his *ūrṇā*, and of future Buddhahood, into his *uṣṇīṣa* (Mukhopadhyaya 1963: 33 = Strong 1983: 202).[3]

Long ago, in a study of these correspondences (Strong 1979: 235–37), I argued that Aśoka's kingship could be seen, like Buddhahood and other types of enlightenment, as a soteriological goal, in that it was vowed for in a past life and predicted by a living Buddha. It is interesting to see a confirmation of this here, in the case of the *Lotus Sūtra*'s and the *Aśokāvadāna*'s variations on the gift of dirt. It may also be that we can find here, in this view of Aśoka as a type of Bodhisattva, a prefiguration of the overlap between Bodhisattvahood, Buddhahood, and kingship that was to be invoked by various Buddhist emperors in China and elsewhere.[4]

The Eighty-Four Thousand *Stūpas*

The gift of dirt is, of course, connected to the deed that makes Aśoka into the most famous paradigm for kingship in the Buddhist world: his construction of 84,000 *stūpas* for the relics of the Buddha. Once again, the *Aśokāvadāna* version of this tale is well known: after collecting the Buddha's relics from the so-called *droṇa stūpas* in which they were originally enshrined after the *parinirvāṇa*, Aśoka redistributes them into 84,000 *dharmarājikas* (*stūpas*) which he has constructed throughout his realm in the small, great, and middle-sized towns, wherever there was a population of one hundred thousand persons (Mukhopadhyaya 1963: 54 = Strong 1983: 219).

So too in the *Lotus Sūtra*, in chapter 22, in a past life as a prince, the future Buddha Bhaiṣajyarāja is said to gather up the relics of the previous Buddha Candravimalasūryaprabhāsaśrī and build for them 84,000 *stūpas* (*Saddharmapuṇḍarīka*, ch. 22, p. 4 = Kern 1884: 383). Kern called attention to the parallelism with the Aśoka story in a note: "Exactly the same number of monasteries was erected by Aśoka according to the *Dīpavaṃsa*" (1884: 383 n.2).

Had Kern been focusing on the story in the *Aśokāvadāna*, he would have noted an even more striking parallel. The Sanskrit legend is quite detailed in specifying that prior to being placed in the *dharmarājikās*, the relics are to be put in urns (*kumbha*) which feature cloth strips (*paṭṭa*) presumably for tying down the lids (Mukhopadhyaya 1963: 54). Exactly the same details are featured in the *Lotus Sūtra*

3 This description of the Buddha's smile is quite common in *avadāna* literature. For a study of some of its ramifications, see Mus 1961 and 1968.

4 See, for instance, the cases of the Emperors Liang Wudi and Wendi, and the Empress Wu Zetian. For discussions of their connections with Aśoka, see the sources listed in Strong 2004: 125, n. 6.

where before enshrining them in the stūpas, the future Bhaiṣajyarāja places the relics in 84,000 *kumbhas* made of the seven precious substances, and further adorns them with *paṭṭa* and bells (*Saddharmapuṇḍarīka*, ch. 22, p. 4 = Kern 1884: 383). Kern does point out that the future Bhaiṣajyarāja here is named Sarvasattvapriyadarśana, noting again that in the *Dīpavaṃsa* (see Oldenberg 1982: 41 [text], 146 [tr.]), Priyadarśana (i.e., Piyadassana, in Pali) is an epithet of Aśoka.

The Edicts

He might also have drawn attention to the fact that Priyadarśana is the prime epithet for Aśoka, i.e., Devānaṃpriya, in the Edicts (see Bloch 1950: passim). The question of the connection of the legend to the edicts at this point is an intriguing one. What Aśoka builds in the *Aśokāvadāna* are called the 84,000 *dharmarājikās*. I have no doubt that this term, which as Edgerton (1953: 281) points out, must mean something like "(an edifice) which belongs to the king of the doctrine (i.e., the Buddha)" should be taken as an equivalent of *stūpa*. Nonetheless, it is worth remembering that Eugène Burnouf (1876: 330), flush with the excitement of James Prinsep's deciphering of the Aśokan edicts, translated *dharmarājikā* as "édit de la loi" (edict of the law), a choice still echoed in the index to Cowell and Neil's edition of the *Divyāvadāna* (1886, index, s.v. *dharmarājikā*).

In a footnote, Burnouf (1876: 330–31n) is further inclined to connect the second half of the term *dharma-rājikā* to the word "*lajjukā*" or "*rājjuka*" which appears in the edicts and is variously translated as "provincial governors" (Nikam and McKeon 1959: 59), "imperial commissioners" (Barua 1968, 1:194), "contrôleur" (Bloch 1950: 169), "magistrate" (Bhattacharya 1960: 45), or "rope-holder," i.e., "revenue and settlement officer" (Bühler, quoted in Mookerji 1928: 133).

Burnouf was most likely wrong in his inclination to make this connection, but it is interesting to pursue his lead a bit further. Since his time, there has been much debate over the responsibilities of the post designated by the term "*lajjukā*." One key passage occurs in Pillar Edict VII (Bloch 1950: 169), where the *lajjukās* are enjoined by Aśoka to instruct the people who are devoted to the *dharma*. In that light, they might be said to be "*dharma-lajjukās*," and Mookerji (1928: 133n), among others, has sought to compare them to the better-known *dharma-mahāmattas*, the agents of Aśoka primarily responsible for propagating his *dharma*.

Even more interestingly, in both Pillar Edict VII and IV (Bloch 1950: 163), the *lajjukās* are granted authority over every 100,000 people. So too, in the *Aśokāvadāna*, the *dharmarājikās* are to be built throughout Jambudvīpa, wherever there is a population of 100,000 people (Mukhopadhyaya 1963: 54 = Strong 1983: 220).[5]

5 Burnouf (1876: 332) fails to see this parallel because he reads the text as meaning "wherever one hundred thousand gold pieces had been amassed." But the Chinese versions (see Przyluski 1923: 243) and other sources make it clear that the figure refers to population and not wealth.

Finally, in Rock Edict III (Bloch 1950: 96), we are told that the *lajjukās* must go out on *dharma*-tours every five years, a specification that Max Deeg (1995: 67) among others has connected to the tradition of the quinquennial festival, the *pañcavārṣika*, which Aśoka, in the legend, undertakes after completing the establishment of the 84,000 *dharmarājikās*.

Back to the *Lotus*

With all of this in mind, I would like, at this point, to return to the *Lotus Sūtra* Distributing the relics of the previous Buddha into 84,000 *stūpas* is not the only devotional act performed by the future Buddha of Medicine, the Bodhisattva Sarvasattva-priyadarśana. Having thus venerated the relics, he goes on to declare that he wants to pay them an even more distinguished honor ("*viśiṣṭatarāṃ pūjāṃ kāriṣyāmi*"; *Saddharmapuṇḍarīka*, ch. 22, p. 4), and he undertakes to set his own arm on fire and hold it aloft as a devotional lamp honoring the *stūpas* for 72,000 years (*Saddharmapuṇḍarīka*, ch. 22, p. 5 = Kern 1884: 383–84).

The *Lotus* is not the only Mahāyāna text that features this act. In the *Samādhirāja Sūtra*, we also read the story of King Śrīghoṣa who erects 84,000 *stūpas* over the relics of the past Buddha Ghoṣadatta, and holds in their honor a great festival. In attendance on this occasion is a very young Bodhisattva named Kṣemadatta, who, seeing the myriads of oil lamps burning, is inspired to do something even greater: wrapping his right hand in his robe, he soaks it in oil and sets it on fire, holding it up as an offering to the *stūpas* (Dutt 1954: 455–57; see also Filliozat 1963: 22–24).

Within the text of Chapter 22 of the *Lotus Sūtra,* however, this fiery act of offering appears to be an echo of an even greater act of self-sacrifice that Sarvasattvapriyadarśana performs for the Buddha in a previous life, when, after ingesting resin and oil for twelve years, he wraps himself in royal garments, bathes in oil and sets his whole body on fire, burning for 12,000 years. This, we are told, is the highest form of giving, better even than the gift of kingship or of giving away one's wife and children (*Saddharmapuṇḍarīka,* ch. 22, pp. 2–3 = Kern 1884: 379–80; see also Burnouf 1852: 244).

As is well known, these acts, which recall *jātaka* stories of the gift of the body (see Ohnuma 2006), become paradigms for later Chinese practices of self-immolation (see Benn 2007). In the context of the *Lotus Sūtra*, however, they are presented as the pinnacle of devotion and sacrifice, the means by which Sarvasattva-priyadarśana seeks to outdo himself in giving. Much the same theme of "upping the ante" may be found in the Sanskrit legendary accounts of Aśoka's *pañcavārṣika*, which, at a minimum, is a festival occasion of supreme great giving (see Deeg 1995; and Strong 1990).

It may also be found in Pali accounts of Aśoka's great festival put on for the 84,000 *stūpas* (*vihāras*) something that, in the *Mahāvaṃsa* is called the "unveiling of the world" (*lokavivaraṇa*) and is described as a time when lavish gifts are given to the *saṅgha*, when the monasteries and streets are adorned with strings of lamps and garlands of flowers, when music is played, sermons are preached and the eight precepts are observed (Strong 2004: 144). Aśoka, standing on the great *stūpa* in his capital gains a vision of the whole of his realm. As I have shown elsewhere (1990: 113–14), this, as well as the *pañcavārṣika*, is a time when the barriers dividing men and gods and kings are broken down and they can see each other face to face, a theme that is echoed, perhaps, in the Brahmagiri/Rupnath inscription (Bloch 1950: 146) in which Aśoka famously declares that, as a result of his zeal, gods and humans now mingle, as Jean Filliozat (1967: 35–55), and others have pointed out.

But most interesting, perhaps, is the further elaboration of this festival scenario in the eleventh-twelfth century Pali text, the *Lokapaññatti,* and later Burmese sources. There, we are told that "Aśoka, wishing to pay even greater *pūjā* to the *Mahāstūpa*, had his own body wrapped in cotton up to his neck and his limbs up to his wrists, and he had himself soaked with five hundred pots of scented oil. Then, standing facing the Great *Stūpa*, with folded hands, his head anointed with oil, and mindful of the Buddha, he had his body set on fire; and the flames rose up in the air to a height of seven persons." In this way, he burns for seven days and nights (Denis 1977, 1: 174 = Strong 1992: 207; see also Strong 1994: 119–20). This seems like a direct echo, if not of the *Lotus Sūtra*, at least of the tradition that got put into the *Lotus Sūtra*.

Conclusion

In conclusion, let me say first that I think it is clear that there are some significant reverberations between the *Lotus Sūtra*, the edicts, and the legends of Aśoka, in both Sanskrit and Pali traditions. What is not clear, however, is how those reverberations came about and which way they rebounded. Our examination of the tropes of the gift of dirt and the 84,000 *stūpas* has led us in textual circles from the *Aśokāvadāna* to the *Lotus Sūtra* to the Edicts to Pali *vaṃsas* to the much later *Lokapaññatti,* and back again. We can hear the echoes but we can't see the echo-chamber—the even greater literary, cultic, and oral context in which these stories are being told and re-told. In this regard, much work still needs to be done on these connections and interconnections and on their significance.

Bibliography

Anguttara Nikāya. 1885–1900. 5 vols. Ed. R. Morris and E. Hardy. London: Pali Text Society.

Ba Kyaw, U. 1980. *Elucidation of the Intrinsic Meaning So Named The Commentary on the Peta-Stories*. London: Pali Text Society.

Barua, B. M. 1968. *Asoka and his Inscriptions*. 2 vols. Calcutta: New Age Publishers.

Benn, J. 2007. *Burning for the Buddha*. Honolulu: University of Hawai'i Press.

Bhattacharya, S. 1960. *Select Asokan Epigraphs*. Calcutta: Firma K. L. Mukhopadhyay.

Bloch, J. 1950. *Les inscriptions d'Asoka*. Paris: Les Belles Lettres.

Burnouf, E. 1852. *Le Lotus de la bonne loi*. Paris: Imprimerie Nationale.

———. 1876. *Introduction à l'histoire du buddhisme indien*. 2nd. ed. Paris: Maisonneuve.

Cowell, E. B. 1895–1907. *The Jātaka or Stories of the Buddha's Former Births*. 6 vols. London: Pali Text Society.

Cowell, E. B. and R. A. Neil. 1886. *Divyāvadāna*. Cambridge: Cambridge University Press.

Deeg, M. 1995. "Origins and Development of the Buddhist Pañcavārṣika–Part I: India and Central Asia." *Nagoya Studies in Indian Culture and Buddhism Saṃbhāṣā* 16: 67–90.

Denis, E. 1977. *La Lokapaññatti et les idées cosmologiques du bouddhisme ancien*. 3 vols. Lille: Université de Lille.

Dutt, N. 1954. *Gilgit Manuscripts*. vol. 2, part iii. Calcutta: Calcutta Oriental Press.

Edgerton, F. 1953. *A Buddhist Hybrid Sanskrit Grammar and Dictionary*. 2 vols. New Haven: Yale University Press.

Filliozat, J. 1963. "La mort volontaire par le feu et la tradition bouddhique ancienne." *Journal asiatique* 251: 21–51.

———. 1967. *Studies in Asokan Inscriptions*. Tr. Mrs. R. K. Menon. Calcutta: Indian Studies Past and Present.

Fuss, M. 1991. *Buddhavacana and Dei Verbum: A Phenomenological and Theological Comparison of Scriptural Inspiration in the Saddharampuṇḍarīka Sūtra and in the Christian Tradition*. Leiden: E. J. Brill.

Gabaude, L. 1979. *Les cetiya de sable au Laos et en Thaïlande*. Paris: Ecole Française d'Extrême-Orient.

Guruge, A. W. P. 1994. "Emperor Aśoka and Buddhism: Unresolved Discrepancies between Buddhist Tradition and Aśokan Inscriptions. " In *King Aśoka and Buddhism. Historical and Literary Studies*. Ed. by A. Seneviratna, pp. 27–66. Kandy: Buddhist Publication Society.

Hirakawa, A. 1990. *A History of Indian Buddhism from Śākyamuni to Early Mahāyāna*. Ed. and tr. P. Groner. Honolulu: University of Hawaii Press.

Jātaka Together with its Commentary. 1877–96. 6 vols. Ed. V. Fausboll. London: Pali Text Society.

Jātakamālā by Ārya Śūra. 1959. Ed. P. L. Vaidya. Darbhanga: Mithila Institute.

Jones, J. J. 1949–56. *The Mahāvastu*. 3 vols. London: Pali Text Society.

Kern, H. 1884. *Saddharma-Puṇḍarīka or the Lotus of the True Law*. Oxford: Clarendon Press.

Khoroche, P. 1989. *Once the Buddha Was a Monkey: Ārya Śūra's Jātakamālā*. Chicago: University of Chicago Press.

Mahāvastu. 1882–97. 3 vols. Ed. E. Sénart. Paris: Imprimerie Nationale.

Mookerji, R. K. [1928] 1972. *Asoka*. Delhi: Motilal Banarsidass.

Mukhopadhyaya, S. 1963. *Aśokāvadāna*. New Delhi: Sahitya Akademi.

Mus, P. 1961. "Le sourire d'Angkor: art, foi et politique bouddhiques sous Jayavarman VII." *Artibus Asiae* 24: 363–81.

Mus, P. 1968. "Où finit Puruṣa?" *Melanges d'indianisme à la mémoire de Louis Renou* (Paris: E. de Boccard). Pp. 539–63.

Nikam, N. A. and R. McKeon. 1959. *The Edicts of Asoka*. Chicago: University of Chicago Press.

Ohnuma, R. 2006. *Head, Eyes, Flesh, and Blood: Giving Away the Body in Indian Buddhist Literature*. New York: Columbia University Press.

Oldenberg, H. 1982. *The Dīpavaṃsa: An Ancient Buddhist Historical Record*. Reprint edition. New Delhi: Asian Educational Services.

Przyluski, J. 1923. *La légende de l'empereur Açoka*. Paris: Paul Geuthner.

Pye, M. 1978. *Skilful Means: A Concept in Mahayana Buddhism*. London: Duckworth.

Saddharmapuṇḍarīkasūtra. On-line edition: http://www.uwest.edu/UWest/sanskritweb/Sutra/roman/Sutra%2036/

Strong, J. S. 1979. "The Transforming Gift." *History of Religions* 18: 221–37.

———. 1983. *The Legend of King Aśoka*. Princeton: Princeton University Press.

———. 1990. "Rich Man, Poor Man, Bhikkhu, King: The Quinquennial Festival and the Nature of Dāna." In *Ethics, Wealth, and Salvation: A Study in Buddhist Social Ethics*. Ed. R. F. Sizemore and D. K. Swearer, pp. 107–23. Columbia, SC: University of South Carolina Press.

———. 1992. *The Legend and Cult of Upagupta*. Princeton: Princeton University Press.

———. 2004. *Relics of the Buddha*. Princeton: Princeton University Press.

Thapar, R. 1994. "Aśoka and Buddhism as Reflected in the Aśokan Edicts." In *King Aśoka and Buddhism. Historical and Literary Studies*. Ed. A. Seneviratna, pp. 11–26. Kandy: Buddhist Publication Society.

Watson, B. 1993. *The Lotus Sutra*. New York: Columbia University Press.

Woodward, F. L. and E. M. Hare. 1932–36. *The Book of the Gradual Sayings*. 5 vols. London: Pali Text Society.

Aśoka and Mauryas: A Graeco-Roman Perspective

KLAUS KARTTUNEN

An inevitable background to the Graeco-Roman perspective on the Mauryas are the Eastern campaigns of Alexander the Great, a marginal event in Indian history, but well documented and remembered in the West. As we all know, Alexander was soon forgotten in India, but not immediately. The Mauryas certainly remembered how far his invasion had extended. Building themselves an empire, they knew the Indian tradition of a universal ruler (*cakravartin*), but the example of Alexander's conquests was much more recent and realistic as a model. An unconfirmed tradition even had Candragupta meeting Alexander in the Pañjāb (Plutarch, *Alexander* 62).

As the main point here is Aśoka, I pass over Megasthenes briefly. The history of this Hellenistic envoy to Pāṭaliputra, from Seleucus to Candragupta, is well known among Indologists since the days of Schwanbeck, Lassen and McCrindle. His work was much read in the Graeco-Roman world and is therefore preserved through many and representative fragments. Many scholars have studied them since the early 19th century.[1] However, the relations between the Mauryas and the Seleucids are problematic in a number of ways.

The problem lies with the nature of the sources. From Mauryan India we have, besides Aśokan edicts and meager archaeological evidence, only late and unreliable legends. Even with the Seleucids, the situation is poor. Nothing is preserved of the flourishing literature of this Hellenistic state save in more or less poor fragments. While the wars with Egypt and especially with Rome are fairly well known, we have only some tantalizing hints of local history and especially of eastern politics.

As it is sometimes wondered why there is a complete silence about Aśoka in Western sources, I think it can be useful to consider the state of our knowledge of Hellenistic historiography a bit more closely. By Hellenism I mean here the period from the death of Alexander to the beginnings of the Roman Empire. The massive collection of fragments published by Felix Jacoby, the *Fragmente Griechischer Historiker*,[2] offers an astonishingly great number of names of historians for this period and shows unquestionably how popular historical writing was. However,

1 See, e.g., my discussion in Karttunen 1997, 69ff.

2 By Jacoby himself, volumes I–II D, Berlin 1923–30 and III A–III C, Leiden 1954–58. There are now some supplementary volumes prepared by others. In addition to Jacoby, I have checked the account of Hellenistic historiography in Lesky 1971, 855ff.

when we turn from fragments to the library of extant works, we see that there is just one single author whose history is still available to us, and even of that, we have only part.[3] This single author is Polybius who wrote in the mid-second century BCE. He wrote a contemporary history, mainly concentrating on Roman exploits, and, although we find some valuable allusions to Indo-Greek history, he cannot help us with Aśoka and the Mauryas.[4]

For the following era, the next extant history is that of Diodorus of Sicily, who wrote in the period of the Roman ascendancy, in the mid-first century BCE. His was a universal history and—with all its defects often and sometimes even exaggeratingly pointed out by modern critics—it could be very valuable to us (I am now speaking from the "Aśokan perspective"), if only we had the entire work, but unfortunately, this is not the case. Of the forty books, we have only fifteen extant in manuscripts; for the remainder, there are only very condensed Byzantine extracts and summaries leaving out most of the valuable details. We have thus the first five books, outlining the history of Egypt and some Asian countries and discussing some points of mythological history. They include the valuable "Epitome of Megasthenes" (2, 35–42), as it is called. After a lacuna of five books, we have books 11–20, covering the period from the Persian wars to 302 BCE. Book 17 is one of the most valuable sources of the so-called Vulgate tradition of Alexander's history and books 18–20 offer a good survey of the wars over Alexander's inheritance. Even Indians are occasionally mentioned.

The extant part of Diodorus stops at 302 BCE and, for the entire third century, our sources for Hellenistic history are extremely sparse. The only good source is Justinus. His third century Latin history is a drastically abridged version of the lost great universal history of Trogus Pompeius. Nevertheless, this brief summary furnishes us with a very interesting version of the Candragupta legend (15, 4, 10–21) and later on (in book 41), there follow some valuable clues to Indo-Greek history. But this is all.

Let us return to the fragments. Literature flourished in the Seleucid state—this much is known—but for some reason, it seems that it produced no great historians. Jacoby offers very few names and even for them, hardly any significant fragments.[5] The most authoritative historians came from Antigonid Macedonia (including Greece) and, to some extent, from Ptolemaic Egypt. Diodorus' main source for the early Hellenistic period, Hieronymus of Kardia (*FGrH* 154), was himself an Antigonid general. His work covered fifty years, starting from the death of Alexander, and we know the first part of it, thanks to Diodorus. Other famous historians of the period, Duris and Phylarchus, were already reproved by classical

3 Only books 1–5 (out of a total of 40) survive complete.

4 Polybius 11, 6 contains the episode of Antiochus III "renewing the friendship" with the Indian king Sôphagasenus, sometimes interpreted as one of the later Mauryas.

5 The most important names to be mentioned here are certainly Megasthenes, Apollodorus of Artemita and Isidorus of Charax. The last two were not Seleucid subjects, but lived in the Parthian Empire.

critics for their predilection for dramatic and rhetorical effects rather than for critical history. We have a few fragments on India from both and must be grateful for that.[6]

The fragments of Hellenistic literature come from authors of the Roman period and their contents reflect the interests of these transmitters rather than those of the original authors. In the Roman Empire, it was Roman history that mattered. The astonishing career of Alexander and the fight over his inheritance were still interesting, but so much had happened in the West—the Pyrrhic Wars, the Punic Wars—that the eastern contacts of the Hellenistic states seemed to be of no importance at all. Had we the universal histories of Diodorus and Trogus Pompeius for the period, we might well meet Aśoka and his ambassadors of *dhamma*, but in the present state of things, the silence of our paltry sources is not to be wondered at.

There is a further point which made India historically and politically uninteresting to the Romans and this was the existence of Parthia. I have mentioned some allusions to Indo-Greek history found in Western literature,[7] but even these were often mentioned in connection with Parthia. The rise of Parthia in the early second century BCE and its very existence as a strong and often dangerous force made India politically uninteresting. Alexander had conquered it, but the emperors could not. Only some poets and rhetoricians were dreaming of a future when Rome will, after having defeated Parthia, even conquer India, while moralists pointed out this would probably already have been done without the plague of the civil wars.[8]

Let me briefly summarize the Hellenistic information about Mauryas. A special place belongs to Megasthenes who—together with some historians of Alexander—was sort of canonized as the standard source on India, on a literary India which always remained the country conquered by Alexander and with no history after that. The remainder of the post-Megasthenian Hellenistic information about India is minimal and wholly accidental in character. There are shadowy envoys such as Daimachus and Dionysius, remembered because they wrote accounts of their travels, but the few fragments give hardly any idea of their works. Hegesander (in Athenaeus, *Deipnosophistae* 14, 652f) picked out an amusing anecdote from the Seleucid diplomatic correspondence about no trade in sophists. The very idea of Aśoka's father supposedly wanting to buy a sophist seems, in my opinion, to go well with the early Greek idea of India as a barbarian country, although this very image was just then radically changing through the accounts of Alexander's historians and Megasthenes. Perhaps this anecdote at least reveals the existence of some interest in Greek thought in India.

Unlike sophists, elephants were traded and with elephants came their keepers. In the Hellenistic West, the word "Indian" soon obtained a new meaning as a

6 Duris, *FGrH* 76, FF 27, 47 and 48, on Dionysus and Prometheus in India and on the supposed origin of fabulous peoples. Phylarchus, *FGrH* 81, FF 35, 36 and 78, on Sandrocottus (below), elephants and Dionysus.

7 Besides Polybius and Justinus mentioned above, should also be mentioned Strabo and Plutarch.

8 "Will do": e.g., *Anthologia Graeca* 4, 3b, 34f; Saint Basil *Letters* 40; Emperor Julian *Epistulae* 75; Libanius *Orationes* 18; Lucianus *Hist. conscrib.* 31; Vergil *Aeneid* 6,794f. and 7, 604f.; "would have done": Lucanus *Pharsalia* 1, 19f. etc.; Plutarch *Pompey* 70.

"mahout."[9] Phylarchus (F 35) mentioned another curiosity: a strong Indian aphrodisiac sent to the Seleucids. In addition, there are a few possible instances of the word *Maurya* in the West.[10]

Now we come at last to Aśoka. Although never mentioned in the extant Western sources at all, king Devānāṃpriya Priyadarśin certainly continued the existing relations between Mauryas and the neighboring Hellenistic states. The Edicts indicate quite clearly that the neighbors were known and the contact continued. These Edicts, however, do not really indicate diplomacy as such. Still, they clearly show the pragmatic side of the emperor. For instance, the jungle tribes are promised peace and forgiveness, only *if* they submit themselves to Aśoka's sovereignty. To the West, he sent his *dhamma* envoys (*dūta*) to preach his message. We do not know it as certain, but it seems likely that he already knew to use monks as diplomats, as was often done later in India as monks and Brahmans were inviolable. In the same way, European princes in the Middle Ages often gave diplomatic tasks to the clergy. According to the Edicts, Aśoka's envoys were sent to the West to preach his *dhamma*, but they probably also had to carry on negotiations. For the Hellenistic kings meeting these envoys, it was the negotiations that mattered. They listened to the moral message as a part of diplomatic good manners and soon forgot it.[11] Unfortunatly, we have no idea of what was discussed.

Every historian of ancient India knows the five Western kings mentioned by Aśoka (R.E. XIII): Antiochus, Ptolemy, Antigonus, Magas, and Alexander (of Epirus).[12] It was a great moment when their names were first read by James Prinsep in the 1830s and published in the pages of the *Journal of the Asiatic Society of Bengal*. They were the first definite point for the establishment of the historical chronology of ancient India.

Another important case is Aśoka's Greek subjects in the Northwest of his empire (R.E. V and XIII). These Yonas, and their neighbors, the Kambojas, did not know Indian religion and social organization. A similar account is found in the Buddhist *Assalāyanasutta* (*Majjhima Nikāya* 93). They must have been descendants of Alexander's colonists, especially in Alexandria in Arachosia (Old Kandahar). With Greek edicts and other inscriptions found in the southeast of Afghanistan, we can no longer claim that Prakrit *yona* could stand for Westerners in general or even be without a connection with Jonian. In fact, the etymology of OIA *yavana* (first in Pāṇini) and MIA *yona* (first in Aśoka) has been well established long ago with the

9 Greek 'Ινδός. See Filliozat (1933) on elephant medicine.

10 Μωριεῖς of Hesychius et al., see Karttunen 1997, 259f.

11 See Thapar 1961, 167f. for a similar interpretation. Mookerji 1963, 29 and 38 seems to take the *dhammavijaya* quite literally.

12 Aṃtiyoka is Antiochus II Theos (261–246), Tulamaya is Ptolemaeus II Philadelphos (285–247), Aṃtekina is Antigonus Gonatas (276–239) and Maka is Magas of Cyrene (died before 250). Only one problem remained and still remains: was the fifth Yona king, Alikasudala, Alexander of Epirus (272–255) or Alexander of Corinth (252–244)? The latter seems to have been somewhat too insignificant, but certainty is not possible to attain. See Karttunen 1997, 266.

intermediate forms, OP *yauna* (and perhaps Akkadian *yamanu*/*yavanu*) from Greek Ἴωνες, Ἰάονες.[13]

These Yonas evidently participated in the Hellenistic civilization as they were the skilled translators of the Greek (and Aramaic) edicts of the emperor. I have earlier pointed out the interesting difference concerning the meaning of *dharma*. In the more or less Buddhist milieu of Aśokan Edicts, the king's *dhamma* was translated as *eusebeia,* but just a century later, *dhārmika* or 'endowed with dharma' was the equivalent of *dikaios* on Indo-Greek coins. It has been suggested that, in a literary work, Greek *aletheia* also stands for *dharma*.[14]

Finally, I must briefly mention the question of the origin of writing in India. Both systems, the Aramaic-based Kharoṣṭhī and the more original Brāhmī, first appear in Aśokan Edicts. The question of their origin has been studied in the 1990s by Oskar von Hinüber and Harry Falk who both suggest a Western origin for both systems. Aramaic as the model for Kharoṣṭhī seems to be quite clear and was already understood in the 19th century; for Brāhmī, they suggest an inspiration from the Greek writing which was certainly known, at least in the extreme Northwest of the Mauryan empire.[15] A certain familiarity with Greek writing is also seen in the reference of Kātyāyana (*yavanānī lipi*) and in the *Mahāvastu*. The Aramaic parallels earlier suggested for Brāhmī by Bühler and others are rather far-fetched. Thus, it seems that we can include that writing was among the few points of contacts between the Mauryas and Hellenism.[16] If we only had more evidence, I am certain that the list would be much longer.[17]

13 The digamma of Ἰάϝονες was lost too early to be relevant for *yavana*. For the history of *yona*/*yavana*, see Karttunen 2003.

14 Clement of Alexandria, see Christol 1983, 37.

15 In addition to the Greek edicts of Aśoka, there is at least one Greek inscription of the early Mauryan period in Kandahar. See Karttunen 1997, 288f. with further references.

16 Not only the writing, but also the idea of inscribing royal proclamations on stone may have a Western, more precisely Achaemenid origin. See, e.g., Thapar 2002, 182. I leave out some hypotheses which—though possible—remain unproven. See e.g., Scharfe 1971.

17 The research for this paper was made possible by the Helsinki Collegium of Advanced Study. Margot Stout Whiting has kindly checked my English.

Bibliography

Text of the Edicts:

Bloch, J. 1950. *Les Inscriptions d'Aśoka.* Collection Émile Senart. Paris: Les Belles Lettres.

Schneider, U. 1978. *Die grossen Felsen-Edikte Aśokas.* Kritische Ausgabe, Übersetzung und Analyse der Texte. Freiburger Beitrège zur Indologie 11. Wiesbaden: Otto Harrassowitz.

Studies:

Christol, A. 1983. "Les édits grecs d'Aśoka: Étude linguistique 1." *Journal Asiatique* 271: 25–42.

———. 1990. "Les édits grecs d'Aśoka: Étude linguistique 2." *Journal Asiatique* 278: 45–70.

Falk, H. 1993. *Schrift im alten Indien: ein Forschungsbericht mit Anmerkungen.* Script Oralia 56. Tübingen: Gunter Narr Verlag.

Filliozat, J. 1933. "Les gajaçāstra et les auteurs grecs, à propos de deux livres récents." *Journal Asiatique* 222: 163–175.

Hinüber, O. von. 1990. *Der Beginn der Schrift und frühe Schriftlichkeit in Indien.* Akademie der Wissenschaften und der Literatur, Abhandlungen der Geistes- und Sozialwissenschaftliche Klasse. Jahrgang 1989: 11. Mainz: Akademie der Wissenschaften und der Literatur/Stuttgart: Franz Steiner Verlag.

Karttunen, K. 1997. *India and the Hellenistic World.* Studia Orientalia 83. Helsinki: Finnish Oriental Society.

———. 2003. "Origin of Yona/Yavana." In *Sarupa Saurabham: Tributes to Indology, Prof. Lakshman Sarup Centenary Volume.* Ed. A. Agrawal, pp. 298–304. New Delhi: Harman Publishing House.

Lesky, A. 1971. *Geschichte der griechischen Literatur.* Dritte neubearbeitete und erweiterte Auflage. Bern and Munich: Francke Verlag.

Mookerji, R. K. 1995 [1963]. *Asoka.* Third revised edition. Delhi: Motilal Banarsidass.

Scharfe, H. 1971. "The Maurya dynasty and the Seleucids." *Zeitschrift für vergleichende Sprachforschung* 85: 211–225.

Thapar, R. 1977 [1961]. *Aśoka and the Decline of the Mauryas.* New Delhi: Oxford University Press.

———. 2003. *The Penguin History of Early India from the Origins to AD 1300.* New Delhi: Penguin Books.

From the Iron-Wheel to Bodhisattvahood: Aśoka in Buddhist Culture and Memory*

MAX DEEG

1. Introduction

In the past few years the term "cultural memory" ("Kulturelles Gedächtnis"), coined by the German Aegyptologist Jan Assmann,[1] has attracted the attention of historians of culture in Germany and in Europe. Assmann has shown how a certain amount of historical information is transformed into a historical memory not of an individual but of a whole cultural entity, a people, and how it is preserved in this very form in order to guarantee stability of cultural and proto-national self-identity which is then—as a kind of cultural *ālaya-vijñāna*—conserved as the "cultural memory." The logical consequence of this concept is that what we can get out of the so-called historical sources is the result of a distillation process, as it were, which says more about the time and the people who preserved them than about the time it pretends to describe.

One of the objects of Buddhist cultural memory—and it appears not only of Buddhist but also of Hindu[2] and Jain culture—has certainly been, and is, the

* This paper is based on my earlier German article Deeg 2001a. It has been changed and extended considerably, especially in the last section about the reception of Aśoka in East Asia. I would like to express my gratitude to Prof. Masahiro Shimoda who invited me to give a lecture on this subject at Tokyo University in October 2005 and thus gave me the occasion of developing my argument and engaging me in discussion with colleagues and students attending this lecture.

1 Assmann 1997.

2 Recently James L. Fitzgerald has argued that the figure of king Yudhiṣṭhira in the *Mahābhārata* had been designed "as a refutation, or at least as a rebuttal, of the emperor Aśoka." (Fitzgerald 2001: 64). Before Nick Sutton had already argued that the concept of kingship found in the *Mahābhārata*—showing a turn from violence to virtue and non-violence—is due to the change of the concept of rulership expressed in Aśoka's own documents and in his legendary representation: Sutton (1997). Both approaches show—however controversial they may be—that a major shift seems to have occurred in the paradigm of kingship during and after Aśoka's reign. I express my gratitude to my colleague Dr. James Hegarty of Cardiff University for having brought these references to my notice.

Mauryan emperor Aśoka. In the Western view he has been viewed as and been called—in a romanticized Orientalist way—the "Indian Constantine" and thus has been compared with the Byzantine emperor who made Christianity the state religion of the Roman Empire.[3] The famous Buddhologist Étienne Lamotte clearly underlines the historical significance of Aśoka: "Buddhism probably would have stayed an insignificant and unknown sect as many other communities had it not benefited of the support of the great emperor Aśoka."[4]

In my view the exclusively positive image of Aśoka as a tolerant ruler engaged in charity already in the third century before Christ comes from Aśoka's own edicts and a wishful-thinking on the side of Western and Asian scholars and, to a certain extent, hinders a fresh look at the great Maurya king and his representation in Buddhist narrative literature. The following pages attempt no more than a first analytic approach to the historical and narrative material on Aśoka, they do not take account of the numerous later and indirect sources from South-East Asia and only bring forward a relatively small amount of evidence from the vast corpus of East-Asian literature.

2. The sources

Chronologically speaking the oldest information on Aśoka comes from his own inscriptions.[5] Much has been written about these inscriptions; so I want to restrict myself to a few comments.

Although the edicts have been treated as invaluable documents for the study of the history of ancient India, two textual traditions on Aśoka in prose have not received the same interest[6] and have not been treated as complex literary corpora,

3 A romanticized position, such as the one of the German historian Fritz Kern, does not subscribe to this parallelization with Constantine—and with other great rulers of the past like Karl the Great, Marcus Aurelius, Salomon, Darius or Akhbar—because: "dieser aus politischer Berechnung an einer schon mächtigen Kirche eine Staatsstütze suchte und sie dafür als Reichskirche privilegierte, Aśoka hingegen aus rein religiösem Motiv eine politisch machtlose Religion wählte, deren Körper er beschirmte, ohne sie dogmatisch vor anderen zu privilegieren" (Kern 1956: 109).

4 Lamotte 1958: "Comme tant d'autres congrégations, le bouddhisme serait sans soute demeuré une secte obscure s'il n'avait bénéficié des sympathies et de l'appui du grand empereur Aśoka." Kern 1956: 109: ". . . der früheste Herrscher der Weltgeschichte, welcher sich voll und ganz dem Dienst an einer Erlösungsreligion verschreiben hat, . . .".

5 As a selection of the innumerous publications on Aśoka's edicts: Lamotte 1958: 245–261; Mookherji 1962. The standard edition is still: Hultzsch 1925; for other editions see: Bloch 1950, and Schneider 1978. The Minor Rock edicts have been edited by Andersen 1990. I will not deal here with the archaeological findings at Laṅgudi hill, Orissa, which have been claimed to include Aśokan inscriptions and two pieces of plastic art which have been identified and promoted as statues representing Aśoka himself by D. R. Pradhan (see for example in CIAA 12.2000, 13–17 and 13.2000, 14–16: see http://www.soas.ac.uk/ciaa/newsarch.htm, access: 29.10.2006). As Prof. H. Falk informed me in an e-mail from 31st October 2006, these pieces have not been published in a reasonable form and are still too "obscure" to be taken into account as historical valuable sources at the moment.

6 An exception is Eugène Burnouf who, in the earliest handbook for the study of Buddhism, Burnouf 1844, refers mainly to the legends as for example the *Aśokāvadāna*, but

but have been used to elucidate unclear passages in the edicts or to bolster interpretations of the edicts.[7]

These two strings of stories on Aśoka are the legends[8]: There is a North Indian Sanskrit version with the title *Aśokāvadāna*, the "Legend of Aśoka."[9] The *terminus ante quem* for the date of this *avadāna* depends on the dating of the complete corpus of legends into which it is incorporated, the *Divyāvadāna*. It seems to be common sense now that this collection or its oldest parts can be roughly dated to the first century CE.

Besides this version written in an Indian language, there are Chinese translations of versions which no longer exist and differ in some points, sometimes even considerably, from the extant Indian text, the *Aśokāvadāna*. The oldest version of the legends preserved in Chinese is the *Ayu-wang-zhuan* 阿育王傳 (T.2042), the "Legend (or Life) of King Aśoka," which was translated by the Parthian monk An Faqin 安法欽 in the year 306; the second Chinese translation dates from the year 513: the *Ayu-wang-jing* 阿育王經 (T.2043[10]), "*Sūtra* of King Aśoka," translated by Saṅghabhara/Sengjiapoluo 僧迦婆羅.[11] Texts of single episodes of the legend are extent, too: T.2044: *Tianzun-shuo-Ayu-wang-piyu-jing* 天尊說阿育王譬喻經, "*Sūtra* of the Heavenly Venerated One [that is: of the Buddha] of the Parable of King Aśoka," translated between 317 and 420; T.2045: *Ayu-wang-xi-huaimu-yinyuan-jing* 阿育王息壞目因緣經, "*Sūtra* on the Karmic Conditions of the Destroyed Eyes of King Aśoka's Son," the Kuṇāla-story translated around the end of the fourth century by Tanmonanti 曇摩難提/ Dharmanandi(n). Parts of the legend were even incorporated into the Chinese *Saṃyuktāgama*/*Za-ahan-jing* 雜阿含經. And there were also texts that are no longer extant, but are nonetheless known to us, for instance, by title from quotation in the Chinese *sūtra* catalogue *Chu-sanzang-jiji* 出三藏集記, "Records on the Compilation of the *Tripiṭaka*," compiled by Sengyou 僧祐: *Ayu-wang-zuo-xiaoer-shi-jing* 阿育王作小兒時經, "*Sūtra* on king Aśoka when he was still a child" (*Chu-sanzang-jiji* 4); *Ayu-wang-di-chujia-zao-shixiang-ji* 阿育王弟出家造石像記, "Report on king Aśoka's brother who became a monk and made a stone statue"[12]; *Jiuli-laoyu-jing* 救離牢獄經, "*Sūtra* on the redemption from prison" (*Chu-sanzang-jiji* 4, 12). This Chinese string of the Aśoka legend is projected into the Buddhist *geographia sacra* of India by the Chinese pilgrims Faxian 法顯, Song Yun 宋雲, Xuanzang 玄奘 and Huichao 慧超.

does not discuss the edicts (except on p.330, note 1, on Prinsep). In this context, it is noteworthy that Alexander Cunningham's edition was published three years after the second edition of Burnouf's book.

7 See Eggermont 1956. This does not mean that it is impossible to extract historical data by comparing the edicts with the legendary sources; see e.g., Bongard-Levin 1971.

8 For a list of texts containing the complete legend or parts of the Aśoka-legend see Bongard-Levin 1971: 124f.

9 Text in: Cowell. Neil 1886, and Mukhopadhyaya 1963; for an English translation and interpretation of the legend see: Strong 1983.

10 T. refers to the numbers in: Takakusu and Watanabe 1924.

11 As a comparative study containing a French translation of the *Ayu-wang-zhuan* 阿育王傳, see Przyluski 1923.

12 For a discussion of the motive of Aśoka's statue see below.

The later Tibetan sources such as found in Tāranātha's *Rgya-gar chos-'byuṅ* ("History of the *dharma* in India")[13] or in Bu-ston's *Chos-'byuṅ* ("History of the *dharma*")[14] belong to the same branch of legendary tradition and—although they may comprise some more details and variants of the Aśoka legend which are not found elsewhere—will not be dealt with here.[15]

Besides this North Indian—I would even go so far to say Northwest Indian[16]—tradition of the legend we find long passages and episodes of Aśoka in the Śrī Laṅkan Pāli chronicles of the Theravādin which were compiled at the earliest from the fourth to the fifth century,[17] the *Dīpavaṃsa*, "Chronicle of the Island [Ceylon]," in the *Mahāvaṃsa*, "Great Chronicle [of the Island Ceylon],"[18] and in the chronicle-like introduction to the huge *Vinaya*-commentary *Samantapāsādikā*, the *Bāhiranidāna*.[19]

Beside translations from the classical Aśoka-legends we find quite a lot of secondary references, direct or indirect, to Aśoka in Central Asian and in Chinese sources.[20]

In the following I will move geographically and will try to work out four basic Buddhist conceptions of Aśoka:

1. The perspective of the edicts themselves: In my eyes, these attempt to integrate Buddhism (and other religions) with a general ideology of the state.
2. The perspective of the Indian sources of, assumedly, Northwestern origin and their (Chinese) descendents: These have a tendency to bring the ruler closer to, or to integrate him into, a monastic ideal concept of rulership. They also have a tendency to keep apart and conserve the spheres of secular rulership and monastic independence.

13 For an English translation see: Chattopadhyaya. Chimpa 1970.

14 Partly translated into German by Obermiller 1932.

15 I also will not discuss here the late Kaśmīran epic poem *Avadānakalpalatā* by Kṣemendra into which different episodes of the legend have been incorporated, e.g., the story of Aśoka's son Kuṇāla or the story of the construction of the *Dharmarājika-stūpas*. But I would like to point out the long continuity of which the fact of the insertion of Aśoka and his *guru* Upagupta (*Mahājātakamālā*, *Guṇakāraṇḍavyūha*, longer recensions of the *Svayaṃbhūpurāṇa*) into late Nepalese texts of the *avadāna* genre clearly give witness: see Hahn 1985: 23ff. and passim; Douglas 2002: 34 (I have to thank Dr. Douglas for sending me an electronic version of his dissertation).

16 So far no direct evidence of the Aśoka legend has been found in the Northwest, but as Richard Salomon has shown during the conference, there are now references to Aśoka in the Kharoṣṭhī documents found in that region, now in the British Library. It cannot be excluded therefore that the presence of the Aśoka legend in the Northwest of the subcontinent will be substantiated by future finds.

17 For the dating and other questions of history of literature see von Hinüber 1996: 87ff. (§182–188: *Dīpavaṃsa* and *Mahāvaṃsa*, second half of the 4th cent. and the end of the 5th cent., 102f. (§208–209: *Sāmantapāsādikā*).

18 Edition: Geiger 1908, and English translation: Geiger 1912.

19 Edition and English translation: Jayawickrama 1986.

20 I will discuss the elements taken from the Aśoka legend in the Buddhist (Tibetan) foundation legend of Khotan in my forthcoming monograph: Deeg forthcoming.

3. The perspective of the South Indian Theravāda sources: These tried to integrate the figure of the king Aśoka completely into the intentions and aims of the Buddhist *saṅgha*.
4. The reception of Aśoka outside of South Asia: In this part, I will examine some examples from Central Asia and China where the legends of the Maurya ruler were mainly used to legitimize the claims for power of allegedly Buddhist dynasties and, at least in China, also found their way in a broader popular context of society.

I should also mention that one could propose a fifth perspective prevalent in Southeast Asia and in Japan, maybe also in Korea about which I do not know enough to make a decisive statement. These very often refer to elements of the Aśoka legend without giving the name of the Maurya emperor[21]; this has also been, for example, the case of the Burmese king Mindon (1852–1878). This seems to suggest that in the historical development of some Theravāda countries position 3 would have been reshaped in such a way that the *saṅgha* was again dominated by the ruler.[22]

3. Integration of the *saṅgha* into the state ideology: Aśoka in his own edicts

Although the edicts and pillar inscriptions appear as objective historical sources at the first sight the question arises of who speaks in these documents: Aśoka as an individual and a committed Buddhist who has even made his religion the state religion, as one can read very often in popular works on the Mauryan king? It should be noticed that such a position obviously has been constructed as a kind of dualist antithesis to the Macchiavellian conception of power reflected in the famous and notorious *Arthaśāstra* of Kauṭilya which was written under the rule of Aśoka's grandfather Candragupta.[23] I myself would rather suggest that Aśoka is speaking of himself as an ideal ruler who propagates an equally ideal policy which is, no question, partly motivated by his individual convictions, convictions, however, not purely religious.

How Aśoka of the inscriptions is interpreted is mainly dependent on the interpretation of the key concept of *dharma*—in the texts the term appears in its Prakrit form *dhaṃmo*. As is well known, the range of meanings of this word covers a broad semantic and connotative area: It is derived from the root (*dhātu*) √*dhṛ*, "to

21 This kind of indirect reference to the Mauryan emperor may be discovered in other Buddhist and other Indian sources as well, as John Strong (*Saddharmapuṇḍarīkasūtra*) and Madhav Deshpande have shown in their contributions to the conference.

22 See Swearer 1995: 64–67 and 72–74; Holt 1996: 18ff.; S. J. Tambiah 1976; Höfer. Prunner. Kaneko. Bezacier. Sarkisyanz. 1975: 465 (on *Mindon*).

23 As a paradigmatic example see Gombrich 1997: 134ff.; but see also Bechert 1988: 23, who contradicts the normal idea that Buddhism had been state religion under Aśoka. Scholars are very often not aware of the fact that this is a kind of vicious hermeneutical circle as everything depends on the definition of state religion.

be stable"[24] and in the oldest Indian texts it may mean "(cosmic) law," but also the secular juridical system and the rules and contents which form the basis of a religion (like in Buddhism). Only this very rough sketch of meanings reflects the problem that the *dhaṃma* which Aśoka propagates could be a religiously founded civil ethics for all state citizens in the Maurya empire as well as a specific religion usually identified as the Buddhist *dharma*. I personally think that Aśoka intentionally aimed for an inclusive understanding of the word *dharma* with all its connotations—even a juridical-normative meaning which would legitimize the use of means of authoritative power in order to achieve the acceptance of his state ideology of ethics. This does not deny the fact that Aśoka refers directly to Buddhism, mainly in the so-called Minor Inscriptions and in the Pillar Edicts,[25] but—and this is very important—never, as far as I see, in the Great Rock Edicts which rather reflect his policy of religion as a statesman.[26]

The Rock Edicts are very clearly imperial decrees in which Aśoka—in spite of all the moral reasons brought forth—gives exhortations and instructions to his people, to laymen as well as to the monastic orders. This can be clearly seen in the style of the edicts by the use of partly negated *participia necessitatis*: edict I: *hida no kichi jīve ālabhitu pajohitaviye, no pi ca samāje kaṭaviye* ("Here no living (beings) are to be killed for the purpose of sacrifice; nor should there be held public (sacrificial?) meetings").[27] A clear order is for example given at the beginning edict III: . . . *me iyaṃ ānapayite:* . . . (". . . has been ordered the (following) by me: . . .").

Aśoka's own role is quite clear: The ruler has transformed from an imperator using military force to a monarch who takes care of his subjects. The best expression of this change is found in edict 13 in which Aśoka regrets the cruelties of his campaign against Kaliṅga (today's Orissa):

> *se āvatake jane tadā kaligesu hate ca maṭe ca apavuḍḍhe ca, tato sata-bhāge vā sahasabhāge vā aja gulumate vā devānaṃpiyasa.*
>
> Therefore—of the many people who were killed in Kaliṅga, died and were deported—even the hundredth, the thousandth part (of them) is taken as a grave (matter) by the Beloved of the Gods. (Schneider, 116f. XIII)

But even when he speaks of the *dharma*, the imperial rhetoric is used when he speaks of "conquest" (*vijaya*) although of "*dharma*-conquest" (*dhaṃmavijaya*),

24 See Mayrhofer 1991: 780, s.v. *dhárman.*

25 Compare the edicts on the pillars of Allahabad-Kosam and Sarnath, the so-called schism-edicts (English translation Hultzsch 1925: 160f.); the Rummindei inscription at Lumbinī referring to a pilgrimage tour to the place of the birth of the Buddha (Hultzsch 1925: 164f.), the inscription of Nigali-Sagar referring to the *stūpa* of the Buddha of the past Konākamana (Kanakamuni) (Hultzsch 1925: 165), the rock-edicts of Rupnath- (Hultzsch 1925: 167ff.), Sahasram- (Hultzsch 1925: 171), Calcutta-Bairat- (Hultzsch 1925: 172f.), Maski-Felsenedikte (Hultzsch 1925: 175.) where Aśoka speaks of himself as a Buddhist layman (*upāsaka*).

26 Cp. Ruegg 1995: 61.

27 I usually follow the synoptic edition and translation of Schneider 1978.

which gains a different dimension when brought together with the references to neighboring and even more distant kingdoms mentioned in edicts II, V and XIII.

It is, of course, difficult to say what kind of concrete politics is standing behind the wording of the edicts if one gives up to use the pattern of the pious ruler. An example of this is found in the passages in which Aśoka speaks of officials who regularly (5 years) tour the empire in order to propagate the *dhaṃma*: See e.g., edict III:

> . . . *savata vijitasi mama yutā lājūke pādesike ca paṃcasu paṃcasu vasesu anusaṃyānaṃ nikhamaṃtu etāye va aṭhāye imāye dhaṃmānusathiye athā aṃnāye pi kaṃmane. . .*
>
> Every five years (and) everywhere in my empire *yutas*, *lājūkas* and *pādesikas* should go out on inspection tours for the purpose of the following *dhaṃma* instructions and also for other activities.[28]

An idealizing interpretation would see here a support and propagation of Buddhism, of the *dharma*. If one accepts the other conception of *dharma* as referring also to civil law, the *mahāmātras*[29] and the other officials can only be controllers who took care of the *dharma* of the king—in the sense of a moral-juridical obligation for the subjects.[30] See edict X:

> . . . *tadatvāye āyatiye ca jane dhaṃmasusūsaṃ sususatu me dhaṃmavutaṃ ca anuvidhiyatu ti. . .*
>
> . . . for the present and for the future people should obey the *dhaṃma* and should follow what I have said on the *dhaṃma*. . . .

The people should, however, also follow and obey the *dharma* of the respective religious groups. Royal regulation[31] and probably also punishment and sanction were supposed to be implied in case of offenses. The statements of the edicts have to be relativized according to the possibility of their execution. It is, for instance, almost certainly not the case that, in the Maurya empire of Aśoka, there were generally no animals killed[32] or hunted[33] as the edicts imply.

And it is rather doubtful that Aśoka could really deliver the social welfare system for the whole empire of which he speaks in his edicts:

> . . . *savatā devānaṃpiyasā piyadasine lājine duve cikisā kaṭā: munisa-*

28 Ed. and German transl. Schneider 1978: 104f., III.

29 In edict V Aśoka mentions that he had instituted as the first ruler these high officers thirteen years after his royal consecration in order to spread the *dharma* in the different regions and populations.

30 Ed. and German transl. Schneider 1978: 112f.

31 Edict VI may indicate this. In it Aśoka reserves his right to be informed directly in case of urgent and disputed matters—an information which implies that Aśoka did also make the final decision in these matters.

32 Cp. edict I (see above, note 28) and the various emphasis that living beings are not to be killed (edicts III, IV, XI).

33 This is to be implied through RE VIII in which Aśoka emphasizes that in former days he went hunting quite often but now performs *dhaṃma*-journeys instead.

> *cikisā ca pasucikisā ca. osadhāni munisopagāni ca pasuopagāni ca, ata atā nathi, savatā hālāpitā ca lopāpitā ca. hemeva mūlāni ca phalāni ca, ata atā nathi, savatā hālāpitā ca lopāpitā ca. magesu lukhāni lopāpitāni udupānāni ca khānāpitāni paṭibhogāye pasu-munisānaṃ.* RE II

> . . . everywhere [and even across the frontiers of the empire] two kinds of healing treatments have been established by king Devānaṃpiya Piyadasin—treatment for humans and treatment for (domestic) animals. [And] on his order herbs beneficent for humans and animals have been procured and planted where they have not been available. In the same way roots and fruits have been procured and planted on his order where they have not been available. On his order trees have been planted and wells have been dug along the roads for the benefit of humans and animals.[34]

The edicts often express themselves in a clear pragmatic and political language when, for example, Aśoka speaks of altruism as the ideal way for political and individual action but then immediately threatens tribes not yet fully controlled:

> *ā pi ca aṭavi devānaṃpiyasa vijitasi hoti, tam pi anunayati anunijha-payati. anutāpe pi ca pabhāve devānaṃpiyasa vucati tesām kiti: avata-peyu no pi ca haṃneyu. ichati hi devānaṃpiye savabhūtānaṃ achati sayamaṃ samacaliyaṃ mādavaṃ.* Edict XIII

> And also the jungle tribes in the empire of the beloved by the gods, he treats them well and causes them to think (about the *dhaṃma*). And in spite of the remorse of the beloved of the gods his might is proclaimed to them so that they restrain themselves and are not killed. Because the beloved of the gods wishes (to perform) non-damage, self-restraint, impartiality and mildness towards living beings.[35]

The *mahāmātra*s have even the right to control the inner chambers of the king's relatives:

> *. . . hidā bāhilesu ca nagalesu savesu olodhanesu bhātinaṃ (. . .) ca me bhagininaṃ ca (va ?) e vā pi aṃne nātike savatā viyāpaṭā. . . .* RE V

> . . . they [the *mahāmātras*] are everywhere, here [that is: in the capital Pāṭaliputra] and in all (the other) cities preoccupied with the private chambers of my brothers and sisters as well as with those of my other relatives. . . .[36]

When we interpret the edicts in the light of a policy of control of religions in

34 Ed. and German transl. Schneider 1978: 104f. The last part of this passage could, of course, be interpreted as measures for the development of the infrastructure of the empire. RE V mentions that the *mahāmātra*s and the other officials should take care of the non-protected and old people (see also RE VIII) and of prisoners who have families.

35 Ed. and German transl. Schneider 1978: 116f.

36 Ed. and German transl. Schneider 1978: 108f.

the Maurya empire, one could see the measures as an attempt to integrate all religious groups into a state ideology. This is not restricted to the Buddhist *saṅgha*. Without assuming a purely utilitarian intention on the side of Aśoka and denying any altruistic motives, this would mean that his tolerance of, and his support for, the religions was firmly integrated in his ultimate aim for, and claim to, imperial power.

4. Balance between ruler and *saṅgha*: the Aśoka in the *Aśokāvadāna*

The origin of the Aśoka legend and the question of where its plot and narratives come from is closely connected with the question of how this legend was still being influenced by the contents of the edicts.[37]

The answer again is very much dependent on another question: To what extent were the edicts still comprehensible in terms of form and content at the time when the legend assumedly was compiled (first cent. of the Christian era)? H. Falk, in his book on Indian scripts, comments:

> The Brāhmī of Aśoka was preserved almost unchanged until the Christian era. . . . The Brāhmī of the Kṣatrapas was given a new style but everyone who was able to read could decipher the old characters at any time. This picture changed with the Guptas as in the South as well as in the North characters were transformed and new forms were developed for aesthetic reasons which made it impossible to recognize their origins.[38]

As the writing of the inscription was still readable up to the first centuries of the Christian era, the language of the documents—which were written in Middle-Indo-Aryan Prakrit—did not cause too much of a problem. We may assume that the content of the edicts was still intelligible to a certain extent in the first and second centuries CE and that it could influence the process of formation of the legend crystallizing around the figure of the king Aśoka[39].

As an example of the connection between the edicts and the legends, I would like to choose the central events surrounding the moral remorse and the "conversion" of Aśoka. In the case of the edicts this was caused by the campaign against Kaliṅga, while in the legend of the *Aśokāvadāna* this is caused through the

37 Cp. Bongard-Levin 1971: 124f.; Ruegg 1995: 63f., seems to think that the Aśoka of the inscription has not left any trace in the legends.

38 Falk 1993: 328: "Die Brāhmī Aśokas hatte sich bis um die Zeitenwende fast unverändert erhalten, . . . Die Brāhmī der Kṣatrapas erhielt zwar einen neuen Duktus, doch konnte jeder des Lesens Kundige jederzeit auch noch die alten Charaktere entziffern. Ab den Guptas änderte sich das Bild, denn im Süden wie im Norden wurden aus Gründen der Ästhetik Zeichen verfremdet und Formen entwickelt, die ihre Ursprünge nicht immer erkennen liem̐en."

39 The reports of the Chinese pilgrims to India, Faxian (5th cent.) and Xuanzang (7th cent.), seem to indicate that in these later periods the inscriptions were not really understood any more (see also below, section 9).

preaching of the Buddhist monk Samudra and later through the instruction of the Buddhist patriarch Upagupta.[40] The violent phase of Aśoka's early reign, which is clearly reflected by Aśoka's comments on his campaign against Kaliṅga and its cruel consequences as reflected in the edicts, is reflected in the *Aśokāvadāna* in the name which the king is given in the first part of the legend: *Caṇḍāśoka*, the "fierce" or "cruel" Aśoka.[41]

However, in the *Aśokāvadāna*, and in the Pāli chronicles as well, there is no concrete event which causes the king to regret his former cruelties. In the *Aśokāvadāna* there is the story of the construction of a hell-like prison by the king where completely innocent people who happen to pass the building were tortured to death by a cruel prison guard/executioner[42]; the destruction of this prison, when Aśoka is taught the *dharma* through the monk Samudra, represents the climax of the fierce and cruel phase of his rulership.[43] Advancing a historical interpretation of the story of the hell-prison, I would suggest that it reflects the detention camps which would certainly have been built after the siege of Kaliṅga and the deportation of a huge number of its population.

The Śrī Laṅkan chronicles only state—somewhat abruptly and without a real narrative motivation—that Aśoka, after having killed his ninety-nine or one hundred half-brothers, rules with justice. There is no moral judgment of his wicked deed of killing his relatives.[44]

40 Cp. the detailed analysis of Strong 1983: 71ff., and Strong 1992: 145ff.

41 In the *Aśokāvadāna* the deliberate killing of five hundred ministers and five hundred ladies of his harem causes Aśoka to be given this name (Strong 1983: 210f). The Śrī Laṅkan chronicle *Mahāvaṃsa* (5.189) only mentions the conversion in very general terms without giving a reason: "He was called Caṇḍāsoka before because of his evil deeds; afterwards he was called Dhammāsoka because of his pious deeds" (*Caṇḍāsoko ti ñāyittha pure pāpena kammunā, Dhammāsoko ti ñāyittha pacchā puññena kammunā*).

42 Aśoka does this after having been advised by his minister Rādhagupta that he should not kill the delinquents personally, as he did with his ministers and the ladies of his serial, but that he should leave this to another person who should also be the master of the prison which bears the euphemistic name "comfortable prison" (*ramaṇīyakaṃ bandhanam*). Ironically this man gets the ideas for his tortures from a Buddhist *sūtra* which Aśoka has burnt after his conversion (Strong 1983: 210ff).

43 Strictly speaking, the conversion of Aśoka in the *Aśokāvadāna*, indicated and symbolized by the title Dharmāśoka, "Aśoka of the law," occurs after Aśoka had erected the 84,000 *dharmarājika-stūpas*: "As soon as king had erected the 84,000 *dharmarājika-stūpas* he became a lawful king of the *dharma* and he was given the name Dharmāśoka. And it will be said: 'The distinguished and noble Maurya erected the *stūpas* for the sake of all living beings in the world.': Previously he had achieved the character of a cruel Aśoka, but he now achieved on earth the character of a lawful Aśoka through this action.'" (*Divyāvadāna* 381f. *yāvac ca rājñāśokena caturaśītidharmarājikāsahasraṃ pratiṣṭhāpitaṃ dharmiko dharmarājā saṃvṛttaḥ; tasya Dharmāśoka iti samjñā jātā; vakṣyati ca: āryamauryaśrīḥ sa prajānāṃ hitārthaṃ kṛtsnaṃ stūpān kārayāmāsa lokam; Caṇḍāśokatvaṃ prāpya pūrvaṃ pṛthivyāṃ Dharmāśokatvaṃ karmaṇā tena lebhe.*). The episode bears burlesque features.

44 *Mahāvaṃsa* 5.18f.: "To Bindusāra one hundred and one sons were born; in terms of virtue, brilliance and power Asoka was the most excellent one of them. When he had slain his 99 stepbrothers [sic!] he gained the sole rulership over Jambudīpa." (*19. Bindusārasutā āsuṃ sataṃ eko ca vissutā, Asoko āsi tesāṃ tu puññatejobaliddhiko. 20. Vemātike bhātaro so hantvā ekūnakaṃ sataṃ sakale Jambudīpasmiṃ ekarajjaṃ apāpuṇi.*). The version in *Dīpavaṃsa* 6.22 is even more extreme: "After Asoka had killed his one hundred brothers

One case in which there is a relative correspondence between the edicts—in this case, the pillar edicts which were found in different Buddhist pilgrimage sites—and the legend is the description of the pilgrimages of Aśoka: The legend reports how Aśoka after his conversion visited the different places famous through events in the life of the Buddha; described in detail is Aśoka's veneration of the *bodhi*-tree at Bodhgayā.[45] One cannot overlook, however, that the focus has shifted from the inscriptions to the legends: While the pillars are found at the places of the Buddha Gautama's birth and at the place where the *stūpa*s of the former Buddha Kanakamuni stand,[46] the legend concentrates on the symbol of the monastic way to salvation, the tree of enlightenment.[47] This difference is not a small one because the Aśoka of the edicts seems to follow the way which is already given by the Buddha in the *Parinirvāṇasūtra*[48]: He venerates the Buddhas and their relics and protects them in his function as a ruler. The legend, in contrast, reflects monastic propaganda insofar as the ruler subordinates himself deliberately under the guide of the *saṅgha*: It is the Buddhist patriarch Upagupta who guides the king on his journey and explains to him the meaning of all the places he visits: Lumbinī, Kapilavastu, Bodhgayā, Sārnāth, Rājagṛha, Sāṃkāśya, Śrāvastī, and Kuśinagarī.[49]

The completion of the task of a contextualizing reading of the two strings of sources, the inscriptions and the legend, should enable us to explain where the differences between both come from and especially where the motivation lies for

and established a dynastic line of his own, he was consecrated king in Mahinda's fourteenth year. After his consecration Asokadhamma (= Dhammāsoka) achieved magical power; he became a turner of the wheel in (Jambu)dīpa, extremely splendid and rich in merit." (*22. hantvā ekasate bhāte vaṃsaṃ katvāna ekato Mahindacuddasame vasse Asokam abhisiñcayuṃ. 23. Asokadhammo 'bhisitto paṭiladdhā ca iddhiyo, mahātejo puññavanto dīpe cakkapavattako.*). *Bāhiranidāna* 44 gives an explanation for the number 99 found in the *Mahāvaṃsa*: "At this time king Bindusāra had one hundred sons. Asoka killed all of them except prince Tissa. After (he) had killed (his brothers) he ruled for four years without having been consecrated [king]; after the fourth year, the two hundred eighteenth year after the extinction of the Tathāgata, he achieved the consecration to be only ruler of the whole Jambudīpa." (*Tena kho pana samayena Bindusārassa rañño ekasataputtā ahesuṃ. Te sabbe Asoko attanā saddhiṃ ekamātikaṃ Tissakumāraṃ ṭhapetvā ghātesi. Ghātento cattāri vassāni anabhisitto 'va rajjaṃ kāretvā catunnaṃ vassānaṃ accayena Tathāgatassa parinibbānato dvinnaṃ vassasatānaṃ upari aṭṭhārasame vasse sakala-Jambudīpe ekarajjābhisekaṃ papuni*. . .).

45 This seems to be the only motive which has found its way into Buddhist art already very early: At one of the *stūpa*s in Sāñcī (2nd cent. BCE) at least two scenes are found which show the attack of queen Tiṣyarakṣitā on the *bodhi*-tree and the bathing of the tree by Aśoka on reliefs of the southern and the eastern gate (Lamotte 1958: 267).

46 RE is usually interpreted as a proof for an actual visit of the *bodhi*-tree (*saṃbodhi*?): . . . *se devānaṃpiye piyadasi lājā dasavasābhisite saṃtaṃ nikhamitha saṃbodhi. Tenatā dhaṃmayātā*. . . . (". . . But king D. P., ten years after his consecration, went out to the *sambodhi*. Thereby, it was a *dharma*-journey. . . .") (Ed. and German transl. Schneider 1978: 110f.). One could question this interpretation (*saṃbodhi* = *mahābodhi* = *bodhivṛksa*; for the problems with such an interpretation, see already Bloch 1950: 112, note 6) and ask if Aśoka had really visited this place and if it really had the significance which it is given in the legend.

47 Strong 1983: 250 (first visit in the company of Upagupta) and 257ff., 265ff.

48 Cp. Waldschmidt 1948: 244ff.; Waldschmidt 1961: 417ff.

49 Strong 1983: 244ff.; Strong 1992: 164f.

the insertion of some narrative episodes into the legend—and this is what I will try to do during the rest of my paper. I would like to start with a general observation: While the Aśoka in the inscriptions is a self-conscious ruler who uses the concept of the *dhaṃma* to express his "ideology of rulership," the legends show a general tendency towards the submission of the king under the *saṅgha*.[50]

Such an image of Aśoka, as reflected in the legends, could not have come from the circles of a ruling elite who, in India as elsewhere, had a great interest in binding and controlling the religious movements and groups. What the legends of Aśoka rather present is the ideal image of a king, a ruler propagated by the *saṅgha*—we finally deal with Buddhist texts—who, above and beyond all his duties as a ruler, committed himself—as an ideal Buddhist layman—to the benefit of the Buddhist order by donations and by constructing *stūpas*, as well as preserving and protecting the Buddhist sacred places like the *bodhi*-tree and the relics of the Buddha (*śarīra*), and by initiating pilgrimages.

But the *Aśokāvadāna* does not only depict Aśoka as a king who is willing to support the *saṅgha*; almost equally important is his role as a paradigmatic Indian world ruler, as a wheel-turning king (*cakravartin*).[51] In the Buddhist framework of the legend this is foretold for him by the Buddha in his former life, when as a child he donated a handful of earth to the Buddha: A prophecy that is, of course, fulfilled. But the monastic authors of the *Aśokāvadāna* are careful enough not to overdo it: In the hierarchy of *cakravartin* as it is found in the *Abhidharmakośa*, for example, Aśoka is only a "turner of the iron wheel" having the lowest position beneath the two other levels of "silver" and "gold." It is thus fair to say that Aśoka is granted a high position as a ruler but he does not, for instance, come close to the type of democratically elected ruler of a Buddhist utopia of the past, represented by the king Mahāsaṃmata.[52] He is also different from the two higher levels of *cakravartin* by not owning the outer and inner qualities of a "great man" (*mahāpuruṣa*), qualities that would bring him closer to the Buddha.[53] Nevertheless the ideal, almost idealistic image of royal rulership in the legend, which was probably meant as a mirror for a real existing ruler, left enough space for political concretization; enough space to legitimize, to a certain extent, the use of imperialistic action and violence.

The tradition of the North Indian *Aśokāvadāna* presents us with an Aśoka who is committed to Buddhism to a very high degree, but there are only a few tendencies in the final portions of the legend that really depict him as dependent on the *saṅgha*. The close connection with the *saṅgha* is expressed through high-ranking monastic individuals such as Upagupta, though the *Aśokāvadāna* leaves enough room for Aśoka to make his own, personal decisions; that may be the

50 According to the Pāli sources at least to the orthodox branch of the Theravādin, while Asoka intervenes at the threat of a schism of the order—but again in favor of the Theravādin.

51 Cp. Strong 1983: 44ff.

52 To this legend which is already found in the canonical literature—in the *Agaññasutta* in the *Dīgha Nikāya*—see also Strong 1983: 44ff., and Ruegg 1995: 59.

53 Strong 1983: 46. Strong considers the thirty-six places which Aśoka has visited on his pilgrimage as a symbolic reference to the thirty six characteristic signs of the Buddha: Strong 1983: 123ff.

reason that we do not find a report on the third Buddhist council in the *Aśokāvadāna*, which is so important for the Pāli sources as we will see. In the *Aśokāvadāna* it is the *dharma*, as a central "organ," to whom both parties, the king and the *saṅgha*,[54] pay tribute; insofar the *Aśokāvadāna* and its tradition seems to be closer to the self-understanding of the Aśoka of the edicts.

If we ask what could be the historical setting of the creation of an ideal ruler as the Aśoka of the *Aśokāvadāna*, I would propose that is was the attempt of a North Indian *saṅgha* to create a Buddhist ideal-typical model of the relationship between state and religion. This reflected the integrative religious policy of the Kuṣāna rulers in this region, the best known of these being Kaniṣka,[55] who is the paradigmatic Buddhist ruler after Aśoka. Through the legendary traditions about this ruler,[56] which are only known in fragments from Indian texts, but which are relatively well preserved in Chinese and Tibetan texts, it becomes clear that some elements were indeed taken from the Aśoka tradition.[57] To give just one example: When it is reported that Kaniṣka especially venerated the relics of the Buddha and even wanted to bring the alms bowl of the Buddha from Central India to Gandhāra,[58] it seems quite clear that this was modeled after Aśoka's distribution of the relics. The difference between the two legends is understandable: While Aśoka had access to primary relics, Kaniṣka could only try to get hold of secondary relics.[59]

The attempt of the historical Kaniṣka to imitate Aśoka can be shown quite clearly by the so-called Kaniṣka-*stūpa* in Shāh-Jī-Kī Ḍherī[60] in Afghanistan. The legend of this site, again, shows a lot of parallels with the Aśoka narratives.[61] Like Aśoka, Kaniṣka was in close contact with the most eminent Buddhist teachers of

54 There may be some significance in the fact that Aśoka in the *Aśokāvadāna* has several monastic teachers (Samudra, Upagupta, Piṇḍola Bharadvāja, Yaśas).

55 The solution of the old dispute about the time of Kaniṣka has become closer by a Bactrian inscription which was discovered in Afghanistan some years ago, so that there are basically only two possibilities left, 100–126 CE or 120–146 CE: see Sims-Williams. Cribb. 1995/96: 105f.

56 Cp. in general: Rosenfield 1967.

57 See Deeg 2004. Another Indian ruler who seemed to have copied Aśoka to a certain extent was Śīlāditya Harṣavardhana on which we have some detailed information through the report of Xuanzang. Harṣa, like Aśoka, organized great *dharma* lectures and discussion and donation assemblies for the *saṅgha*. Again these assemblies correspond to the *pañcavārṣika* of the legend which themselves go back to the quinquennial envoys' tours: see Deeg 1995, and Deeg 1997. It is remarkable that in Xuanzang's *Xiyu-ji*, Harṣa is not at all submissive to the *saṅgha*, but controls the monastic community in an almost autocratic way. This may on the one hand reflect the "sinisized" position of Xuanzang, but it may also show the real attitude of an Indian autocratic ruler towards religious communities, which demonstrates that the figure of Aśoka could also been used as a legitimization for dominating the *saṅgha*.

58 This is confirmed by the Chinese pilgrims (Faxian, Xuanzang) but also through other Chinese sources; see Zürcher 1968.

59 See in general: Verardi 1983.

60 Dobbins 1971; Kuwayama 1997; for an analysis of the legend of this *stūpa* and the connections with the Aśoka legend see Deeg 2004.

61 A parallelization of the monuments: Aśoka-*stūpa*s; Kaniṣka-*stūpa*; Kaniṣka-*vihāra*: Aśoka-*ārāma*.

his time; according to the legend, he tried to get in contact with the famous monk and poet Aśvaghoṣa. In the legendary reports on the Buddhist council in Kaśmīr, which was organized by Kaniṣka, Aśvaghoṣa plays a dominant role[62]; it is he who is also said to have converted Kaniṣka.[63] It was with the Sanskritization of the canons of the Sarvāstivādin and the Mahāsāṅghika[64] that a process began which aimed to make Buddhism fit for the struggle with the Brahmanical counter-reform and other heretical teachings.

It is probably the Kuṣana period in which the Aśoka legend of the North gained its shape[65] and this is, I would claim, not a coincidence: The parallels between certain narrative elements in the Aśoka and Kaniṣka legends make it plausible that the Aśoka legend, in the form preserved in the *Aśokāvadāna*, took its shape in Buddhist circles of this period. Certain intentions were responsible for the way in which this legend describes the Mauryan emperor, intentions which were closely connected with the political and social situation of the time. The lack of, as far as I am aware, art historical evidence of the Aśoka legend,[66] especially in the narrative art of Gandhāra, may fit in this time scenario.

This all accepted may shed some new light on the *Aśokāvadāna*. It is, primarily, not a text describing a historical personality Aśoka. From inscriptional, numismatic and archaeological sources we know that the Kuṣana rulers supported Buddhism, but also that their religious polity was a rather pluralistic one.[67] There may have been a certain tendency to use Buddhism which, as a monastic institution, had the best infrastructural system in comparison with other religions for other

62 According to the Tibetan tradition this was the Third Council, e.g., in Tārānātha's *Chos-'byuṅ* (Chattopadhyaya. Chimpa 1970: 92ff).

63 A reflex of this imitation of Aśoka may also be the epithet of Kaniṣka, Chin. Zhantan < *Caṇḍa(na) (?), in the episode of the conquest of Pāṭaliputra, the old capital of Aśoka (sic!), which could then refer to Aśoka's epithet *Caṇḍa-*: It is only after the conquest of this city and the subsequent delivery of Aśvaghoṣa and the alms bowl relic that Kaniṣka is converted and becomes a just king: see the English translation resp. paraphrases by Zürcher 1968: 384 and 386. A detailed study of the legend of Kaniṣka in the light of and in comparison with the legend of Aśoka has still to be done.

64 See Janos Harmatta's "Religions in the Kushan Empire" in Harmatta. Puri. Etemadi 1994: 324.

65 I think that this falls in the reign of the Kuṣāna kings Kaniṣka or Huviṣka and this conclusion seems to be affirmed by the earliest translation of the Aśoka legend into Chinese and the complete lack of depiction of the legend in Buddhist art (e.g., in Gandhāra). This is not directly connected with the question of the time of origin and school affiliation of the *Divyāvadāna*, which now seems to be brought together rather with the school of the Mūlasarvāstivādin than with that of the Sarvāstivādin (Heinz Bechert 1985: 49, and Jens-Uwe Hartmann, "Zur Frage der Schulzugehörigkeit des Avadānaśataka," in Bechert 1985: 219 and 224). The *Aśokāvadāna* certainly was an independent text before it was incorporated into the *Divyāvadāna*.

66 There is, however, earlier evidence of Aśoka in Buddhist art: one relief on the gate of Sāñcī (Marshall. Foucher I, 212, and II, plate XL).

67 See the overview in Harmatta 1994: 313ff. Strangely enough in the already mentioned inscription from Rabatak, Afghanistan, no reference to Buddhism is found although Kaniṣka sees his reign supported by different gods (Nana, Umma, Ahura Mazda).

reasons than purely religious ones.[68] The *Aśokāvadāna* is, in my opinion, a Buddhist reaction to such a situation insofar as it attributes to the ruler a role which is in accordance with the interest of the *saṅgha*: He should further and support *dharma* in the form of the Buddhist community and receives advice and instruction from the side of the *saṅgha*; the *saṅgha* for its side did, however, not go so far as to dominate the ruler in matters outside of the range of the Buddhist *dharma*—a kind of "Middle Way" in the relationship between religion and state.

5. Integration of the ruler into the dominance of the *saṅgha*: the Pāli-Chronicles

In the *Aśokāvadāna* the contact of Aśoka with the *saṅgha* was mainly restricted to individual monks. This kind of non-institutional relationship changes when we have a look at the Aśoka tradition of the Southern Theravāda. There it is not a single and individual monk to whom Aśoka pays respect, whose pupil he becomes and through whose teaching he becomes an ideal Buddhist ruler. In the Theravāda chronicles *Dīpavaṃsa* and *Mahāvaṃsa* it is rather the *saṅgha* in its institutional integrity that dominates the action and the thought of the ruler.

As I have already mentioned one of the most important differences between the *Aśokāvadāna* and the Ceylonese sources is that in the latter sources the third Buddhist council is the central episode while the *Aśokāvadāna* does not even mention it. The historical basis for this council is certainly the so-called schism-edict of Aśoka. It may be assumed that the *Aśokāvadāna* did not integrate this episode because of its tendency toward a well-balanced relationship between *saṅgha* and ruler in which there was an active role for Aśoka. This would have meant an involvement of the king in the matters of the *saṅgha* which, in real terms, would have been contrary to what the *saṅgha* in the Kuṣāna empire would have preferred.

The *Aśokāvadāna* gives Aśoka a certain freedom to act as the eminent monks, the *sthaviras*/P. *theras*,[69] not only advise him but also because he asks for instructions from different monks on different occasions. In the Theravāda tradition, it is clear that the ruler has come into a relation with the *saṅgha* which could almost be called a complete dependence.

This goes well with the time of origin of the sources, the *vaṃsas*, during which the monks of the Mahāvihāra monastery, which had become most influential on the island, tried to have the kings support their orthodox denomination by presenting them with the model of the great Maurya ruler through an idealized image of the early Ceylonese king Devānāṃ Piyatissa.[70] According to the *vaṃsas*

68 In this context I would like to point out a project of the University of California, Berkeley, which tries to collect data for this theory: see the abstract by Mehendale. Williams 2000.

69 With the exception of the name of Aśoka, I subsequently will use mainly Pāli terms and names.

70 Cp. Geiger 1986: 203.

some Siṃhalese kings recognized the authority of the *saṅgha* even in state affairs to an extent which is not found in other sources.[71]

I would like to take two examples that show this treatment of Aśoka in the *vaṃsa*s: the first contact of the king with the *saṅgha* and the report about the schism of the order under the reign of Aśoka.

The episode of the first encounter of Aśoka with Buddhism[72] is found in *Dīpavaṃsa* 6.23ff., *Mahāvaṃsa* 5.34ff., and *Bāhiranidāna* 46ff.: After the king has asked all heretics—in the view of Buddhists, of course—to expound their teachings in order to grant them a seat in his royal hall according to the ranking of their religion, he is struck by the charismatic appearance of the young Buddhist monk Nigrodha and he invites him to sit down at a privileged place. Nigrodha seizes Aśoka's hand and sits down on the throne to expound the *dharma*.[73] This episode clearly reflects the standpoint of the Theravāda *saṅgha* about the relation between *saṅgha* and king: The king has to be subdued to the *saṅgha*—here represented in the form of a young monk and not a patriarch as in the *Aśokāvadāna*—and Aśoka accepts this position.[74] It is remarkable that Nigrodha does not have the same

71 That this has not been the general point of view of Theravāda-dominated cultures is shown by the Aśoka legend in the cosmological text *Lokapaññatti*, compiled in Burma around the 11th or 12th cent. by a monk Saddhammaghosa—for the date and the history of this text see von Hinüber 1996: 182f. (§394–395)—which shows mainly parallels with the North Indian version of the legend (see Strong 1992: 186–208). It almost seems that the later South Asian *saṅgha* returned to a kind of Middle Way after the extreme position in the *vaṃsas*—a Middle Way which was much more able to cope with the real structures of power in Southeast Asia; for such conceptions and historical examples of kings in Buddhist Southeast Asia, see Swearer 1995: 63ff., and for the "reorganizer" of Ceylonese Buddhist culture, king Kīrti Śrī, see Holt 1996: 18ff.; for the Burmese king Mindon and his direct reference to Aśoka, see Höfer. Prunner. Kaneko. Bezacier. Sarkisyanz 1975: 465. Mindon obviously used both the edicts and the chronicles and other legends. His autocratic interpretation of Aśoka is also reflected by the reaction of the *saṅgha* which reconstructed its origin back to the mission of the two monks Soṇa and Uttara to the region Suvaṇṇabhāmi (Skt. Suvarṇabhūmi) under Aśoka, an account mentioned in *Dīpavaṃsa* 8.12 and *Mahāvaṃsa* 12.44–54. This region is identified with Burma or with Thailand, depending on the standpoint: see (1975), 451, 456 (Burma), 505 (Thailand).

72 For this episode see Ruegg 1995: 64f., who only discusses the relation between the monk and the king in the sense of kingly preceptor and royal donator (*dānapati*) without reflecting the difference between the traditions of the *Aśokāvadāna* and the *vaṃsas*.

73 *Dīpavaṃsa* 6.47f. lays a special emphasis on this: "Thinking thus (the king) further said: 'A well-prepared seat is spread; may you sit down on the seat reserved for an ordinated (monk). I will bestow upon you what you wish.' After he had heard the words of the king he seized the right (hand of the king?), went up to the seat and sat down on the most excellent throne like Sakka, the king of the gods, (sits down) on (his seat) Paṇḍukambala." (47. *vīmaṃsamāno punad evaṃ abravī: supaññattaṃ āsanaṃ. . . patthataṃ, nisīdayī pabbajitatthaṃ āsane, mayā anuññātaṃ tassābhipatthitaṃ*. 48 *ādāya rañño vacanaṃ padakkhiṇaṃ. . . gahetvā abhirūhi āsane, nisīdi pallaṅkavare asantāso Sakko va devarājā Paṇḍukambale.*).

74 Cp. *Bāhiranidāna* 47 (Jayawickrama 1986: 169, l.17ff.): "When the king saw him (Nigrodha) approaching the throne he thought: 'Today even this novice will be lord of the house (of the king).'" (*Rājā taṃ pallaṅkasamīpaṃ upagacchantaṃ eva disvā cintesi: ajj' eva dāni ayaṃ sāmaṇero imassa gehassa sāmiko bhavissatīti.*). Compare with *Mahāvaṃsa* 5.64ff., where Nigrodha suspends himself on the hand of the king (*ālambitvā karaṃ rañño so pallaṅkaṃ samāruhi. . .*) when he mounts the throne.

function as the patriarchs of the *Aśokāvadāna*, Upagupta and Piṇḍola Bharadvāja: He is—and it is expressed quite clearly[75]—only the motivator for the king to come into contact with the whole *saṅgha* and to support it; the instruction of Aśoka which the king orders after his meeting with Nigrodha is not preformed by an individual monk but through the whole *saṅgha* (*Dīpavaṃsa* 6.73ff., *Mahāvaṃsa* 5.73ff., *Bāhiranidāna* 49ff.).

The schism episode clearly shows then how much Aśoka has to depend on the instructions of the *saṅgha*. It is the elder (*thera*) Tissa Moggaliputta—a name which does not occur at all in the *Aśokāvadāna*—who has to tell the ignorant Aśoka which are the heterodox elements in the *saṅgha* (which the king finally has to fight and to oust: *Dīpavaṃsa* 7.52ff.). In *Mahāvaṃsa* 5.247ff. and *Bāhiranidāna* 58f. this scene is presented in a different way, now in favor of the position of the monk: Moggaliputta refuses two orders of Aśoka to come to him and help him with his advice and it is not until the king sends a boat up the river Gaṅgā and prevails upon him to prevent the decline of the Buddhist teaching that Moggaliputta is ready to visit the king. Aśoka even humiliates himself to the degree of welcoming the monk standing in the water, supporting him with his hand and washing and anointing his feet.[76] The king is only able to decide which faction's teaching is orthodox and which is heterodox with the help of Moggaliputta. Aśoka and the monk sit behind a curtain while the different parties of the *saṅgha* present their arguments so that the king does not lose face in revealing that he needs the support of a monk and is thus not capable of deciding these issues on his own. The episode is a reflection of a monastic power play to instrumentalize the king in a moment of danger for the integrity of the *saṅgha*.

The *Dīpavaṃsa* does not even conceal the pragmatic reasons for the attempts at influencing the ruler in favor of the orthodox part of the *saṅgha*: When Aśoka after having given donations to the *saṅgha* boasts of his Buddhist faith, he is immediately rebuked by Moggaliputta who asks him to have his son Mahinda—the future missionary of Ceylon—and his daughter Saṅghamittā ordained (*Dīpavaṃsa* 7.16f.); as a motive for this the text frankly states: ". . . to secure a comfortable existence for the *saṅgha*, for the spread of the *dharma* and because [Moggaliputta] as a wise man knew about the future of the *saṅgha*."[77]

75 *Mahāvaṃsa* 5.69ff., where Nigrodha passes the presents received from Aśoka to his teacher (*upajjhāya*) and to the *saṅgha*. *Bāhiranidāna* 48 expresses the intention of Nigrodha to pass the king's attention to the *saṅgha* even more clearly because here it is Aśoka who asks who is the teacher of the *saṅgha* and Nigrodha then points out the dominating position of the *saṅgha* as an institution: "'Who is this so-called *saṅgha* of the monks, my dear?' (It is the one) on which depend the ordination and consecration of my teachers and masters and even my own.'" (*Ko ayaṃ tāta bhikkhusaṅgho nāmāti. Yam nissāya mahārāja amhākaṃ ācariy'upajjhāyānañ ca mamañ ca pabbajjā ca upasampadā cāti.*).

76 The *Mahāvaṃsa* remarks that it is only by compassion that Moggaliputta really took the hand offered by the king (5.255f.). *Bāhiranidāna* is even more expressive: The king gives up his royal privileges and becomes the student of the representative of the orthodox *saṅgha* accepting even his orders (59).

77 *Dīpavaṃsa* 7.15: . . . *saṃghassa tesu vihāraṃ anuggahatthāya sāsanaṃ, anāgate ca addhāne pavattiṃ sutvā vicakkhaṇo;* . . . . This passage about the benefit of the *saṅgha* is lacking in the *Mahāvaṃsa* (5.194ff.).

Another striking difference of the *vaṃsas*' Aśoka is that his "career" is not divided into a violent and evil first period and a following period in accordance with the *dharma*. This seems to be a tendency to shift the first half of Aśoka's rule as a despot to the background. The *Dīpavaṃsa* (6.21f.) and the *Mahāvaṃsa* (5.18ff.) merely mention that Aśoka killed his brothers 214 years after the *nirvāṇa* of the Buddha; according to *Dīpavaṃsa* 7.31, this had happened one year after his meeting with Nigrodha, that is, after his conversion to Buddhism. Four years later, he was consecrated king[78] or rather consecrated himself (*Mahāvaṃsa* 5.22f.) and from there on he ruled successfully by the support of all heavenly beings (*devas* and *nāgas*: *Dīpavaṃsa* 6.1–15; *Mahāvaṃsa* 5.24) as the world conqueror Asokadhamma[79] over Jambud(v)īpa.[80] What is emphasized here is not so much the positive action of the ruler for the benefit of his dynasty and his subjects[81] but his relation with the *saṅgha* which could almost be called submissive.[82]

As I have already mentioned, it is the Ceylonese king Devānāṃ Piyatissa—who, according to the tradition, is like a successor of Aśoka—who possessed the requisites of a protector and preserver of the *dharma*, the relics of the Buddha and a sapling of the *bodhi*-tree, and transferred them to the island in order to guarantee the successful transmission of the *dharma*. In this context it is important that the primordiality of the *saṅgha* in the texts is clearly expressed by the order of events: First the teaching and monastic ordination line is brought to Ceylon through Aśoka's son Mahinda (*Mahāvaṃsa* 13ff.; *Dīpavaṃsa* 12ff.; *Bāhiranidāna* 73ff.) and then the transmission is terminated by the semi-political act of the transfer of the relics to king Devānāṃ Piyatissa (*Mahāvaṃsa* 17ff.; *Dīpavaṃsa* 15f.; *Bāhiranidāna* 88ff.).

78 This means that his earlier ruling period of four years must be understood as regent.

79 In my opinion the name in Pāli reflects the different standpoints of both legend traditions: While Aśoka is always called by this name in the *Aśokāvadāna* and is varied by the attributes *caṇḍa*- or *dharma*-, the king in the Pāli chronicles is given a name which looks like a variation of the epithet of the edicts *devānaṃ piyadāsin*: *piyadassana*, "the one with a beautiful appearance" (this contradicts the statement of the *Aśokāvadāna* according to which Aśoka was so ugly that even the ladies in his serail detested him). In strict terms Asokadhamma can only be taken as a *bahuvrīhi*: "whose *dharma* is without infliction."

80 *Dīpavaṃsa* 6.2: *āgata rājaiddhiyo abhisitte Piyadassane, pharati puññatejañ ca uddhaṃ adho ca yojanaṃ, Jambudīpe mahārajje balacakke pavattati*. ("The royal power went over to Piyadassana after he had been consecrated; he distributed the splendor of his merits one *yojana* above and beneath (earth and he) toured (his) great kingdom of Jambudīpa on his wheel of strength.").

81 In this context the shift of the motive of construction of the 84,000 *dharmarājika-stūpas* becomes intelligible: In the *vaṃsa*s the king constructs 84,000 monasteries in the 84,000 cities of Jambudīpa for the *saṅgha* (*Dīpavaṃsa* 6.98)—a definite shift from the Buddha (*Aśokāvadāna*: relics) in favor of the *saṅgha*.

82 Clearly expressed in *Dīpavaṃsa* 7.47 (resp. in *Dīpavaṃsa* 7.12): Three quarters of the daily donations of Aśoka are distributed to the order in its threefold structure (*cetiya*, *stūpa*-like monuments for the Buddha, sermons for the *dhamma* and the *saṅgha*), only one quarter is reserved for charity purposes (treatment of the diseased). This indicates that the chronicles were not so much concerned about depicting an "Aśokan paradigm of righteous rule"—as expressed by Trainor 1997: 76—rather the contrary: The balance which is found in the so-called tolerance edicts of the emperor is to be changed in favor of the *saṅgha*.

6. Aśoka in Central Asia

I want to touch on the Central Asian reception of Aśoka which should get a separate and detailed description only briefly and with two examples. The popularity of the Mauryan emperor is already shown by the existence of translations of the Aśoka legend or part of it in various Central Asian languages.[83]

My first concrete example is the description of a five-years-assembly, the *pañcavārṣika* ceremonies of the *Aśokāvadāna*, in a country called Jiecha 竭叉[84] by the Chinese pilgrim Faxian in which the ruler of the kingdom acts exactly as described in the great donation parties in the Aśoka-legend. This seems to indicate that in the early fifth century the model of Aśoka had been ideologically and ritually adopted by Central Asian rulers.[85]

The second example is found in the foundation legend of the kingdom of Khotan, preserved in a Tibetan version. Here Aśoka is indirectly involved in the foundation of the kingdom of Khotan. According to the Tibetan chronicle on Khotan, the founder of the royal dynasty of Khotan was the son of Aśoka, Tib. Sa-nu, meaning "Earth-Breast." He was given a miraculous birth in which his father and mother were traveling near Khotan and, because the child was predicted a bright future as a ruler, his father Aśoka, out of fear of his son, abandoned him in the wilderness. I would argue that we see in this legend a clear representation of Aśoka the Fierce, Caṇḍāśoka, with the potential of a pious *dharma*-ruler transferred to his abandoned son, the first Khotanese ruler Sa-nu, whose fate shows similarities with another son of Aśoka, Kuṇāla.

7. Aśoka in China: Bodhisattvahood and Legitimation of Power

We have already seen that the first translations of texts concerning Aśoka go back to the second century of the Christian era. It is remarkable that episodes from the Aśoka legend are also inserted into the Chinese *Saṃyuktāgama/Za-ahan-jing* 雜阿含經 (T.99.161b.10ff.)[86] from the end of the fourth century. This could be explained in two ways: If the episode was already there in the Indian original, this would go together very well with the scenario of the *Aśokāvadāna* that I have described above. If the episode was not extant in the Indian original, it has to be assumed that it was an interpolation by a Chinese redactor of the *Saṃyuktāgama*. If we accept the last possibility the intention of the monastic redactor would probably have been to show the Chinese authorities the ideal of a Buddhist ruler and to highlight this very intention through the integration of Aśoka-episodes into a canonical and therefore highly authoritative text.

83 See, for example, the Kuṇāla story and other references in Khotan-Saka: Bailey 1966.

84 On the location of Jiecha in the Karakorum rather than the northern part of the Pamir as usually stated, see Deeg 2001b.

85 See Deeg 1995; Deeg 2005: 99ff.

86 See Przyluski 1923: 55f.

The reception of Aśoka and his legend in China is, however, not restricted to so-called canonical Buddhist sources. There are Chinese sources showing that the ruling class and not only the *saṅgha* utilized the Mauryan king. The *saṅgha* has a rather secondary role—it has, at best, the task of confirming the rulers' interpretation of Aśoka.

Early Chinese sources consist of reports of Aśoka-*stūpa*s and inscriptions which had been found in China[87]; historically speaking these reports, of course, presuppose the knowledge of the Aśoka legend. In this period of Chinese Buddhism—let us say from the 3rd to the 6th century—this proto-archaeology certainly was a means of integrating China into the Buddhist *oikumene* by referring to the 84,000 *śarīrastūpa*s which Aśoka had distributed all over Jambudvīpa.[88] As to the inscriptions, it is an unsolvable riddle which language these were written in, but at least these reports show that the Chinese at a very early date knew about inscriptions of the Mauryan ruler—although the legend texts do not mention them.[89] From the middle of the fourth century over a period of around two centuries we find nineteen such proto-archaeological "sites" in Buddhist sources.[90] In all cases we can identify the political intention of the reports: They were supposed to provide the local non-Han rulers with the possibility of identifying themselves with Aśoka and thereby legitimizing their own rule by means of reference to the model of Aśoka's universal rulership as a *cakravartin*.

Compared with India this is a clear shift from the proper interest of the *saṅgha* to a subsidiary aim: The central consideration was not so much the positive attitude and action of the ruler towards the monastic community as in the *Aśokāvadāna* and in the Pāli chronicles, but the claim for universal rulership through reference to the authority of the Mauryan king which was transferred to Chinese soil by proto-archaeological finds.

The best known and most striking example of a direct imitation of Aśoka is, however, not found in the barbarian North of the Nanbei-chao period but in the Southern empire of the Liang dynasty. It was Liang Wudi 梁武帝 (502–549)[91] who is accused by the conservative Chinese historiographers of ruining the empire as a consequence of his Buddhist zeal. Many elements in the acts of emperor Wu clearly show the influence of the Buddhist model-ruler Aśoka although the name is never directly used in the sources, neither in the sources by Wu himself nor in the other sources. It is not, however, by chance that the second translation of the Aśoka-legend, the *Ayu-wang-jing*, was made under the rule of emperor Wu who is said to have personally written parts of the translated text.[92]

87 See Zürcher 1972: 277–280; Shinohara 1992, and Shinohara 1999.

88 Five of these were believed to be at mount Qishan 岐山: see Chen 2002a: 38f.

89 Theoretically it is conceivable that the Chinese with their inherited emphasis on scripts and writing did just assume that there had to be inscriptions on monuments created by such a great king. Practically speaking the Chinese knew from Indian monks since at least the fourth century that such inscriptions especially on the pillars really existed.

90 Zürcher 1972: 277.

91 See Chen 2006a.

92 See Nishiwaki 1992: 96ff.

Wu also organized huge Buddhist donation ceremonies which refer to the Aśoka of the legend (*Aśokāvadāna*): Like his great ideal Wu donated himself several times to the *saṅgha* during the so-called "quinquennial meetings," *wunian-hui* 五年會, or "meetings without restrictions," *wuzhe-hui* 無遮會, and asked his ministers and officials to redeem him with huge amounts of money.[93] The example of emperor Wu does, however, also show that there was no acceptance of a balanced relation between the state authorities and the *saṅgha* from the ruling class: Wu saw himself not so much as a *cakravartin* but more as a Bodhisattva-king, a spiritually privileged position which allowed him to interfere with the matters of the *saṅgha*.[94]

It should be mentioned that the German sinologist Annette Kieser[95] in her book on the tombs of the Chinese gentry in Southern China between the 3rd and the 6th century has stressed the theory[96] that the pillars which Wu has erected in the precincts of the Liang family graveyard were meant to be copies of the Aśoka pillars first mentioned by Faxian in his report on Buddhist India. As attractive as this thesis may be in the light of the strong Buddhist inclinations of emperor Wu, the evidences—shape,[97] context[98] and function[99] of the pillars—are too weak to convince me of Kieser's argument of a direct involvement of emperor Wu and even more of a direct influence by Faxian's report. I do not, however, exclude the possibility that, giving due credit to the uniqueness of these pillars in Chinese sepulchral culture[100] and their sudden appearance in the context of the tombs of the imperial Xiao 蕭 family of emperor Wu, records on India which included reports on the Aśokan pillars (and others identified as such) in general shaped the idea that pillars with items (animals, epigraphic stone plates with the names and functions of the buried) on top of the capitals are connected with royalty in general.

Wu clearly thought of himself as a Bodhisattva ruler and thus seems to go beyond the framework of an Aśoka-like *cakravartin*. There are indications that in China the image of Aśoka changed from one of a pious Buddhist king to a more religious and soteriologically important figure. This may have happened under the influence of emperor Wu's Bodhisattva-ruler conception or earlier.

93 See Deeg 1997. On the Bodhisattva-aspect of emperor Wu's action, see Jansen 2001; Janousch 1999. It is striking that Janousch completely overlooked or left out the influence of the Aśoka tradition on Wudi. See further Chen Jinhua 2006b.

94 See Janousch 1999: 136ff.

95 Kieser 2002: 147f.

96 According to Kieser 2002: 147, first brought forward by the Chinese scholar Teng Gu in 1935.

97 The pillars are very short with fluted bodies and stand on stone bases with animal motives (tiger, dragon): see Kieser 2002: 143, and the photos and drawings on pp. 221, Abb.4.9, 223, Abb.4.14, 227, 4.25, 229, 4.29 and 4.32, 230, 4.34, 231, 4.38.

98 There is no direct evidence of Buddhist influence on the tombs (except some lotus motifs).

99 Kieser is not able—and she seems to be aware of this—to explain how the clear eulogical function of the pillars which is reflected in Faxian's report came to be transferred to the function of flanking the spirit paths (*shendao* 神道).

100 See Kieser 2002: 147: "Die Säulen hingegen wirken völlig unchinesisch."

In T.279, the *Dafangdeng-fo-huayan-jing* 大方廣佛華嚴經, the translation of the *Avataṃsaka-sūtra* by the Khotanese Śikṣānanda/Shichanantuo 實叉難陀 (652–710), Aśoka is presented as the paradigm of a Bodhisattva who donated everything, even parts of his body:

> Sons of the Buddha, Bodhisattvas, *mahāsattvas* donate their hands and feet to the living beings like the Bodhisattva Nityodyukta ('Constant Energy,' Chang-jingjin), the Bodhisattva king Aśoka (Wuyou-wang) and all the other incalculable Bodhisattvas, in (all) forms of existence and in different lives donated their hands and feet, made their belief their faith and caused beneficial conduct, were reborn in *saṃsāra*, diligently practiced the true *dharma*, made vows to achieve jewel-hands, donated their hands; their actions are not in vain; the way of the Bodhisattvas always keeps their hands open; they bestow great kindness, walk around calmly, are brave and no cowards; with the force of their pure faith they strive energetically, eliminate the evil forms of existence and attain enlightenment (*bodhi*, *puti*).[101]

It is clear that the ideology of Mahāyāna Buddhism had opened the traditional religious opposition of the monastic *saṅgha* and the laity: Donation (*dāna*, *shi* 施) was a means by which a layperson could excel over an ordained monk who had not entered the Bodhisattva-path in terms of Buddhist virtues, as it is the first stage (*bhūmi*, *jie* 界 or *di* 地) of the *pāramitās*, *boluomiduo* 波羅蜜多, of a Bodhisattva. Donation pushed to the utmost in the form of giving away one's self—or, in an extreme form, of sacrificing parts of the body—could bring Aśoka into a new pattern of interpretation: His donations to the *saṅgha*, especially giving his own person to the *saṅgha* to be redeemed by his ministers and relatives, was the ideal representation of the first *bodhisattva-bhūmi*, the *dāna-pāramitā*.

A proof for a popular belief in Aśoka as a soteriological Buddhist figure under the rule of Liang Wudi has been unearthed in the year 1995 in Chengdu 成都 (Xi'an-lu 西安路), Province Sichuan 四川: It shows a standing statue of Aśoka, made of sandstone and partly gilted, astonishingly with all features of a full-fledged Buddha wearing, however, a Kuṣāna-style moustache. The identification of the statue as Aśoka, despite its Buddha-like appearance, is clearly proved by the inscription on the reverse:

> On the thirteenth day of the ninth month of the fifth year of the era Taiqing[102] the disciple of the Buddha, the monk Du, for the sake of his deceased child Li made a donation to the Buddha and made a statue of (A)yu-wang (Aśoka-rājā) and donated (it). He made a vow (on behalf

101 T.279.146a.22ff. 佛子。菩薩摩訶薩。以其手足。施諸眾生。如常精進菩薩。無憂王菩薩。及餘無量。諸菩薩等。於諸趣中。種種生處。布施手足。以信為手。起饒益行。往返周旋。勤修正法。願得寶手。以手為施。所行不空。具菩薩道。常舒其手。擬將廣惠。安步遊行。勇猛無怯。以淨信力。具精進行。除滅惡道。成就菩提。

102 This date is strange as the era Taiqing lasted from 547–549. It may well be, however, that the donator of the stele continued the era although it had already ended three years before.

> of) his still living and deceased relatives and those who will be born so that they (will be able) to directly hear the *dharma* from the Buddha, attain early enlightenment and not experience (re)birth and death, that . . . he proclaimed this same vow. . .[103]

Statues of Aśoka, some of them with miraculous powers which could justify the Buddha-like appearance of the Chengdu-statue at least in the range of folk belief, seem to have been a very early phenomenon and have been more popular than it is known from the extant Chinese Buddhist sources.

The encyclopedic *Taiping-guangji* 太平廣記 quotes a report from a lost *Zhugong-yishi* 渚宮遺事, "Miraculous Events of the Lake Palace,"[104] of such a statue (fasc. 99):

> In the Changsha-si there was a statue of king Aśoka, and according to the tradition this was made by the daughter of king Aśoka. In the era Taiyuan (of the Eastern Jin: 376–396), when the night hovered towards the river ford, a fisherman saw a strange light as if it was high noon and all people of the monastery—a thousand of them—(went) to welcome it (but) it stood out very high and did not move. The *dharma*-master (Tan)yi of the Changsha-si in order to practice austerity took ten (other) monks, went there and prayed there with all his heart; he went there with a sedan-chair. Until they were finished (with their practice) the statue moved around every night. When (once) an ignorant person (tried) to cut it with a halberd, it gave a bronze sound and (the ignorant person) fell down. Whenever there are great events or disasters or upheavals in the Southern Dynasty, (the statue) certainly will sweat some days before. From what has been taught about this statue (it is clear) that it is a highly miraculous matter.[105]

103 Catalogue of the exhibition Chūgoku-bunmei-ten/Chinese Civilization (Sekai-shidaibunmei) 中国文明展 (世界四大文明) (8.2000–12.2001) 2000: 158, no.100:

太清五年
九月卅日
佛弟子杜僧逸為亡兒李
仏施敬造育王像供養
願存亡眷屬在所生(滅)
值仏聞法早悟无生亡
□因緣及六道含令普
□同斯誓謹
□□

104 Zhugong 遺事 originally refers to the palace of the Chu-kings (楚) in the Chunqiu-period (春秋), but is also used generally for a palace standing on the shore of a lake or a river.

105 長沙寺有阿育王像，相傳是阿育王女所造。太元中，夜浮至江津。漁人見異光如晝，而諸寺以千人迎之，嶷然不動。長沙寺翼法師者，操行精苦，乃率十僧，至誠祈啟，即時就輦。至齊末，像常夜行。不知者以槊刺之，作銅聲而倒。每南朝大事及災役，必先流汗數日。自像教以來，最為靈應也。

The biography of Tanyi in the *Gaoseng-zhuan* 高僧傳, the "Biographies of Eminent Monks," gives more details about the statue which is said to have been inscribed with Indian letters.[106]

The use of Aśoka in legitimation processes in the first centuries of Chinese Buddhism was mainly restricted to North Chinese rulers of barbarian origin—Liang Wudi was rather an exception. These rulers tried to find a tool for legitimation of their rule which could not so easily be done in the framework of the traditional Chinese imperial ideology of the "mandate of Heaven," *tianming* 天命. But it has to be emphasized that the paradigm of Aśoka claiming imperial legitimation was also used in the unified empire of the Sui and the Tang. An obvious symbolic representation of this is the existence of so-called *daochang* 道場 in the inner palace of a lot of these rulers. *Daochang* is the Chinese translation word for *bodhimaṇḍa(na)*, the "place of enlightenment," and although it is normally used in the sense of "spot of (Buddhist) practice" for monasteries and other institutional places, when brought into connection with a Chinese ruler, it certainly bears some connotation with Aśoka's fondness for the *bodhi*-tree.

The continued appeal of the Bodhisattva-ruler Aśoka as a model for rulership is clearly found in the figure of the first emperor of the short-lived Sui 隋 dynasty (581–617), Wendi 文帝 (r. 581–604), who had been born in a Buddhist monastery and been raised by a Buddhist nun. Wendi showed a real "obsession with the political and religious ideal embodied by Aśoka"[107]: In the sources he is called the Great Donor (*mahādānapati*)—a clear reminiscence to the *pañcavārṣika*-ceremonies of the Mauryan emperor—and a *cakravartin*, but at the same time he is called "Bodhisattva Son of Heaven" (*pusa-tianzi* 菩薩天子), combining a Buddhist

106 T.2059.355c.28ff. 翼常歎。寺立僧足。而形像尚少。阿育王所造容儀神瑞皆多布在諸方。何其無感不能招致。乃專精懇惻請求誠應。以晉太元十九年甲午之歲二月八日。忽有一像現于城北。光相衝天。時白馬寺僧眾先往迎接不能令動。翼乃往祇禮。謂眾人曰。當是阿育王像降我長沙寺焉。即令弟子三人捧接。飄然而起迎還本寺。道俗奔赴車馬轟填。後罽賓禪師僧伽難陀。從蜀下入寺禮拜。見像光上有梵字。便曰。是阿育王像。何時來此。時人聞者方知翼之不謬。年八十二而終。終日像圓光奄然靈化。莫知所之。道俗咸謂翼之通感焉。 ("(Tan)yi always sighed that there were enough residents in the monastery but still only a few images. The ominous signs of appearances which king Aśoka had made were all spread in (different) regions. In the nineteenth year of (the era) Taiyuan of the Jin(-dynasty), the 31st year (of the sexagenary calendar), in the second month, on the eighth day a statue suddenly appeared north of the city (whose) auspicious light (beamed) towards the sky. At that time the *saṅgha* of the Baimasi first went to welcome (the statue but) could not move it. (Tan)yi went there to venerate (it) and said to the people: 'Now this statue of king Aśoka has come down to our Changsha-si.' And he had three of his disciples go and pick up the statue. They raised it (as easily) as if it was floating (in the air) and brought it back to their monastery. Monks and laypeople rushed there, wagons and horses were completely crowded. Then the meditation master Saṅghānanda from Kaśmīr (Jibin) came from Sichuan (Chu) to the monastery to pay his reverence and he saw that on the light of the statue there were Indian characters. Thereupon he said: 'This is a statue of king Aśoka. When did it come here?' At that time people realized that (Tan)yi had not (been) wrong about (this statue). When he died at the age of eighty-two, at the day of his death the halo of the statue was suddenly transformed in a miraculous way and nobody knew the reason. Everybody, the monks and the laypeople, called this the wonderful power of (Tan)yi.")

107 Chen 2002b: 76.

soteriological ideal and the traditional Chinese ideal of rulership.[108] In the year 601, after he had conquered the southern empire of the short Chen 陳 dynasty, Wendi initiated three great campaigns to distribute Buddhist relics all over the newly unified empire; in the document related to these campaigns—the *Sheli-ganying-ji* 舍利感應記, "Report on the Miraculous Signs of the Relics"—we find a legendary report about how Wendi, before his accession to the throne, had received these relics from a mysterious Indian monk (*poluomen-shamen* 婆羅們沙門) and that the nun fostering him in his childhood had earlier told him that he would stop the decline of the *dharma*.[109] In another document—the *Qing-sheli-ganying-biao bing da* 慶舍利感應表並答, "Memorial Celebrating the Miraculous Signs of the Relics and (Imperial) Reply" by Sui-prince Ande 安德—it is clearly stated that these actions of the emperor were seen as a repetition of Aśoka's act of relic-distribution: "Since Indra had asked for the ashes (from the cremation of the Buddha) and since king Aśoka had constructed the *stūpas*, nobody has distributed the relics (any more) and promoted these excellent actions."[110]

Wendi's son Yangdi 陽帝 (604–617) continued this tradition of a Buddhist ruler, supporting the *saṅgha* and already receiving the Bodhisattva-vows and the title *zongchi-pusa* 總持菩薩, "Bodhisattva of absolute control," from the Tiantai-patriarch Zhiyi 智顗 in the year 591.[111]

Although the Tang dynasty did not openly support Buddhism in the way that the Sui rulers did, we have one fascinating example of reference to Aśoka in the symbolism of the only ruling empress which China had during her 3000 years of imperial history. The interim dynasty of the Zhou founded by empress Wu Zetian 武則天 (690–705)[112] shows elements of Aśoka-symbolism as had already been seen under Liang Wudi: She organized donation ceremonies for the *saṅgha*.[113] By extending her official title to *jinlun-shengshen-huangdi* 金輪聖神皇帝, "Wise and holy emperor of the golden wheel," in the year 693 she indicates what syncretistic model of rulership she had in mind: Besides the title of the Chinese emperor (*huangdi*) she is a wise and holy *cakravartin* of the golden wheel—*shengshen*[114] and *jinlun*. She labeled herself as a kind of super-*cakravartin*,[115] thus even

108 See Wright 1979: 76f.

109 Text preserved in the *Guang-hongming-ji* 廣弘明記 (T.2103); English translation in Chen 2002b: 89f.

110 T.2103.216c.12 自釋提請灰之後，育王建塔以來，未有分布舍利，紹隆勝業。My translation differs slightly from Chen 2002b: 101f..

111 See Wright 1979: 117.

112 On the policy of religion of Wu Zetian, see Deeg 2001c.

113 For this Buddhist festival, see Deeg 1995, and for Wu Zetian 82f.

114 Weinstein 1987: 164, note 27, speaks of "a curious mixture of Indian and Chinese terminology," but it should be taken into account that some Chinese translations of the title *cakravartin* already contain elements of the traditional Chinese titles: *zhuan-lun-shengwang* 轉輪聖王, "Wise King Wheel-Turner," *zhuanlun-shengdi-wang* 轉輪聖帝王, "Wise Imperial King Wheel-Turner": see (W)ogihara. Tsuji 1940. vol.1: 452b., s.v. *cakravartin*. In this case the title would have been chosen very skillfully because it would combine both fields of connotation, the traditional Chinese and the Buddhist.

115 The expression *jinlun* 金輪, lit. "Golden Wheel," is obviously an abbreviation of **Zhuan-jinlun-wang* corresponding to a Skt. *suvarṇacakravartin(-rājā)*. *Jinlun*—according to Hirakawa 1997: 167a. s.v.—can also correspond to *kāñcanamayī mahāpṛthivī*, the "great

excelling Aśoka. This was, however, only an intermediate step before, in the year 694, she identified herself officially with the Bodhisattva of the future, Maitreya (Cishi 慈氏).[116]

Another imitation—though at the same time an exaltation—of the model of Aśoka can be found integrated into the famous commentary to the *Dayun-jing* 大雲經, the "*Sūtra* of Great Clouds," of 690, produced by a group of ten monks in which it was stated that Wu had made a vow to distribute eight million and forty thousand relics all over the world.[117] Antonino Forte goes even so far as to propose that the great construction project of empress Wu, the "Axis of the Sky" (*tianshu* 天樞), should be seen as "reminiscent of the pillars of Aśoka."[118]

That the figure of Aśoka still played a role in Wu's self-projection as a Buddhist ruler is clear from the passage of the *Avataṃsakasūtra* quoted above. The translation of the text between 695 and 699 was sponsored by the empress who ordered the text to be brought from Khotan and who served personally as a copyist and wrote a preface.[119] The passage on the Bodhisattva-king Aśoka is, of course, not found in the older translation by Buddhabhadra from the beginning of the 5th century.

Empress Wu seems to have continued and brought to completion a tendency already obvious in the case of Liang Wudi: For empress Wu, Aśoka was the model ruler for the early period of her rule after which she finally became "emancipated" and a superhuman Bodhisattva-ruler.[120]

world circle consisting of gold." The little nuance in her choice of the name in relation to Aśoka is certainly not without intention. The empress claims a higher rank than the Indian emperor who, according to the Buddhist texts, had only been an "Iron Wheel-Turner." This brings in two other aspects: According to the Buddhist categories of the *cakravartin*—e.g., in Vasubandhu's *Abhidharmakośa*—of the four classes the ruler of the Golden Wheel is the top, while the ruler of the Iron Wheel holds the last rank. The ruler of the Golden Wheel rules over four continents through his "own vehicle" (*svayaṃyāna*), while the ruler of the Iron Wheel is only ruler over Jambudvīpa through the power of weapons (*śastrajita*): see Strong 1983: 51f.. Forte 1976: 136ff. discusses in detail the different types of *cakravartin* in connection with the *Mahāmeghasūtra/Dayun-jing* 大雲經 used by Wu Zetian in order to legitimize her usurpation of the throne, but does not refer to the legend of Aśoka. A consistent report of the historiographical sources in comparison with the Buddhist ones is not to expected; the *Jiutang-shu* 舊唐書 for instance says that it was prophesized in the amulet (*fuming* 符命) produced by the monks who fabricated the *Mahāmeghasūtra* that Wu would be "ruler over Jambudvīpa" (*Yanfuti-zhu* 閻浮提主): Weinstein 1987: 163, note 16 (translates: "World Ruler").

116 See Weinstein 1987: 43; Forte 1988: 264f.

117 See Chen 2002a.: 61f.; Chen 2002b.: 127f.

118 Forte 1988: 243.

119 See Weinstein 1987: 45.

120 See Chen 2002a.: 80 and esp. 124f., who sees Sui Wendi 隋文帝 as another model for empress Wu. There is probably a connection with the erection of a statue of king Aśoka in the *Famen-si* 法門寺 (659), the former Ayuwang-si 阿育王寺, bearing the face of Gaozong 高宗 (initiated by Wu?): Weinstein 1987: 37.

8. The Chinese pilgrims and their image of Aśoka

After the great persecutions of Buddhism under the Tang-emperor Wuzong 武宗 in the years 842–45, Buddhism lost its attraction for the political thinking and acting of the ruling class. It was not the universal image of a Buddhist ideal ruler of Aśoka's type but rather the ideal of a Bodhisattva-ruler which could be made compatible with the Chinese traditional conceptions of a sacral ruler in the person of the "Son of Heaven" (*tianzi* 天子). The Chinese *saṅgha* had almost completely lost its always more or less disputed influence on politics and the higher ranges of society. A foreign ruler like Aśoka was obviously found useless for legitimation processes. Rulers like empress Wu had certainly played their role in such a devaluation of Aśoka's (ruler-)paradigmatic status, but it should not be overlooked that there is another aspect of influence which one would probably not expect: the famous pilgrim monk Xuanzang—and this brings us back to where my story started, to India.

In the light of the legend it is quite expectable that the Chinese pilgrims' accounts are full of Aśoka-*stūpa*s in India,[121] but it is strange that they do not report on the rock edicts. This seems to indicate that in India these inscriptions, if their existence was known at all, were not connected with the great Mauryan emperor. This is definitely a point which has to be investigated in more detail.

The Chinese pilgrims do, however, report on the pillars. The first time that the pillars are mentioned in Chinese sources is in the report of the earliest pilgrim, Faxian 法顯, who was in India in the first decade of the 5th century. As is very often the case, when there are differences between Faxian's and Xuanzang's descriptions, scholars in general have treated Xuanzang as the more reliable source without taking into account the context and intention of his report.

The first pillar which Faxian clearly identifies as Aśọkan is the one at Saṃkāśya[122]:

> Behind the monastery [of the staircase of the Buddha's descent from the Trayastriṃśa heaven] (Aśoka) erected a pillar which has a height of about twenty (*zhou* = *hasta*: ca. 45 cm). (He) had (the image of) a lion made (to put it) on (top of the pillar). On all four corners of the pillar there were images of the Buddha which reflected inside and outside like lapis lazuli. Once heretic scholars disputed with the (Buddhist) *śramaṇas* who should be allowed to stay at this (place) and the arguments of the *śramaṇas* were crushed. Thereupon, they made the following vow: 'If this is the place where the *śramaṇas* should dwell, there will be a miracle.' (Immediately) after they had said this, the lion

121 The way in which Xuanzang describes the *stūpas* with their relics is very stereotypical: Most of them are 200 or 100 *chi* 尺 (ca. 23 cm) high, in the latter case sunk into the earth. Some of them have pillars standing beside them. Besides there is an increase of Aśoka-*stūpas* compared with those mentioned in Faxian's report.

122 861ff. 精舍後立石柱，高二十肘，上作師子，柱內四邊有佛像，內外映徹，淨若琉璃。有外道論師，與沙門諍此住處；時沙門理屈，於是共立誓言："此處，若是沙門住處者，今當有靈驗。"作是言已柱頭師子乃大鳴吼，見證。於是外道懼怖心伏而退。

on top of the pillar rose his roar and (thus) the miracle was evident. Hereafter the heretics became afraid, acknowledged (the result) and retired.

Xuanzang's description is more or less the same as Faxian's, but he does not tell the story of the defeated heretics.[123] It should be mentioned that strangely enough on top of the pillar found near Sāṃkāśya there was the image of an elephant.[124]

Faxian[125] and Xuanzang[126] describe two pillars standing at the gate of the famous Jetavana in Śrāvasti, which have not been found to the day. It is worth mentioning that Faxian does not mention who erected the pillars, which in my opinion—up to now such a pair of Aśoka-pillars has not been found—raises some suspicion about Xuanzang's ascription of the pillars to Aśoka.

Another pair of pillars—this time unanimously ascribed to Aśoka—are located in Pāṭaliputra. Both pillars are said to bear inscriptions documenting the cause of their erection: One is related to the three great donation parties and one mentions the construction and the date of Aśoka's prison before the time he was converted to Buddhism. Strangely enough Faxian[127] is much more detailed in his description of the pillars than Xuanzang; in his reports both pillars were inscribed

123 XJ 4 (Ji 1985: 418) 傍有石柱高七十餘尺，無憂王所建。色紺光潤，質堅密理。上作師子蹲踞向階，彫鏤奇形。周其方面，隨人罪福，影現柱中。 ("Beside (the monastery) there is a stone pillar, about seventy *chi* (ca. 23 cm) high, erected by king Aśoka. Its color is of a deep blue and it shines as if anointed (with an oily substance); (the stone) is very hard and has a delicate pattern. On top of it they put a lion, which sits on his hind legs and looks in the direction of the staircase. All around on the surface (of the pillar) special figures are chiseled whose shapes become visible on the pillar according to the sins and merits of the people (looking at them).")

124 Description in Cunningham 1871: 274f. (reconstructed sketch of the capital on Plate XLVI).

125 860b.15f. 精舍東向開門，門戶兩邊有二石柱；左柱上作輪形，右柱上作牛形。("The (main) gate is pointed towards the East and on the sides of both doors of the gate there are two stone pillars; on top of the left pillar they have put (a statue) in the shape of a wheel, on the right pillar one in the shape of a cow.")

126 XJ 6 (Ji 1985: 489) 東門左右各建石柱，高七十餘尺。左柱鏤輪相於其端，右柱刻牛形於其上，並無憂王之所建也。("To the right and to the left of the Eastern Gate (of Jetavana monastery) two pillars were erected, about seventy *chi* high. Into the left pillar the symbol of a wheel is chiseled and on top of the right pillar is put the image of a cow carved of stone; both (pillars) were erected by king Aśoka.")

127 862b. 塔南有一石柱，圍丈四，五，高三丈餘。上有銘題，云：阿育王以閻浮提布施四方僧，還以錢贖；如是三反。塔北三四百步，阿育王本於此作泥梨城。中央有石柱亦高三丈餘，上有師子。柱上有銘，記作泥梨城因緣及年數，日，月。 ("To the south (of the first relic *stūpa* erected by Aśoka) stands a stone pillar, 1,4 or 1,5 *zhang* (2.3 m) in perimeter and more than 3 *zhang* high. It bears an inscription saying: 'King Aśoka donated Jambudvīpa to the *saṅgha* of the four directions and ransomed it: This he did three times.' Three or four hundred paces to the north of the *stūpa* king Aśoka had once constructed the fortress Niraya. In this fortress there is a stone pillar which is also more than three *zhang* high and is topped by a lion. On the pillar is inscribed the reason why the fortress Niraya was (constructed) and it gives the date (of its construction).")

while according to Xuanzang only the first pillar had an inscription.[128] The first pillar may be the one which was discovered in pieces by L. A. Wadell in the year 1903 near Kumrahar. The fragments, however, do not show any traces of an inscription.[129]

There is another inscribed pillar mentioned by Faxian between Kuśinagara and Vaiśālī[130] which he, however, does not ascribe to Aśoka and which is not mentioned by Xuanzang.[131]

Xuanzang provides accounts of more Aśoka pillars than Faxian: He precisely describes those of Kanakamuni and Krakucchanda near Kapilavastu and the famous Lumbinī pillar at the birth place of the Buddha, which Faxian strangely does not mention at all. For Kuśinagara, Xuanzang records two pillars with inscriptions about the *nirvāṇa* of the Buddha[132] and his cremation.[133]

Another place where according to Xuanzang two pillars were found was Vārāṇasī.[134] He mentions another inscribed pillar that was shortly south before

128 XJ 8 (Ji 1985: 635) 佛跡精舍側不遠有大石柱，高三十餘尺。書記殘缺。其大略曰；"無憂王信根貞固，三以贍部洲施佛，法，僧，三以諸珍寶重自酬贖。" 其辭云云，大略斯在。("Not far away, beside the monastery of the traces of the Buddha's feet, there is a big stone pillar, about thirty *chi* high, with a fragmentary inscription saying roughly: 'King Aśoka, in firm faith, has donated Jambudvīpa to the Buddha, the *dharma* and the *saṅgha* three times and ransomed it with all his treasure.' This is roughly the wording which is extant.") XJ 8 (Ji 1985: 627ff.) 王故宮北有石柱，高數十尺，是無憂王作地獄處。. . . ("To the north of the old royal palace there is a stone pillar, several ten *chi* high. This is the place where king Aśoka had constructed his 'hell'. . . .")

129 See Mizutani 1971: 247a., note 1; Ji 1985: 635, note 1; Mookherji 1962: 86.

130 861c. 到諸梨車欲逐佛般泥洹處。而佛不聽，戀佛不肯去。佛化作大深塹，不得度。佛與鉢作信遣還。其處立石柱，上有銘題。("Proceeding twelve *yojana* to the Southeast (from Kuśinagara) one comes to the place where the Licchāvi wanted to follow the Buddha to the place of his *parinirvāṇa*. The Buddha, however, did not want to hear this, but because of their affection towards the Buddha they did not want to leave. The Buddha made a very deep pit which they could not cross. The Buddha gave them his alms bowl as a sign of memory and sent them back home. At this place one has erected an inscribed stone pillar.")

131 XJ 7 (Ji 1985: 598).

132 T.2087.903b.20ff. 前建石柱以記如來寂滅之事。雖有文記不書日月。("In front of (the *stūpa* Aśoka) had built a stone pillar on which were recorded the events of the extinction of the Tathāgata. Although there is a record, no date is written down.")

133 T.2087.904c.3f. 無憂王所建也。是八王分舍利處。前建石柱刻記其事。("(This *stūpa*) was built by king Aśoka and it is the place where the eight kings dispersed the relics. In front of it (Aśoka) had a stone pillar built with a record of the events.")

134 905b.12ff. 大城東北婆羅痆河西有窣堵波。無憂王之所建也。高百餘尺前建石柱。碧鮮若鏡光潤凝流。其中常現如來影像。("To the northeast of the big city and to the east of the river Vāraṇī, there is a *stūpa* erected by king Aśoka. It is more than one hundred *chi* high and in front of it he had built a stone pillar whose stone looks fresh like a mirror whose light flows out like oil. The form of the shadow of the Tathāgata can often be seen on it.") 905b.22ff. 精舍西南有石窣堵波。無憂王建也。基雖傾陷尚餘百尺。前建石柱。高七十餘尺。石含玉潤鑒照映徹。慇懃祈請影見眾像。善惡之相時有見者。是如來成正覺已初轉法輪處也。("To the southwest of the monastery there is a stone *stūpa* built by king Aśoka. Although its foundation is already sunk into the earth, it still measures more than one hundred *chi* in height. In front of it a stone pillar is erected, more than seventy *chi* high. The stone is as bright as jade, is glistening and has a penetrating light. If one prays diligently, the shadow (of the light) shows all kinds of shapes and the good or evil signs appear sometimes. This is the

Vaiśālī[135] and one that was in Vaiśālī near the Markaṭahrada.[136] Still another pillar is located in New Rājagṛha near the famous Veṇuvana monastery.[137] In general it can be stated that these pillar descriptions are very stereotyped and show all signs of an inflation of the *geographia sacra* common in Xuanzang's report. At the same time they lack the narrative motives rebinding them with the Aśoka legend.

As can be shown in an overwhelming number of examples, Xuanzang in the *Xiyuji* 西域記 does not skip a chance to describe Buddhist India in eulogizing terms. He uses India as a speculum, as a mirror to show the Chinese what an ideal Buddhist kingdom does look like. Why then, could one ask, does he not take the opportunity to project a Bodhisattva-like Aśoka?

The answer is, in my opinion, that finally the *Xiyuji* was a description of India written for the Tang emperor Gaozong 高宗 (649–683), who had just consolidated rule of the Tang dynasty. There was no way of describing an Indian ruler excelling the Chinese emperor in virtue and rulership. This is beside the fact that the Indian tradition itself could not provide such an image.

Xuanzang often presents us with an amalgam of traditional Chinese world-views and Indian Buddhist conceptions. In the case of Aśoka, however, he seems to reduce the Mauryan ruler once again to the function and role which is ascribed to him in the legends: a true Buddhist layperson and king, donator to the *saṅgha* and the one who spread the relics and built *stūpa*s all over Jambudvīpa. The reason for this is, I think, a political one: The Chinese emperor should not be confronted with an idealized and apotheosized Indian ruler of the past like Aśoka, but rather be brought diplomatically into contact with the actual ruler of India, Śīlāditya Harṣavardhana, who, in the *Xiyuji*, expresses himself as aware of and impressed by the greatness of the Chinese monarch. Xuanzang had brought home to China an Aśoka that had been previously constructed by the South Asian legends about the Mauryan emperor: a pious Buddhist who could be an individual model for a Chinese ruler but could not, however, serve as an ideal for a "Son of Heaven" who was responsible for his dynasty and his country. At the same time he also reconstructed the image of a superhuman Buddhist *cakravartin* whose model had become Aśoka and whose representatives in China were rulers like Liang Wudi or Sui Wendi.

place where the Tathāgata, after he had attained full enlightenment, turned the wheel of the *dharma*.")

135 908a.7ff. 那羅延天祠東行三十餘里有窣堵波。無憂王之所建也。太半陷地前建石柱高餘二丈。上作師子之像。刻記伏鬼之事。("If one goes more than thirty *li* from the Nārāyaṇa temple to the East, there is a *stūpa* built by king Aśoka. More than half of it is sunk into the earth and in front of it stands a stone pillar, more than two *zhang* high. On top of it there is the statue of a lion and it is inscribed with the events surrounding the defeat of the demons.")

136 908b.14ff. 其西北有窣堵波。無憂王之所建也。傍有石柱。高五六十尺。("To the Northwest there is a *stūpa* erected by king Aśoka. On (its) side is a stone pillar, fifty or sixty *chi* high.")

137 923a.13ff. 迦蘭陀池西北行二三里有窣堵波。無憂王所建也。高六十餘尺。傍有石柱刻記立窣堵波事。高五十餘尺。上作象形。("If one goes from the Karaṇḍahrada two or three *li* to the Northwest, there is a *stūpa* erected by king Aśoka, more than sixty *chi* high. On (its) side there is a stone pillar on which is inscribed the cause of the erection of the *stūpa*; it is more than fifty *chi* high and has the image of a lion on top of it.")

Bibliography

Andersen, P. K. 1990. *Studies in the Minor Rock Edicts of Aśoka. I. Critical Edition*. Freiburg: Verlag Hedwig Falk (Freiburger Beiträge zur Indologie, Bd.)

Assmann, J. 1997. *Das kulturelle Gedächtnis. Schrift, Erinnerung und politische Identität in frühen Hochkulturen*. München: C. H. Beck.

Bailey, H. W. 1966. "A Tale of Aśoka." *Bulletin of Tibetology* 3.1: 5–11.

Bechert H. ed. 1985. *Zur Schulzugehörigkeit von Werken der Hīnayāna-Literatur*. Göttingen: Vandenhoeck and Ruprecht.

———. 1988. *Buddhismus, Staat und Gesellschaft in den Ländern des Theravāda-Buddhismus, Band I: Grundlagen. Ceylon (Sri Lanka)*. Veröfftentlichungen des Seminars für Indologie und Buddhismuskunde der Universität Göttingen. Göttingen: Seminar für Indologie und Buddhismuskunde der Universität Göttingen.

Bloch, J. 1950. *Les inscriptions d'Asoka. Traduites et commentées*. Paris: Societé d'Édition.

Bongard-Levin, G. M. 1971. "The Historicity of the Ancient Indian Avadānas." In *Studies in Ancient India and Central Asia*. Ed. G. M. Bongard-Levin, pp. 123–11. Calcutta: Indian Studies.

Burnouf, E. 1844. *Introduction à l'histoire du Buddhisme indien*. Second edition 1876. Paris: Imprimérie Royale.

Catalogue of the exhibition Chūgoku-bunmei-ten/Chinese Civilization (Sekai-shidaibunmei) 中国文明展 (世界四大文明) *(8.2000–12.2001)*. 2000. Tokyo:

Chattopadhyaya, A. and L. Chimpa. 1970. *Tāranātha's History of Buddhism in India*. Simla: Indian Institute of Advanced Study.

Chen, J. 2002a. "Śarīra and Scepter: Empress Wu's Political Use of Buddhist Relics." *Journal of the International Association of Buddhist Studies* 25.1, 2: 33–150.

———. 2002b. *Monks and Monarchs, Kinship and Kingship. Tanqian in Sui Buddhism and Politics*. Essays: Volume 3. Kyoto: Italian School of East Asian Studies.

———. 2006a. "Buddhist Establishments within Liang Wudi's (r. 502–549) Imperial Park." In *Engaged Buddhism, Its History, Doctrines and Practices: Essays in Memory of Master Yinshun (1906–2005)*. Ed. M. Hsu and L. Meeks. Hua-lien: Ciji Daxue chubanshe.

———. 2006b. "*Pañcavārṣika* Assemblies in Liang Wudi's Buddhist Palace Chapel." *Harvard Journal of Asiatic Studies* 66.1: 43–103.

Cowell, E. B. and R. A. Neil. 1970 [1886]. *The Divyâvadâna—A Collection of Early Buddhist Legends*. Reprint. Amsterdam: Oriental Press.

Cunningham, A. 1871. *The Ancient Geography of India, I. The Buddhist Period Including the Campaigns of Alexander, and the Travels of Hwen-Thsang*, London: Trubner and Co. [reprint Delhi: Munshiram Manoharlal Publishers 1990].

———. 1879. *Inscriptions of Asoka*. Calcutta: Office of the Superintendent of Government Printing (Corpus Inscriptionum Indicarum, Vol.1).

Deeg, M. 1995. "Origins and Development of the Buddhist Pañcavārṣika—Part I: India and Central Asia." *Nagoya Studies in Indian Culture and Buddhism—Saṃbhāṣā* 16: 67–90

———. 1997. "Origins and Development of the Buddhist Pañcavārṣika—Part II: China". *Nagoya Studies in Indian Culture and Buddhism—Saṃbhāṣā* 18: 63–96.

———. 2001a. "Von Integration zur Legitimation—Die Aśoka-Legende (Aśokāvadāna) im buddhistischen Indien und in China." In *Religiöser Text und soziale Struktur*. Hallesche Beiträge zur Orientwissenschaft 31/2001. Ed. W. Beltz and J. Tubach, pp. 111–146. Halle (Saale): Druckerei der Martin-Luther-Universität Halle-Wittenberg.

———. 2001b. "On the localisation of Faxian's kingdom of Jiecha." In *South Asian Archaeology, Papers of the 14th International Conference of the European Association of South Asian Archaeologists in Rome* (7.7.–11.7.1997). Ed. M. Taddei and G. de Marco, pp. 877–88. Rome: Istituto Italiano per il Medio ed Estremo Oriente.

———. 2001c. "Der religiöse ‚Synkretismus' der chinesischen Kaiserin Wu Zetian - Versuch einer Staatsreligion?" In *Religion und Staat in der asiatischen Religionsgeschichte*. Acta Universitatis Upsaliensis, Historia Religionum. Ed. P. Schalk, M. Deeg, O. Freiberger, and C. Kleine, pp. 119–138. Uppsala: Uppsala University.

———. 2004. "Legend and Cult—Contributions to the History of Indian Buddhist Stūpas—Part 1: the Stūpa of Kaniṣka." *Buddhist Studies Review* 21.1: 1–34.

———. 2005. *Das Gaoseng-Faxian-zhuan als religionsgeschichtliche Quelle. Der älteste Bericht eines chinesischen buddhistischen Pilgermönchs über seine Reise nach Indien mit Übersetzung des Textes*. Studies in Oriental Religions 52. Wiesbaden: Harrassowitz.

———. forthcoming. *Miscellanae Nepalicae: Early Chinese Reports on Nepal—The Foundation Legend of Nepal in its Trans-Himalayan Context*. Lumbinī: The Lumbinī International Research Institute.

Dobbins, K. W. 1971. *The Stūpa and Vihāra of Kanishka I*. The Asiatic Society of Bengal Monograph Series, Vol. XVIII. Calcutta: The Asiatic Society.

Eggermont, P. H. L. 1956. *The Chronology of the Reign of Asoka Moriya. A Comparison of the Data of the Asoka Inscriptions and the Data of the Tradition*. Leiden: E. J. Brill.

Falk, H. 1993. *Schrift im alten Indien—Ein Forschungsbericht mit Anmerkungen*. Tübingen: Gunter Narr Verlag.

Fitzgerald, J. L. 2001. "Making Yudhiṣṭhira the King: the Dialectics and the Politics of Violence in the Mahābhārata." *Rocznik Orientalistyczny* 54.1: 63–92.

Forte, A. 1976. *Political Propaganda and Ideology in China at the End of the Seventh Century. Inquiry into the Nature, Author and Function of the Tunhuang Document S.6502, Followed by an Annotated Translation*. Napoli: Istituto Universitario Orientale.

———. 1988. *Mingtang and Buddhist Utopias in the History of the Astronomical Clock. The Tower, Statue and Armillary Sphere Constructed by Empress Wu*. Roma, Paris: Istituto Italiano per il Medio ed Estremo Oriente, Ecole française d'Extrême-Orient.

Geiger, W. 1908. *The Mahāvaṃsa*. London: Pali Text Society.

———. 1912. *The Mahāvaṃsa or The Great Chronicle of Ceylon*. London: Pali Text Society.

———. (ed. H. Bechert) 1986. *Culture of Ceylon in Medieval Times*. Stuttgart: Steiner.

Gombrich, R. 1997. *Der Theravāda-Buddhismus. Vom alten Indien bis zum modernen Sri Lanka*. Stuttgart: W. Kohlhammer Verlag.

Hahn, M. 1985. *Der Grosse Legendenkranz (Mahājjātakamālā), Eine mittelalterliche Legendensammlung aus Nepal* (Nach Vorarbeiten von Gudrun Bühnemann und Michael Hahn herausgegeben und eingeleitet). Asiatische Forschungen, Monographienreihe zur Geschichte, Kultur und Sprache der Völker Ost- und Zentralasiens. Bd.88. Wiesbaden: Harrassowitz.

Harmatta, J., B. N. Puri, and G. F. Etemadi. ed. 1994. *History of Civilizations of Central Asia, Volume II: The development of sedentary and nomadic civilizations: 700 B.C. to A.D. 250*. Paris: UNESCO Publishing.

von Hinüber, O. 1996. *A Handbook of Pāli Literature*. Berlin, New York: de Gruyter.

Hirakawa, A. 1997. *Buddhist-Chinese Sanskrit Dictionary—Bukkyo-kanbon-daijiten*. Tokyo: The Reiyukai.

Höfer, A., G. Prunner, E. Kaneko, L. Bezacier, and M. Sarkisyanz. 1975. *Die Religionen Südostasiens*. Stuttgart, Berlin, Köln, Mainz: Kohlhammer Verlag.

Holt, J. C. 1996. *The Religious World of Kīrti Śrī. Buddhism, Art, and Politics in Late Medieval Sri Lanka*. New York, Oxford: SUNY Press.

Hultzsch, E. 1925. *Inscriptions of Asoka (New Edition)*. Corpus Inscriptionum Indicarum, Vol. I. Oxford: Clarendon Press.

Janousch, A. "The emperor as bodhisattva: the bodhisattva ordination and ritual assemblies of Emperor Wu of the Liang dynasty." In *State and court ritual in China*. Ed. J. P. McDermott, pp. 112–49. Cambridge: Cambridge University Press.

Jansen, T. 2001. "Der chinesische Kaiser Liang Wudi (reg. 502–549) und der Buddhismus." In *Religion urd Staat in der asiatischen Religionsgeschichte*. Acta Universitatis Upsaliensis, Historia Religionum. Ed. P. Schalk, M. Deeg, O. Freiberger, and C. Kleine. Uppsala: Uppsala University.

Jayawickrama, N. A. 1986. *The Inception of Discipline and the Vinaya Nidāna—Being a Translation and Edition of the Bāhiranidāna of Bhuddhaghosa's Samantapāsādikā, the Vinaya Commentary*. London: Pali Text Society.

Ji Xianlin季羡林. ed. 1985. *Datang-xiyuji-xiaozhu* 大唐西域記校注. Beijing: Zhonghua-shuju 中華書局.

Kern, F. 1956. *Aśoka—Kaiser und Missionar* (hrsg. v. Willibald Kirfel). Bern: Franke.

Kieser, A. 2002. *Landadel—Emigranten—Emporkömmlinge: Familienfriedhöfe des 3.–6. Jahrhunderts n.Chr. in Südchina*. Asiatische Forschungen, Monographienreihe Band 144. Wiesbaden: Harrassowitz.

Kuwayama, S. 1997. *The Main Stūpa of Shāh-Jī-Kī Ḍherī—A Chronological Outlook*. Kyoto: Jinbun-kagaku-kenkyujo.

Lamotte, É. 1958. *Histoire du Bouddhisme indien des origines à l'ère Śaka*. Louvain: Publications Universitaires.

Marshall, J. and A. Foucher. 1940. *The Monuments of Sāñcī*. 2 vols. Delhi: Government of India Press.

Mayrhofer, M. 1991. *Etymologisches Wörterbuch des Altindoarischen, vol.1*. Heidelberg: Winter.

Mehendale, S. and B. Williams. 2000. "Kushan Polity and Buddhism Monasteries." In *2000 PNC, Annual Conference and Joint Meetings, University of California, Berkeley and Stanford University, January 11–17 2000, Abstracts*. Berkeley: 105.

Mizutani Shinjō 水谷真成. 1971. *Daitō-saiiki-ki* 大唐西域記. Tokyo: Heibonsha 平凡社(Chūgoku-koten-bungaku-daikei 中國古典文學大系 22).

Mookherji, R. 1962. *Asoka*. Delhi: Motilal Banarsidass.

Mukhopadhyaya, S. 1963. *The Aśokāvadāna. Sanskrit Text Compared with Chinese Versions*. Delhi: Sahitya Akademi.

Nishiwaki, T. 1992. "Die Reliquienverehrung (*śarīra*) und ihre Beschreibung in den Mönchsbiographien." *Monumenta Serica* 40: 87–120.

Obermiller, E. 1932. *History of Buddhism (Chos-ḥbyung) by Bu-ston. II. Part: The History of Buddhism in India and Tibet*. Heidelberg: Carl Winter.

Przyluski, J. 1923. *La légende de l'empereur Açoka (Açoka-Avadāna) dans les textes indiens et chinois*. Paris: P. Geuthner.

Rosenfield, J. M. 1967. *The Dynastic Arts of the Kushans*. Berkeley: University of California Press [Indian reprint Delhi: 1993].

Ruegg, D. S. 1995. *Ordre spirituel et ordre temporel dans la pensée bouddhique de l'Inde et du Tibet (Quatres conférences au Collège de France)*. Collège de France, Publications de l'Institut de Civilisation Indienne, Fascicule 64. Paris: Publications de l'Institut de la Civilisation Indienne.

Schneider, U. 1978. *Die grossen Felsen-Edikte Aśokas. Kritische Ausgabe, Übersetzung und Analyse der Texte*. Freiburger Beiträge zur Indologie, Bd.11. Wiesbaden: Otto Harrassowitz.

Shinohara, K. 1992. "Guanding's Biography of Zhiyi (Appendix: Stories about Asoka images)." In *Speaking of Monks—Religious Biography in India and China*. Ed. P. Granoff and K. Shinohara, pp. 201–213. Oakville, Ontario: Mosaic Press.

———. "Literary Construction of Buddhist Sacred Places: The Record of Mt. Lu by Chen Shenyu." *Asiatische Studien/Études Asiatiques* 53: 937–964.

Sims-Williams, N. and J. Cribb. 1995/96. "A New Bactrian Inscription of Kanishka the Great." *Silk Road Art and Archaeology* 4: 75–142.

Strong, J. S. 1983. *The Legend of King Aśoka—A Study and Translation of the Aśokāvadāna*. Princeton: Princeton University Press.

———. 1992. *The Legend and Cult of Upagupta. Sanskrit Buddhism in North India and Southeast Asia*. Princeton: Princeton University Press.

Sutton, N. 1997. "Aśoka and Yudhiṣṭhira: A Historical Setting for the Ideological Tensions of the Mahābhārata?" *Religion* 27: 333–341.

Swearer, D. K. 1995. *The Buddhist World of Southeast Asia*. Albany: SUNY University Press.

Takakusu J. and K. Watanabe. ed. 1924. *Taisho-shinshu-daizokyo (The Tripitaka in Chinese)*. Tokyo: Kankōkai.

Tambiah, S. J. 1978. *World Conqueror and World Renouncer. A Study of Buddhism and Polity in Thailand against a Historical Background*. Cambridge: Cambridge University Press.

Trainor, K. 1997. *Relics, Ritual, and Representation in Buddhism—Rematerializing the Sri Lankan Theravāda Tradition*. Cambridge: Cambrigde University Press.

Tuladhar-Douglas, W. 2006. *Remaking Buddhism for Medieval Nepal. The Fifteenth-Century Reformation of Newar Buddhism*. London, New York: Routledge.

Waldschmidt, E. 1948. *Die Überlieferung vom Lebensende des Buddha. Eine vergleichende Analyse des Mahāparinirvāṇasūtra und seiner Textentsprechungen, Zweiter Teil: Vorgangsgruppe V–VI*. Abhandlungen der

Akademie der Wissenschaften in Göttingen, Philologisch-Historische Klasse, Dritte Folge Nr. 30. Göttingen: Vandernhoeck and Ruprecht.

———. 1961. *Der Buddha preist die Verehrungswürdigkeit seiner Reliquien. Sondertext I des Mahāparinirvāṇasūtra*. Nachrichten der Göttinger Akademie der Wissenschaften. Göttingen: Vandernhoeck and Ruprecht. = (quoted after) Waldschmidt, E. 1967. *Von Ceylon bis Turfan. Schriften zur Geschichte, Literatur, Religion und Kunst des indischen Kulturraumes. Festgabe zum 70. Geburtstag am 15. Juli 1967*. Göttingen: Vandernhoeck and Ruprecht.

Weinstein, S. 1987. *Buddhism under the T'ang*. Cambridge: Cambridge University Press.

Wogihara, U. and S. Tsuji. 1940. *Kanyaku-taishō-Bonwa-daijiten*. Tokyo: Kōdansha.

Wright, A. F. 1979. "The Sui dynasty (581–617)." In *The Cambridge History of China, Volume 3: Sui and T'ang China, 589–906, Part 1*. Ed. D. Twitchett and J. K. Fairbank, pp. 48–149. Cambridge: Cambridge University Press.

Verardi, G. 1983. "The Kusana Emperors as Cakravartins, dynastic art and cults in India and Central Asia: history of a theory, clarifications and refutations." *East and West*: 125–194.

Zürcher, E. 1968. "The Yüeh-chih and Kaniṣka in the Chinese Sources." In *Papers on the Date of Kaniṣka*. Ed. A. L. Basham, pp. 346–390. Leiden: E. J. Brill.

———. 1972. *The Buddhist Conquest of China—The Spread and Adaptation of Buddhism in Early Medieval China*. Leiden: E. J. Brill.

Index